A Duke a Dozen

The Survivors: Book VI

Shana Galen

A DUKE A DOZEN
Copyright © 2019 by Shana Galen

Cover Design by The Killion Group, Inc.

All rights reserved. Except for use in any review, the reproduction or utilization of this work in whole or in part in any form by any electronic, mechanical or other means, now known or hereafter invented, including xerography, photocopying and recording, or in any information storage or retrieval system, is forbidden without the written permission of the author.

All characters in this book have no existence outside the imagination of the author and have no relation whatsoever to anyone bearing the same name or names. They are not even distantly inspired by any individual known or unknown to the author, and all incidents are pure invention.

Also by Shana Galen

REGENCY SPIES
While You Were Spying
When Dashing Met Danger
Pride and Petticoats

MISADVENTURES IN MATRIMONY
No Man's Bride
Good Groom Hunting
Blackthorne's Bride
The Pirate Takes a Bride

SONS OF THE REVOLUTION
The Making of a Duchess
The Making of a Gentleman
The Rogue Pirate's Bride

JEWELS OF THE TON
If You Give a Duke a Diamond
If You Give a Rake a Ruby
Sapphires are an Earl's Best Friend

LORD AND LADY SPY
Lord and Lady Spy
The Spy Wore Blue (novella)
True Spies
Love and Let Spy
All I Want for Christmas is Blue (novella)
The Spy Beneath the Mistletoe (novella)

COVENT GARDEN CUBS
Viscount of Vice (novella)
Earls Just Want to Have Fun
The Rogue You Know
I Kissed a Rogue

THE SURVIVORS
Third Son's a Charm
No Earls Allowed
An Affair with a Spare
Unmask Me if You Can
The Claiming of the Shrew

THE SCARLET CHRONICLES
Traitor in Her Arms
To Ruin a Gentleman
Taken by the Rake
To Tempt a Rebel

STANDALONES AND ANTHOLOGIES
Mrs. Bvrodie's Academy for Extraordinary Young Ladies (duo)
Stealing the Duke's Heart (duet)
A Royal Christmas (duet)
The Dukes of Vauxhall (anthology)
A Grosvenor Square Christmas (anthology)

One

With four brothers dead and in their graves, Phineas Leopold Duncombe, the ninth Duke of Mayne, had reason to wonder if he would be next. As he walked along King Street in St. James, he took care to look up, lest an errant piano crash onto his head. He kept one eye on the street at all times, vigilant in case a horse bolted and an out of control carriage flattened him. And he was mindful of where he stepped. He'd never heard of quicksand in London, but considering his family's luck, one could not be too careful.

He sighed with relief when he reached the Draven Club. Porter, the Master of the House, greeted him, taking his overcoat. "Your Grace, nice to see you back," the silver-haired man said. "May I offer my condolences on the passing of your brother."

"Thank you." Phin's gaze swept about the familiar wood-paneled vestibule. The large chandelier overhead illuminated a suit of armor on one side of the room and Scottish broadswords on the other. Directly opposite him was a large shield bisected by a medieval sword. Phin didn't need to move any closer to know fleurs-de-lis embellished the sword's pommel and a skull was at the cross guard. Around the perimeter of the shield, eighteen fleurs-de-lis symbolized the men of the troop who had died during the war. Phin was one of the twelve to come home.

"Is Lieutenant Draven here?" he asked, referring to the leader of the troop.

"Not yet."

Phin started toward the winding staircase carpeted in royal blue, Porter followed, his wooden leg thumping as he moved. "Do you want dinner, Your Grace?"

"No, but I could use a drink. I have a rather distasteful errand to complete and could use fortification."

"I see. I have a French brandy from ninety-five saved for just such an occasion."

"Perfect. I'll be in the reading room." Phin climbed the stairs to the small room with bookshelves on three sides. A large hearth dominated the fourth side and a fire blazed within. Phin settled into one of the large leather armchairs set before the fire, leaned his head back, and closed his eyes. The wings of the chair were so large, he was all but obscured. He didn't bother to light a lamp as he didn't intend to read. He wanted time to think. He'd been in the country with his grieving mother and sisters for three weeks. He'd had barely a moment to himself. Not since his brother Richard had turned up dead on Christmas Day.

Happy Christmas, Phin thought. You are the Duke of Mayne. Worst Christmas present he had ever received.

But finally, he had quiet, peace, solitude.

"What are you doing back in town?"

Phin's eyes opened at the man's voice, though he managed to avoid jumping with fright. It took him a moment before he placed the drawl and the slight sarcastic tone. "Fortescue?" he asked, though he was almost certain he'd guessed correctly.

Stratford Fortescue, with his high forehead and piercing blue eyes, leaned forward from the chair on Phin's left.

"Duncombe. No, wait. You're Mayne now. Congratulations, Duke. And here we all thought you were expendable." He was referring, of course, to one of the reasons the men of Draven's troop had been chosen to join what amounted to a suicide team. They were the best and the brightest, but also younger sons who were considered expendable.

"It turns out I'm surprisingly indispensable."

Fortescue raised a brow. "I'm still dispensable."

"Congratulations?"

"That was my line. What happened to this brother? Did he drown?"

Phin wished Porter would hurry with that drink. "That was the fifth Duke of Mayne."

Fortescue didn't say it, but Phin knew what he was thinking. Everyone said the dukedom was cursed. How else did one explain the early demise of so many Dukes of Mayne? There was Phineas's brother Phillip, the fifth duke of Mayne and the one Fortescue referenced. Phillip had drowned in a pond on the family estate in West Sussex. The boys had swum there as children hundreds of times.

"He fell on ice then? Or was that the sixth duke?"

"It was the seventh. The sixth was killed in a duel."

That had been George. Admittedly, the sixth Duke of Mayne had had a bit of a temper, so his untimely death was not wholly unexpected. But how did one explain the death of the seventh Duke of Mayne, Ernest? Ernest was a quiet, cautious sort of fellow. He'd died after falling on ice and hitting his head.

"What killed the eighth?"

Richard. The Idiot, as Phineas thought of him. "It seems my brother Richard was so drunk he fell off his horse on the way to the family pile. According to the coroner, he hit his head and died instantly."

All unfortunate, premature, accidental deaths. Bad luck, Phin's brother-in-law John had said when they'd found the body. Bad luck for Phin as now the curse had fallen on him.

"Curious."

Phin looked at Fortescue. "Do you think so?"

"Four older brothers and four early deaths. It *is* curious. You don't think so?"

Phin sat back in his chair. Herein lay the problem. He did think the deaths strange, but he couldn't put a finger on any reason to believe them anything other than accidents or the result of poor choices.

"You asked why I'm back in Town."

Fortescue sipped his drink. "It was a rhetorical question. I assumed you wanted to escape your mother and sisters."

"There's that, but I also want to question the woman who was with my brother the night before he traveled to West Sussex."

Fortescue narrowed his eyes, looking every bit the strategist, which had been his assignment in the troop. "Was she the last person to see him alive?"

"No. He stopped at a farmhouse to visit our neighbors. The ladies there are quite… friendly to gentlemen. But they've lived on that land for decades. They're a bit loose with their charms, but they're harmless."

"You questioned them, of course."

"Until they were brought to tears. They said he was perfectly well, although exceedingly drunk, when he left them for Southmeade Cottage."

"If you believe the ladies, the circumstances seem relatively straight forward."

"I know." So why was he here?

"And yet, the lady who was with him the before he left for West Sussex might have information you haven't taken into consideration."

Fortescue had vocalized Phineas's own thoughts. "Exactly. I shouldn't leave that stone unturned."

"Who is she?"

"They call her the Wanton Widow." Phin had seen her only once, and the image of her was burned into his mind. "Do you know anything about her?"

"No." Fortescue looked almost disappointed that he didn't have any information.

"I do."

Phineas did jump now then turned in his chair to stare at the chair on his right. Colin FitzRoy leaned forward, his dark curls falling over his forehead.

"How long have you been sitting there?" Phin demanded.

FitzRoy seemed to ponder this question. "Longer than either of you."

Phin looked to his left. "Did you know he was there, Stratford?"

"No. He must have disguised himself as a chair."

"I don't need a disguise. You two are wholly oblivious."

Porter entered with the bottle of brandy and three snifters on a silver tray. He set the tray on the table beside Phineas. "Anything else, Your Grace?"

Phin gestured to the brandy. "Three snifters?"

"In case you would like to share." He turned and left them.

Phin poured three fingers for Fortescue and three for FitzRoy. FitzRoy waved it away, so Phin took it. The brandy was smooth and had an earthy flavor.

"You asked about the Wanton Widow."

Phin stared at FitzRoy, a burning beginning in his chest. He'd felt this burning before, the night he'd first seen her. "You know her?"

"We're not acquainted, but I know of her."

"Go on," Phin said, the burning cooling a bit. Must have been the brandy, he decided.

"She married the Earl of Longstowe twenty-five or more years ago. My grandfather had dealings with him and always said he was the worst sort. It gave him pleasure to be cruel. When the earl died, no one could blame the countess for seeking a diversion or two."

"But this is the *ton*," Fortescue said darkly.

FitzRoy eyed him. "So they did blame her. Thus, the sobriquet."

"Her standards can't be very high if she took Richard to her bed," Phin said, annoyed at how much that one fact bothered him. "I don't necessarily think she had anything to do with his death, but I'll feel better having spoken to her."

Colin met his gaze with light green eyes framed by dark lashes. "Is that what you've told yourself?"

Phin finished his brandy. "Explain."

"She's a beautiful woman."

The burning in his chest began again. "And?"

"Maybe you hope to take her to bed."

Phin laughed, but the laugh sounded false even to him. "I don't want Richard's seconds." He turned to Fortescue for support, but the man was eyeing him curiously over his snifter.

Phin rose. "It's late. I should go."

As he stalked toward the door, Colin called after him. "A word of advice?"

"I don't need *your* advice on women."

FitzRoy put a hand to where his heart should beat. "Ouch," he said without emotion. "Lady Longstowe is not like the debutantes your mother foists upon you at dinner parties. She won't be awed by your title or your money."

"Good. I'll like her all the more for it."

An hour later, after summoning his carriage and braving the cold again, he peered out the window of the conveyance and studied the cold, barren streets of Mayfair. The *ton* was in the country for the Christmas holidays, and the town houses were shuttered and dark on this late January evening.

Phin sat back, disliking the pretension of the Mayne ducal coach, but with four older brothers dead in less than a decade, his mother had asked him not to risk riding in the dark on horseback. What she did not say was, "Don't give the curse a chance at you, dear." But that's what she'd meant.

After all, a tree branch might fall on his head, killing him instantly. Or perhaps a deranged squirrel would attack him. Did squirrels hibernate in the winter? Phin had no idea. He felt like he'd been losing his mind for the past three weeks. He couldn't even walk to his club without fretting about falling pianos.

The coach slowed and stopped in front of a modest town house on the outskirts of Mayfair. The address was still fashionable, but Phin knew the property would lease for far less than its sisters in Berkeley Square. Still, the building was well-maintained. With all the coal in use in Town, it didn't take long for the limestone buildings to become gray with soot. But this house was white, which meant the paint was fresh. He also noted the windows were clean, and the walk had been swept free of the leaves and trash that tended to gather when the winds kicked up as they had lately. He thought he saw a curtain on the ground floor twitch, but other than that, the house looked quiet.

The coach door opened, and a footman lowered the steps. Phin could have jumped out easily, but he was the duke now. He was supposed to act ducal. And so he made use of the steps and, holding his hat on his head so it wouldn't blow away, made his way to the door. His solicitor, who Phin paid to gather information, had said Lady Longstowe was in Town. Her knocker was still in place, so Phineas had reason to hope his visit tonight would prove fruitful. A proper duke would have sent a note to the lady requesting a meeting, but Phin hadn't wanted to give the lady time to think of answers to his questions. He hoped to surprise her and observe her reactions. It wasn't that he did not want to give her a chance to reject the meeting. No one would dare turn down an audience with a duke.

Except someone unimpressed by dukes.

Damn Colin.

Phin turned to look back at his coach. The footman looked quickly away, pretending he hadn't been watching him. He was being ridiculous. Of course, she would see him. He had legitimate questions. He didn't know what, precisely, they were, but they would come to him. Because he hadn't come to seduce the countess. He didn't want to seduce her at all. He knew many beautiful women, and *he* wasn't impressed by a woman like her.

Before he could knock on the door, it was opened by an elderly man with only one good eye. Phineas looked into the cloudy blue of the other eye then at the sharp blue one fixed on him. "Yes?" the butler said, peering down his long nose at Phineas. "Were you planning to knock? I'm too old to stand here all evening."

Phin ignored the insolence. The man did look like he was about to fall over. "I'm here to see Lady Longstowe."

"She's not expecting you." The butler began to close the door, but Phineas stuck his boot between the door and jamb. The old butler looked feeble enough that Phineas could have pushed inward on the door and knocked him over, but that wouldn't have been very ducal.

"If you would be so kind, please tell her I'm here and ask if she'll see me." He held out his gloved hand, his cream-colored calling card extended between two fingers. The butler took the card reluctantly, looked closely at the writing with his good eye then at Phineas then back at the card. "Tell her I apologize for arriving unannounced. It's a matter of some urgency."

"Very well." The butler opened the door enough that Phin could squeeze into the foyer. "Wait here." Taking a cane from where it rested against a wall, the butler hobbled away.

Interesting. A butler with one good eye and a bad leg. He'd thought Lady Longstowe a widow of some means, but perhaps he'd been incorrect if she could not afford a more proper servant. He made a mental note to have his solicitor look into it. He'd never had a solicitor before. The man came with the ducal title, it seemed, but Phineas was finding him quite useful.

He looked about the vestibule with curiosity. He'd expected the house to be, if not gaudy, overdone. After all, the countess was known as the Wanton Widow. The term wanton was not usually applied to a woman with good taste, but Phin could find nothing in what he saw to disapprove. The foyer was lit brightly by two wall sconces. It was neither too big nor too small, and it was furnished with a small table topped with a silver dish, no doubt for calling cards, and a stand for coats. There was no chair about, and Phineas deduced callers were not usually left to stand in the foyer waiting.

"Oh, there you are!"

Phineas looked up to see a girl—no, a woman—of indeterminate age descending the steps rapidly.

"Crotchett told me we had a guest, but I didn't know it would be a gentleman. He should not have made you wait here." She stopped before him and looked up. He was a man only a little taller than average, but this woman—the housekeeper, he assumed—was the size of a child. The height of one of his young nieces. "Let me help you with your coat, my lord."

Phineas removed the garment, and she reached for it then brought it to the coat rack, where she managed to hang it high enough so it didn't touch the floor. Phineas had the urge to help her, but he did not think his offer of assistance would be welcome. She then took his scarf and hat and bade him to follow her.

"I am Mrs. Slightley. The missus is ornamental. I've never been married. I don't know why Crotchett didn't show you to the drawing room. He's been in a foul mood the last ten years."

Phineas stifled a chuckle. He liked her pleasant demeanor much better than the dour butler. "Did something happen ten years ago?"

"Oh, no!" Mrs. Slightley waved a hand then opened the doors to the drawing room. "I just didn't know him before that. I suspect he's been in a bad mood all his life." She put a finger to her lips. "But don't tell him I said that. Now, I'll fetch tea, and you make yourself comfortable. Her ladyship will be down shortly."

Phineas turned from the center of the drawing room, where he was contemplating which pale blue seat to take. "She will see me then?"

"I can't think why not. You're a far sight more handsome than that stack of books she spends all her time with."

Phineas inclined his head in thanks. Mrs. Slightley closed the doors, and he heard the patter of her feet as she rushed off to fetch tea. The Wanton Widow spent her spare time not in illicit trysts but reading? What had she seen in his idiot brother?

Phineas looked about the drawing room. Like the foyer it was well-appointed. The furnishings were modest but attractive. There was a pianoforte in one corner by the windows and a grouping of chairs in cream and pale blue in another corner near the hearth. A few paintings of seascapes hung on the walls. He didn't recognize the artist, but they were attractive enough.

Phineas took a seat beside the hearth, which had been banked but still gave off some warmth, and decided this was not at all what he had expected. The Wanton Widow did not appear very, well, wanton. But then just because she had good taste in household furnishings did not mean she was not a libertine who was free with her favors. Not to mention, he had met her. That wasn't entirely accurate as he hadn't been introduced to her, but he had locked eyes with her and felt…the effects of too much alcohol, surely.

He doubted she was even as beautiful as he remembered. Regardless, the fact was he had not traveled all this way to admire Lady Longstowe. He had questions, damn it. He wanted answers, and the best way to accomplish that was to speak to the woman directly. He didn't want to take her to bed. She probably had the pox.

The door opened, and Phin jumped up as the pox-ridden woman herself was there. Phin had a moment to think she looked quite well for a woman suffering from the pox.

"Lady Longstowe, the Duke of Mayne," the butler said as though the words required tremendous effort. Phin felt his knees buckle and wished he could sit down.

Two

"Thank you, Crotchett." Lady Longstowe stepped into the drawing room and walked directly toward him. The room seemed to tilt, and Phineas shifted to maintain his balance. He hardly had time to find his bearings and then she was before him, grasping both his hands in hers. He looked down at them. She wore gloves, and he desperately wished he could touch her bare skin.

"Your Grace, I am so sorry for your loss. Your brother's death was quite a shock to me. How is your family?"

He looked almost directly into her eyes. He hadn't realized she was so tall, only a few inches shorter than he. Phin also hadn't expected her to be so gracious. He'd arrived unannounced, interrupted her evening, and she did not seem annoyed in the least. Finally, he found his voice. "They are as well as can be expected. Thank you for inquiring."

"Please sit down. I'll ring for tea."

"Your housekeeper has already gone to fetch it."

"Oh. You met Mrs. Slightley?" She hesitated for a moment before taking a seat across from the chair he'd occupied. She obviously expected him to mention the housekeeper's diminutive size.

"I did. She seems quite capable."

She offered a slight smile and sat, gesturing for Phin to follow. For a long moment, they sat in silence. Phineas knew he should say something, but seeing her again made his head spin. The first time he'd seen her, he'd had several glasses of champagne, but he had no such excuse tonight. No excuse for the way his chest tightened and his breaths came short when he looked at her. She looked much as she had that first night. Her auburn hair was swept off her face in a simple style that highlighted her bright blue eyes. Her skin was pale, and now that he was closer he saw she had a few freckles scattered over her nose and cheeks. She was dressed in a simple blue gown with a high neck that did not reveal her bosom, but he remembered it well enough from the ball where he'd first glimpsed it. A man didn't forget something that magnificent.

She was older than he. At least ten years and possibly more. There were faint lines at her mouth and eyes, but they didn't diminish her beauty or his attraction to her. An unwanted attraction that apparently had nothing whatsoever to do with too much drink. But he could, and would, ignore the attraction and press on.

"Again, I am sorry about your brother," she said, finally breaking the silence. Phin felt like a fool for allowing it to go on so long. "I am sure it must have been a shock to your family."

"Yes, well, we have become used to the shock, I'm afraid."

"Your family has suffered more than its share of tragedy." She offered him a sad smile, but he could see in her eyes the beginnings of confusion. She really did not know why he was here.

"I called on you tonight, my lady, because I wondered if you might answer a few questions for me."

Her eyes narrowed slightly with suspicion. "Of course."

"Thank you." How to begin? Phin cleared his throat. He had studied law at Oxford. He could ask a woman questions, even a beautiful woman. "What was the, ah…nature of your relationship with my brother?" His voice sounded bitter, and he felt surprisingly bitter. He'd never envied Richard anything until he'd seen his brother with the Wanton Widow.

"The nature of my relationship with your brother?"

"That was my question."

For a moment, she hesitated and Phineas wondered if she might refuse to answer the question. And then she said, stiffly, "I danced with the late duke at Lady Houghton's ball. That was the nature of my relationship."

Phin blew out a breath. "Come, my lady. Even I know it was more than that. I saw you with him."

Phineas would not have been surprised to look behind him and see someone had opened the window, letting the January air inside. The room was suddenly several degrees colder, as were Lady Longstowe's icy blue eyes.

"Are you implying that—"

The door opened again, and Mrs. Slightley pushed the tea cart inside. "Here we are then," she said in a cheery tone that did nothing to dispel the chill in the room. "A bit of tea and those ginger biscuits you like so much, my lady."

"That will be all, Mrs. Slightley," Lady Longstowe said when the tray was beside her chair. As she didn't reach for the tea pot or make any move to offer her guest tea, the housekeeper hesitated.

"Do you want me to pour, my lady?"

"No, thank you."

Mrs. Slightley gave Phineas an assessing look and then walked slowly out of the room. She closed the door behind her, but Phin would have wagered a fiver she was on the other side, listening.

"Why don't we dispense with the pleasantries," Lady Longstowe said, flicking a hand at the tea tray and the biscuits, which did look rather appetizing. "What exactly do you wish to know, Your Grace?"

"I want to know what my brother's last hours were like. I want to piece them together." He stood. "I didn't want to be the duke, but I am, and I suppose I want to understand why." He hadn't meant to tell her all of that or any of it, and he closed his mouth and paced away to stare at the polished wood of the pianoforte.

"And why would I know anything about your brother's last hours?"

Phin was facing away from her and resorted to the childish gesture of rolling his eyes. He turned, leaning against the piano. "Lady Longstowe, I know your reputation. My brother knew your reputation. When I left the ball, you and he looked quite friendly, and he did not return until dawn the next morning. Are you saying he did not leave the ball with you?"

She sat so straight Phin's shoulders actually ached for her. It couldn't be comfortable to sit so stiffly. "What does it matter what I say? You have made up your mind."

"I want the truth."

She blew out a breath. "No, you want confirmation."

Phin pushed away from the instrument. "Are you saying you did not take my brother to your bed?"

She sat very still, and Phin began to wonder if she would not answer. Worse, he began to wonder if this wasn't the question he'd wanted answered all along. Really, how could she know anything about Richard's last hours? But when he thought of her with Richard, the burning in his chest began again. He hadn't been able to escape it every time he thought of her. He was angry that Richard, the Idiot, had bedded her. Because Phin had wanted her as he'd rarely ever wanted any other woman.

Too late, he realized coming here had been a mistake. FitzRoy was right. He had come to seduce her.

And she knew it.

As he watched, she seemed to change. The stiff posture melted away, and she leaned casually on the arm of her chair. Her mouth, which had been tight with what he'd thought was indignation, softened. Her eyes lowered then looked up at him from under her auburn lashes. "Is that why you came?" she asked—no, it was more of a purr, actually. Her voice had become lower and lusher and she spoke slowly. "To hear all about what I did with your brother? In bed?" She rose and walked toward him, her hips swaying in a manner he had difficulty tearing his gaze from.

"Not those details necessarily." He had to clear his throat as his mouth had gone dry. He should leave. Now. He should go. But how could he walk away from a woman who could move like that?

She stopped before him, standing far closer than was necessary. He tried to step back, but the pianoforte stood behind him. "I read he was found in West Sussex on the twenty-fifth of December. Our"—she lifted her hand and placed a finger lightly over the top button of his waistcoat—"night of sin took place in the early hours of December twenty-four." Her finger trailed down to the next button. He should remove it, but he couldn't seem to move. Or breathe. Or look away from her lush mouth.

The way she'd said *sin* had caused a flash of heat so strong he'd thought he might ignite.

"You're not a suspect." His voice was little more than a rasp.

"Then perhaps you came because you were curious." She looked up at him as her finger trailed to the next button, coming increasingly closer to his waist and his burgeoning erection. "Perhaps you want a sample of what I gave your brother."

He shook his head.

"No." She licked her lips. "You don't want me to take you in my mouth?" She lowered her finger again, and he was painfully aware of how close her hand was to his erection. "You don't want to slip between my thighs with that hard cock until you're sated and spent?"

He swallowed. "That's not why I came?" It sounded much more like a question than he liked.

She stepped back, and her eyes were icy again. All the sensuality of a moment ago was gone with a chill. "Then why did you come, Duke? Did you want to see if I was really as wanton as my sobriquet suggests? Were you curious about my house? Perhaps I would have naughty toys about or lascivious paintings. You could gossip about me at your club and tell everyone how you bent me over a chair and—let's see—" She put a finger to her lips, considering. "Are you the sort of man who would say he 'rogered' a wench or do you prefer 'fuck'?"

He moved away from her then, his face hot and his head spinning.

"You don't like me saying that. Only men can speak like that, and we ladies are supposed to pretend we don't know what you are talking about. You may not know why you came, Your Grace, but I do. And I don't care if you are the king himself, you'll never see my bed chamber."

"That's not why I came!" He was lying. She knew it and so did he. Phin felt more like a scolded schoolboy, and he knew he deserved to feel far worse.

"No, you came to ask me questions." She rolled her eyes as though this was the silliest thing she had ever heard. "I won't answer them. I'll have Crotchett show you out now." She started for the door, walking rigidly now and showing none of the grace she had earlier.

"I can send the magistrate to ask you." Phin didn't know why he said it. Perhaps he disliked having been so thoroughly thrashed.

She paused and looked back at him, and he felt his face redden. It was a childish thing to say, and he was ashamed to have thrown the threat at her. She was obviously not a woman to be threatened.

"Go ahead. I am not afraid of magistrates or dukes nor do I care what Society says about me. When you have faced real demons, all other threats seem paltry in comparison." She swept out in a swath of watery blue silk.

Phineas stood in the empty drawing room for several more seconds then, without waiting for the butler, left the chamber behind, and made his way down the steps to the ground floor. He found his coat and hat where the housekeeper had put them and pulled them on hastily.

But not hastily enough.

The housekeeper hurried down the steps. Phin held up a hand. "No need to throw me out. I am leaving."

"Good." Mrs. Slightley stopped at the base of the stairs, arms crossed and brows lowered. "I can't say what I want being that you're a duke and might throw me in the stocks—"

"The stocks? I wouldn't throw an innocent woman in the stocks."

"Good. Then I'll say you should be ashamed of yourself."

Phin finished buttoning his coat and set his hat on his head. He wasn't ashamed of himself, but he didn't feel exactly proud at the moment either. He opened the door. "Good night, Mrs. Slightley."

"It was a good night until you made my mistress cry."

Phin turned around. "Made her cry? Lady Longstowe is crying?"

"What do you care?"

"I don't." Phin stepped outside and flinched when the door slammed behind him.

He walked to the waiting coach, keeping his head down to avoid the bite of the wind. Once inside the coach, he directed the coachman to drive to the City and the office of his solicitor, then he poured himself another brandy and determined not to think of Lady Longstowe again.

Which was easier said than done. Because he did care.

He cared that he had upset her. He cared that he had made a fool of himself.

He cared that she was right. He had come out of curiosity and out of lust. He did have an interest in his brother's last hours, but all evidence pointed to the fact that he'd spent the evening before Christmas with one of the Johnson sisters at a farmhouse not far from Southmead Cottage. The magistrate had spoken to the Johnson girls, and they'd confirmed he'd been there and left quite intoxicated. The next day he'd been found dead.

Lady Longstowe was most definitely not a suspect. Nor were the Johnson girls. Nor was anyone as The Idiot could, and obviously did, manage to get himself killed all on his own.

And though Phin had all of this information at his disposal, there was one fact of which he was not certain. Had his brother gone to bed with Lady Longstowe?

It didn't matter. It was irrelevant. Yet still, he'd wanted to know.

And now he knew.

Or did he?

Before he could pour more brandy, the carriage stopped, and he descended again to enter his solicitor's establishment. It was a tidy building on Gresham Street, an area of the city known for housing financial establishments. It was late, but Phineas had been solicitous of his man's time and sent a note earlier in the day informing the man he was coming. It was more than he'd done with lady Longstowe.

A clerk greeted Phin as soon as he entered and showed him to the office of Mr. Clarence Moggerton. When Moggerton stood and shuffled around his desk to shake Phin's hand, the duke had a moment to reflect that Clarence Moggerton, unlike Lady Longstowe, was exactly what he'd expected. Moggerton appeared ageless with his white hair, his rheumy eyes, his large spectacles, and his black clothing. His hand, when Phin shook it, felt frail, the skin papery. "Good evening, Your Grace." Moggerton spoke as though with some effort, his voice sounding like he had not used it in the last decade.

"Good evening." Phin removed his hat and took the seat Moggerton offered.

"May I congratulate you on your elevation to the title of duke?" Moggerton said.

"No, you may not," Phineas answered, making Moggerton's eyes widen behind the spectacles. "I want no congratulations or condolences. I'm not here for that."

"Of course, Your Grace." Moggerton lifted a stack of ledgers, the weight of which seemed more than he could manage. He slid them across his desk so they resided in front of Phineas. "Here are the estate accounts from the last three years, as requested. I have placed Southmead on top and then the other estates underneath in descending order of size. Would you like some tea or perhaps something stronger before we begin?"

Phineas stared at the ledgers. He had asked Moggerton to give him a full accounting of the dukedom. He wanted to know what debts he owed, what his holdings were, which were profitable and which were not. Moreover, he wanted to know how badly Richard and George had depleted the family coffers. He'd always received his allowance on time, and neither his mother nor unmarried sister complained at not receiving theirs, but that did not mean he was a wealthy man. Peers often mortgaged property or lived on credit to afford the appearance of having more blunt than they knew what to do with.

"No refreshments for me, Mr. Moggerton. Begin."

Moggerton went about his task with alacrity, and Phin tried to listen, he really did. When he heard nothing to alarm him and more to reassure him, his thoughts wandered. They wandered right back to Lady Longstowe. What was it about her that made him want her so desperately? Even when he'd known she was playing the role of temptress, he couldn't seem to tamp down his arousal. He'd liked that she put her hand on his waistcoat. He'd wanted her to touch him all over, to touch his bare skin. He'd wanted to touch her.

Clearly, she was disgusted by him. But why should she be disgusted by him and enthralled by Richard? Unless she hadn't slept with Richard? Had he merely assumed because she was called the Wanton Widow, she offered her favors to every man?

"Mr. Moggerton," Phineas said, interrupting Moggerton's droning on about the prices of wheat. "What do you know about Lady Longstowe?

Moggerton looked up from the documents before him, his eyes magnified by the spectacles he wore. "I beg your pardon, Your Grace."

"Lady Longstowe. What do you know about her?"

"I have never heard of the woman, Your Grace." Moggerton took a piece of foolscap and dipped his pen in ink. "What would you like to know?"

Phineas stared at the pen suspended above the paper. What did he want to know? Everything, truth be told. But hadn't he already invaded the woman's privacy enough? What kind of man continued to investigate a woman who had made it clear she disdained him? Phin had never wanted to be the Duke of Mayne, and now that he was he would not abuse the title by sending his lackeys to spy on an innocent woman.

Phin sighed. Richard had always called him Perfect Phineas. It was difficult being so perfect all the time. "On second thought, Moggerton, I don't want to know about the lady."

Moggerton, obviously used to the vacillations of the upper classes, merely set his pen down and waited patiently for further instructions. "Certainly, Your Grace."

"Indeed, I would like to hear more about that estate in— er, the country. Do enlighten me further."

"Of course, Your Grace." Moggerton shifted to look at his stack of documents again. "The estate yielded quite a supply of corn and wheat, but the barley harvest was not what it once was…"

Phin looked down at his waistcoat—the garment the Wanton Widow had touched—and resigned himself to never seeing her again.

Three

"Why on earth would you call on him?" Lady Buntlebury asked the next day. After a sleepless night Annabel, Lady Longstowe, had called on her friend and related the story of the visit of the Duke of Mayne, then told her friend the idea that had kept her awake most of the night. "He is a pompous ass—a handsome pompous ass, but you and I know appearances can be deceiving."

As if to punctuate this point, the sound of raucous male laughter rose from the dining room below where Mary said her husband and his friends had been playing cards for the last eighteen hours. Lord Buntlebury had been handsome when he was younger. Mary had fallen head over heels in love with him. But he'd turned out to be interested in little other than cards and drink, and Mary was glad to stay in Town where she could spend as little time with her husband as possible.

"I am not deceived by his appearance," Annabel said. "I know exactly why he called on me yesterday."

The duke might have told himself he had questions about his brother, but the way he'd looked at her was unmistakable. She knew lust when she saw it.

"Did he really think you had something to do with his brother's death?"

Annabel offered a delicate shrug. "No, but he did believe I took his brother to my bed."

"That lout!" Lady Buntlebury set her tea cup down with enough indignation to cause it to rattle. "Why would you want such a man?"

"Because I'm the Wanton Widow."

Mary sighed. "That old scandal? I doubt anyone even remembers how it began."

Annabel agreed. She'd made mistakes when she'd been young and newly widowed, and though no one might remember what exactly she had done, her reputation would never recover. She knew men called her the Wanton Widow. She didn't care—unless they came to her door, sat in her drawing room, and threw it in her face.

The new Duke of Mayne had surprised her with his visit. She had, of course, read of the death of his brother and been saddened, but not surprised, by the news. The family was probably better off with that member of the family out of the way. She didn't know the new duke, but he couldn't have been any worse than his brother, who'd stepped on her toes and leered at her bosom while dancing with her at the Houghton's ball.

Except she realized she did know the new Duke of Mayne.

As soon as Annabel had walked into her drawing room, she realized she knew the ninth Duke of Mayne by sight. He'd been at the Houghton ball, and she'd locked eyes with him. He was a handsome man, with his honey colored hair and green eyes. He was slim and fit and had an easy smile. She imagined all the ladies were in love with him. She herself had admired him, but in the way one admires an actor on stage or the husband of a friend. He was not for her. He was a young man, barely thirty if she had to guess, and she would be fifty in a few years.

He was not for her.

And then he was in her drawing room, and he made her so angry that she wanted to shock him. She'd shocked him—at least she thought she had—but she'd shocked herself too because she'd almost wanted to take the little act she played further. She'd been tempted to kiss his full, soft lips and reach between his legs to feel the hard outline of his erection.

He might have told himself he came for answers about his brother, but he wanted a closer look at the Wanton

Widow. Perhaps he even wanted her to show him just how wanton she could be. But Annabel had no interest in tutoring boys in the art of bedsport.

"I assume you sent the impudent boy away with a scolding." Mary lifted her tea cup again.

Annabel sipped her tea. "Something like that."

"Then I don't understand why you think he will help you."

"I don't know if he will, but it's not as though I know any other dukes. I need a man with some power and weight behind his name to get the answers I've been seeking all these years."

And that was the idea that had awakened her in the middle of the night. The Duke of Mayne might be able to help her. Since the earl had died, she had made a point of never asking any man for help. But now she had run out of options. Her stomach tightened at the idea of putting herself at a man's mercy, especially a powerful man like a duke. But what other choice did she have? And if she did not, what would become of Theadosia? What *had* become of Theadosia?

Mary ran a hand over the soft fur of the little pug asleep on the settee beside her. The dog snorted and went back to sleep. "He will want some form of payment," Mary said, her eyes on the dog.

Annabel had thought of this as well. She knew how the world worked and what men wanted from a woman. "I imagine he will."

"And you're prepared to give that to him?"

Annabel's chest tightened. She did not want to offer herself to him as payment for his help, but she had nothing else to persuade him. He didn't need her money or her title. "It's not as though I'm a virgin or I haven't done whatever he might ask before."

"Yes, but you said—"

Annabel raised a hand. "I know what I said, but I don't see another way." She gave her friend a faint smile. "And as you said, at least he is handsome." Though that really did not matter. She had said she would never lay with a man she did not want again. She'd spent years in a marriage where her body had not been her own. She never wanted to give up control of it again. But she could bear it for Theadosia.

"When will you go?" Mary asked.

"This afternoon."

Mary rose and went to her friend, clasping Annabel's hand. "You don't have to do this."

"I have to do something," Annabel whispered. "I can't let her think I've abandoned her. What if she is suffering? What if the place where she lives is horrible?"

Mary squeezed her hand. "You're right, of course. Send for me if you need me tonight." She cleared her throat. "After."

"You don't have plans?"

Mary rolled her eyes. "I can cancel them. Buntlebury will no doubt be sleeping off the excesses of last night and today. Send for me if you need me."

***

Annabel wore a gown the color of sunset. Red was far too obvious a choice for seduction and black would only highlight how much older she was than the duke or make him think of mourning. The bright orange with tulle at the shoulder and hem was striking but not gaudy. The bosom was round but showed only a hint of décolletage. The skirt was slightly fuller than the current style, but then Annabel had come of age when fuller skirts were fashionable, and she still preferred them.

As she stepped out of her carriage and released her footman's gloved hand, she looked up at the imposing edifice of Mayne House, the town house of the Duncombe family. She was not expected and as far as she knew, neither of the duke's sisters were in residence. Propriety dictated that she should not be alone with a man not her husband or close relative. Her breach of propriety would not be lost on Mayne.

She was counting on that.

As she started for the front door, she touched her head to adjust her hat then realized it was evening and she hadn't worn a hat. Her auburn hair was secured loosely at the back of her head in a sophisticated chignon. She could release it by pulling just a few pins free. She didn't know why she should be so nervous. It wasn't as though she was some young, ingenue walking into the lion's den. She knew exactly what she was doing and why.

And she didn't have to go through with it. She was not desperate, though it did feel like the duke might be her only hope. No one who had been willing to help her these last twenty years had possessed enough clout and authority. The few she encountered who did have those qualities had not been interested in her plight.

But her knees shook and her heart thudded and her hands in her gloves felt moist. She was thankful she had not eaten, for she would surely cast up her accounts if she had anything in her belly. Taking a deep breath, Annabel knocked on the door then lowered her hands and smoothed her pelisse over her skirts. The pelisse was white, and she thought it an amusing contrast to her scarlet reputation.

The door opened and a man who must be the butler—he looked exactly as a butler should—stared at her. "May I help you…" He paused for just a moment. "My lady?"

"Lady Longstowe to call on His Grace." She held out her card. Her hand shook almost as much as her voice.

The butler produced a silver tray, and she laid the card on it as though it were a sacrifice.

"The duke is not at home to callers," the butler said. "But I will give him your card, my lady." How proper he was. He did not even admit her, thus preserving respectability.

"The duke will be home to me," Annabel said. "May I wait inside while you inform him I am here?"

The butler looked down at the card and then back at her. Annabel looked him directly in the eye. Oh, yes, she knew what she was about and what she was asking. Bile rose in her throat, but she swallowed it and her fears. She had to be strong. She had to do this.

"Of course. Do come in." The butler held the door wide then closed it behind her. "Please wait here."

Still carrying the tray, he ascended the wide marble stairs. As she watched, a maid hurried toward her, took her coat, and offered her a seat in a comfortable chair far enough away from the door so she would not feel a draft. Her legs appreciated the respite. They felt as weak as a new foal's.

The vestibule was enormous. She'd expected no less from a house in Grosvenor Square. It was easily the size of her drawing room and built of so much marble she imagined it had taken an entire quarry to equip it. There were marble columns, marble busts, a marble floor, and of course, those marble steps. Above her, everything was lit by a crystal chandelier. It was barely evening, and most households would have tried to cut expenses by waiting until almost dark before lighting the thirty or so candles in the chandelier. Apparently, the duke was not concerned with expenses because it burned brightly even as the last rays of the sun disappeared behind the taller buildings of London.

Annabel had just begun to study the paintings in the vestibule when the butler descended the steps again. He gave her a short bow. "His Grace will see you."

That hadn't taken long.

She rose and followed the butler back up the steps, lifting her skirts so she would not tread on them. She expected to be shown into the drawing room; instead, the butler opened a door that entered into a dark-paneled room with a billiard table and two card tables.

The Duke of Mayne was seated at one of the tables.

He rose when she entered, and her breath hitched. Her heart had been beating rapidly since she'd set foot in her carriage, but now it began to gallop. He was taller than she remembered. She was as tall as many men, but he was at least six feet and perhaps an inch taller. And he was lean but not skinny. Beneath his clothes, she imagined he was fit and muscled. He could easily overpower her.

But putting fear aside, if that was possible, it was impossible to deny that the duke was exceptionally handsome. She liked his honey-colored blond hair and his crooked smile. The room was lit by only a few candles, and the shadows seemed to lend him an air of danger she hadn't sensed when she'd seen him before. Then he'd been like an adorable puppy. Now he seemed more formidable, more powerful. She made an effort to stand still and not turn and run.

"Thank you, Banks. That will be all."

The butler closed the door, leaving them alone. Annabel felt she should cross the room and offer her hand, but she did not move. Or perhaps she could not move.

"I didn't expect to see you," the duke said, his eyes never leaving her face. He had beautiful eyes, the color of emeralds. Green was her favorite color, and those eyes were the perfect shade. "I am glad you've come. May I offer you refreshment?"

"Thank you," she said. Now that the time had come to tell him her story, ask for his help, she wasn't sure where or how to begin. She had told so few people this tale. It was very personal. "Tea would be lovely."

How stupid she sounded! *Tea would be lovely.* As though this was a garden party. She didn't want tea. She wanted this over with.

He started toward a bell pull. "I'll ring for the tea tray."

"Please, don't bother! I don't really want tea."

He paused and looked at her as though she had gone a bit mad. He was not wrong. But she went on because there was no turning back now. "I won't drink it and it will grow cold, and besides I'd rather not be interrupted."

He paused, his gaze returning to her face. He'd been very careful not to look below her face. "You wish for privacy?"

"I do."

"Do sit down then." He indicated a chair at one of the card tables.

"I'd rather stand."

"Very well." He clasped his hands behind his back. "I am ready. Go ahead with your tirade." He straightened his shoulders and seemed to steel himself.

"My tirade? You think I came to deliver a tirade?"

"Why else? My behavior yesterday was inexcusable. You have every right to berate me."

"I didn't come to berate you." Despite her assertion that she wanted to stand, she sank into a chair at the table.

"Why not? I deserve it. I was impudent and pompous and behaved like an arse—forgive the language." He ran a hand through his hair, which was rather long for a duke, and it flopped right back into disarray.

"Don't you think you are being a little hard on yourself?" She couldn't help but smile. She did not know him well enough to know whether he spoke in jest or seriousness, but he had certainly put her at ease with his dramatics.

"Oh, not nearly hard enough, I'm afraid. I imagine you have some harsh words for me or perhaps some names?" He looked almost hopeful.

"What would you suggest?" she asked.

"Scoundrel?" he offered.

"Surely, you aren't that bad."

"You're right." He scratched his chin. "Lout?" He raised a brow. "Too mild?"

"Actually, I think you behaved as one would expect considering your title. You came in making demands and assumptions and were annoyed when you did not get your way." It was a description she felt would fit most men.

He sat in the chair across from her. "You are calling me a duke then?"

"Yes."

He closed his eyes and pressed his hand to his chest. "It hurts, but the wound is not mortal. Do you want to add an adjective? Arrogant, perhaps?"

"No. In fact, while I appreciate your apology—I assume this is your way of apologizing—that isn't why I came."

"No?" He looked genuinely surprised. "Then why have you come?"

"I wanted to ask you for a favor."

His brow furrowed in confusion. "Really? I suppose I owe you that much at least, after the way I treated you. I am sorry, by the way. I forgot that part."

Oh, she wanted to like him. That made him dangerous. But he would soon enough show her he was like every other man. Then she could despise him, grit her teeth, and suffer through what was to come.

"Your Grace, there's no need to continue apologizing. I didn't expect an apology, and I don't feel as though you owe me anything. You were not wholly incorrect in your assumption that I am a wanton widow—that is my sobriquet, is it not?"

"I wouldn't know." He blinked innocently.

"You lie very prettily, but I am well aware I have a sordid past and that people—men—like to discuss it. No doubt that was why your brother showed an interest of me at the Houghton ball. He wanted an easy—"

The duke rose unexpectedly. "I need a drink. Would you like a drink?"

Oh, yes. "Do you have anything stronger than tea?"

He went to a cart pushed against a wall and lifted a crystal decanter. "Brandy. Yes?"

"Yes."

As she watched, he poured two glasses, filling them to the rim. A novel idea occurred to her. "Do I make you nervous, Your Grace?"

"I don't know that 'nervous' is the correct term." He set her brandy before her and took a long sip of his own.

"What is the correct term?"

"I'd rather not say as it might result in my having to apologize again."

That was interesting, interesting enough she forgot her own nervousness for a moment. Did she arouse him? Horrify him? Disgust him?

"Putting all talk of your brother and our previous encounter aside—"

"Thank God," he muttered.

"As I said, I have a favor to ask you."

He sipped his brandy again. "Whatever you need, my lady."

"You should hear it before you agree, Your Grace." Now she sipped her own brandy, desperate for the fortification.

He held up a finger. "If you're to ask for favors, Lady Longstowe, and I am to agree to them"—he waved a hand—"yes, I know, after I have heard them. Might we dispense with all the *your graces* and *my ladys*? I do grow tired of peppering my speech with them, and I worry if I've used the honorific too much or not enough and then worry whether I should throw one in or stop throwing them in—"

"I think I understand, Your Grace—er, Duke. Or what would you have me call you?"

"I'm not suggesting we use Christian names."

He looked so proper in that moment that she stifled a smile. "No, of course not."

"But would you be comfortable calling me Mayne?"

"Yes. And do you wish to call me Longstowe then?"

He seemed to ponder this. "That's a bit of a mouthful. How do you feel about Long or would you prefer Stowe? Or Countess?"

"Long is fine."

"Good. So then, Long, you have a favor to ask of me?"

"Yes." She took another sip of her brandy, aware he was watching her and probably noting that her hand shook. "I can't properly ask for the favor without telling you why I ask. You see, I have a secret."

His green eyes glittered. "We all have secrets."

"Not like this one, Mayne. I have a child no one knows about."

"An illegitimate child," he said with a nod.

"No, she is the late earl's child and born within the bonds of marriage."

He leaned forward. "Long, I don't mean to criticize, but secrets are usually rather salacious tidbits. I don't think your so-called secret qualifies."

She sighed. "You haven't much patience, have you?"

"Oh, it gets better then?"

She laughed. She couldn't remember when she had smiled or laughed quite this much. He was really quite adorable, or perhaps that was simply a mask he wore to put her at ease. She imagined he would not be so adorable when she told him the rest of the tale. "There is more. We did not tell anyone about the child when she was born. Her name is Theadosia, by the way. She is named after my mother. We didn't tell anyone because the child was born with obvious…differences."

To his credit, he did not interrupt.

"Her face did not look as it should." She would not use the word *deformed*. That was the word the doctor had used. She would not repeat it. "And the doctor said her brain was damaged, and she would not develop as other children."

"I'm sorry," the duke said simply.

She nodded, grateful she did not feel the prick of tears. She could speak of this now without weeping. "The earl sent the two of us away to the country, and I cared for her. She was a sweet baby, though even after a year and a half she had not learned to crawl. The doctor had been right that she was slower to develop. It did not matter to me, of course. She was my child. I loved her. But the earl made arrangements for her to be cared for by hired servants. She was sent away at only two years of age."

She pushed away the anguish that the memory of walking into the nursery and finding it empty conjured in her.

He hadn't asked her, hadn't even told her until the deed was done. And when she'd wept and pleaded and begged on her knees to go with her daughter or at least have the opportunity to say goodbye, he'd coldly told her they would return to Town and she was to speak no more of Theadosia. He'd told everyone the girl had died.

"I was never able to learn any more about Theadosia while he lived," she said, still dry eyed and voice steady. The brandy helped, but she would need much more tonight if she was to sleep. This retelling had brought up too many memories. "But after he died I was able to discover that she had been sent to a hospital of sorts. A place for those who have gone mad or who cannot care for themselves. She would have been six or seven then."

"How did you learn this?" Mayne asked.

"The earl's solicitor told me. He wouldn't give me the name of the place or any further information, just that she was well cared for and money had been set aside to ensure her care for the rest of her life. Of course, I tried everything I could to find her. I went to everyone who might have any information, even the smallest tidbit. I have never given up."

"I see. How long ago was this?"

"The earl has been dead sixteen years."

"And how old is the child now?"

"She would be twenty."

He stared at her then drank the rest of his brandy.

She looked down at the table, ran a hand over the green baize covering it. "As I said, I asked others to help me, but though a few have been willing none have been successful. You see, with no heir, the earldom has passed to the earl's grandnephew. He was but one when the earl died, and he is quite under his mother's thumb. If Lady Wavenwell has access to the late earl's papers, she will not tell me or give me any information to help in my search."

"And this is why you need me," the duke said.

"Yes. Lady Wavenwell has no respect for lawyers or doctors and my pleas fall on deaf ears. But she does respect power."

"And you think that if I ask, she will give me what you want."

"I think if the Duke of Mayne demands the information, she will give it. Furthermore, I believe if the Duke of Mayne goes to the hospital and signs the papers for the release of Theadosia, she will be released." She looked at him directly. "It is a lot to ask, and I am willing to offer payment. But that is the favor I request."

Four

Phin sat very still for a long moment. He wanted to argue with Long. He was a skilled negotiator, and he had no doubt he could gather the information she wanted from the Earl of Longstowe's mother. But he had no right to the information and no legal claim on the child—woman, now, it would seem—in the hospital. And while that should make a difference, should make him refuse her offer, he couldn't help but remember that he'd been born the son of a duke. He knew the privilege that carried. He could have almost anything he wanted but for the asking.

Long had said she would offer payment. Perhaps with his title and a bribe, they might just have a chance to—

She stood then and Phin was shaken out of his thoughts. He'd been trying to keep his eyes on her face, but it was difficult not to allow them to dip to the generous swell of her breasts just peeking above the top of her bodice. She was even more beautiful tonight than when he'd seen her at the ball. Her skin was flushed, her lips red, and her eyes so blue it seemed impossible they were real. He liked that she was tall and curvaceous. He had the feeling if he pulled her into his arms, she would be soft and fit him perfectly.

"I have a little money," she said, her voice shaking slightly.

Phin frowned. "I don't need your money." Dash it but he certainly had enough to bribe a doctor at a hospital. He wouldn't ask for hers.

"I didn't think it would appeal to you," she said, sounding resigned. "I hope I can interest you in something else as payment." She reached up and plucked a hairpin out of her hair and then another and then another until her hair fell down about her shoulders in auburn waves. Her hair was glorious. He'd never seen a shade like that. He hadn't realized how much he wanted to see it loose. But what the devil was she doing taking it down?

And what the hell was he supposed to do now? His every instinct was to go to her and touch that hair. He wondered how it would look in his hands, how it would feel against his skin, how it would smell if he buried his nose in it. But he had to pull his thoughts together. One minute they'd been talking about paying the doctors at the hospital. The next she was…undressing?

She'd reached for her bodice and, as she had with her hair a moment before, plucked out a pin.

Phin stood up. He couldn't allow this to go on. Could he? Perhaps just one more pin?

No. No. He had to stop her. Damn it, but he had to behave as a gentleman.

"As much as I like the direction you are taking, Long, I must ask what the hell you are doing."

She looked up at him from under her lashes as her hand moved to remove the next pin.

God, yes. He wanted that pin gone.

"I'm undressing, Mayne."

Thank God. *Take it all off*, he wanted to say. Instead, he said, "I see that. And I cannot believe I am saying this, but do stop."

"Stop?" She frowned at him.

"Don't make me say it again. I don't know if I can manage."

She gave him an uncertain smile. "You don't want me to take my dress off?"

"Of course, I want you to take your dress off." What did she take him for? He very much wanted her to take her dress off. "But I don't want you to disrobe like this."

"You prefer to move to your bed chamber then?"

He had to grip the table at that suggestion. Long in his bed chamber. Naked. Oh, he liked that image.

"You should stop talking," he grit out between his clenched jaw. "You are not helping." Deep breath. Do not think about her bent over the bed. "There's been a mistake," he announced. "Some confusion. I think I missed a step. You asked me for a favor and then started to disrobe. I'm at sixes and sevens here."

She stared at him for a long time, her gaze suspicious. Finally, she said, "I don't believe you. I don't believe you don't understand what's happening."

He hadn't really thought about it. His thoughts had been…elsewhere. He swallowed. "Are you thinking I want…"

She raised her brows at his pause. He would not use some coarse euphemism. That was what she expected. He was a duke, goddamn it.

He cleared his throat. "Do you think I want to take you to bed in exchange for helping you find your daughter?"

"I assumed you would want a favor from me. I don't have to repay you in a bed."

"Oh God." His knees felt weak. He was a duke. He really could have whatever he wanted. He understood perfectly now. He could tell her to disrobe, and she would do it. He could make her get on her knees and…oh, best not to think of that.

He was a duke.

But he did not want to be the sort of duke, the sort of man, who asked a woman to pleasure him in return for helping her find her daughter. He couldn't think of anything viler.

"I do want to take you to bed," he said. She reached for that pin again.

Yes, *please.*

But no. Not that sort of duke. "Just wait! Don't do that." He hated being a duke. He really hated it. "I do want to take you to bed but only if you want me to take you to bed."

"I want you, Mayne," she said in a sultry voice that he remembered from the day before in her drawing room. He wanted to believe her. He tried very hard to believe her, but deep down in the part of himself that would never let him forgive himself if he ignored its whining, he heard a voice that said, *she doesn't mean it.* This was an act. She was playing a role as she had the day before.

"No, you don't." He pointed at her. "You think you have to give me a favor for me to give you a favor, but I don't want your favors."

"You don't?"

"Of course, I do!" He wanted every single favor she had and then some.

Her brows came together in confusion. This was not good. He raked a hand through his hair. "But not like this. You don't have to do anything. I will help you find your daughter. In fact, if you continue taking off your clothing, I will *not* help you. I'll only help you if you understand I expect nothing in return." There. That had been the right thing to say. Now, he wanted a knife so he might stab himself through the eye. It would be less painful than denying himself the view of her breasts. This was the last time he behaved himself.

"You want nothing?" She raised her brows.

"Fine. You may write me a note of thanks."

"A note."

"On vellum," he specified.

"That's all?"

"That's all I can think of at the moment. I'm distracted." He gestured to her loose hair and her bodice with its one missing pin.

She looked down at her bodice, where his eyes had strayed, and while he looked away, she presumably replaced the pin. When he looked back at her, she had pulled her hair back and was presentable again.

"I don't know what to say. Thank you."

He curled his lip. Now she was thanking him. She was grateful. He was a disgusting toad for still wishing he could toss her skirts up. "Do not thank me. You have no idea the lascivious thoughts swirling about in my mind right now." She put a hand over her mouth, ostensibly to hide a smile.

"I'll limit my appreciation to written form."

"Good. Now, let us return to the matter at hand. Your daughter."

She took a deep breath and squared her shoulders. It was obviously not a topic she enjoyed discussing. After the events of the last few moments, Phin wasn't entirely comfortable himself. He needed a long swim in a freezing cold pond. "First, I believe we need more brandy."

"I still have most of mine." She gestured to her glass, which looked as though it had barely been touched.

"I need more brandy," he said, lifting the decanter. Then he reconsidered. "Actually, if I'm truthful, I'm famished. It's dreadfully gauche, but I've become used to country hours and early dinners. Would you be averse to joining me?"

Her lovely blue eyes widened. "I don't think that's proper."

"It's a good deal more proper than you and I fornicating on the floor." Her lips turned up in amusement. "Besides how can a man be expected to concentrate on anything with an empty belly? We'll eat and you can tell me all about...what is the name of the chit I must intimidate?"

"Lady Wavenwell, and I assure you she's no mere chit."

Phineas was unconcerned. He had been known as the Negotiator when he was part of Draven's Dozen, the suicide troop charged with defeating Napoleon at any cost. He and the other eleven men of the troop who had come home from the Continent alive called themselves the Survivors. Phin had no doubt they would have lost more than eighteen if he hadn't negotiated their way out of several risky situations.

He could handle Lady Wavenwell.

He pulled the bell for a servant then walked to the billiard table. "Do you play?" he asked.

"It's not considered a game for women," she answered.

"That was not my question. Do you play?"

"From time to time, but I don't remember the rules very well."

He shrugged and lifted a cue. "I never liked the rules anyway. I made up my own game, and the rules are simple. Shall we play?"

"If you like."

He collected three red balls and a white and placed them in the middle of the table in a diamond shape with the white ball at the head. A servant tapped on the door and entered. "Would you like tea, Your Grace?" Banks asked, anticipating his request. That would have been the more reasonable request. Long was correct that their dining alone together was not wholly proper. But what use was being a duke if one could not do as one liked?

"No, Banks." Phin crouched to examine the angle of the white ball. "I'd like dinner. Something simple as I'm sure Cook wasn't expecting to have to serve this early. Oh, and set the table for two. Lady Longstowe will be joining me."

"I see." The butler stood in the doorway. Phin looked away from the shot he contemplated.

"Was there something else?"

"No, Your Grace. I'll inform Cook." The door closed and Phin looked back at the table.

"I told you this was improper. The silent disapproval emanating from your butler was deafening."

Phin beckoned to Long. "Don't worry about Banks. He's like his name—a veritable institution. We can rely on his discretion, not that either of us need it. I am unmarried, and you are a widow. If the *ton* discovers we dined together, it will be no great scandal."

"It won't help my reputation either."

"If you prefer, I will take you for a ride in the park tomorrow, and you can tell me all about Lady Waddlesworth then."

"It's Lady Wavenwell, and I'd rather not ride about Hyde Park in a carriage in this cold. I will stay for dinner." She sipped her brandy.

"Excellent. Then let us play the game while we wait for Cook." He gestured to her again, and this time to she moved to stand beside him. "You are the guest, and I think it only polite you are allowed to break."

She nodded. "I hit that white ball against the others and scatter them."

"Correct."

"And then?"

Now that she was close to him, he could smell her light perfume. It was something sensual and musky. Perhaps he could help her hold the cue and better identify the tantalizing scent. "And then it is my turn. You give me the cue and tell me which ball I must sink, using the white ball of course."

She gave him a patient look. "And I suppose if you sink it, I must remove an article of clothing."

He gave her an impassive look even while his heart kicked at the thought. "I have never met a woman so eager to take off her clothes or one who would force me to keep telling her to keep them on."

She laughed. "I do apologize, Mayne."

"Good. There is no disrobing in billiards." Not in this game, at any rate. Now that she'd mentioned it, he rather liked the idea. "If I sink the ball, it is your turn. I tell you which ball you must sink. If I miss the shot, then you are allowed to ask me one question, and I must answer it."

She raised a brow. "Any question?"

"Any question. What do you think?"

She took the cue stick and leaned over the table, positioning it for a test shot. "I think that despite your protestations at my attempts to disrobe, you are a very naughty boy."

"I'm hardly a boy."

"We'll see." She bent over the stick.

"Would you like me to show you how to hit the ball?" He could already imagine fitting his body to hers, feeling her bottom press against his thighs.

"No."

So much for that fantasy. He stepped back and attempted not to stare at her round bottom.

"How do we determine who wins this game?" she asked.

"Good question. I suppose the winner is the player who sinks the most balls."

She straightened and looked at him over her shoulder. "I thought you had invented this game."

"I did. Just now."

"Just now? Here? With me?"

"Exactly. Do you think I want to play with the men at my club? I would fall half asleep at the sort of answers they might give to my questions."

"If you have questions to ask me, why not just ask?"

He looked heavenward. As though he had not thought of that. "Because you won't answer them. This way, you must."

"And you must answer my questions."

He wiggled his brows. "That's the fun. Now, will you break?"

She turned back to the table and lowered the stick. He expected her to hit the white ball lightly and barely break up the diamond. But she made a solid attempt, and the balls scattered nicely.

"Well done," he said and held out his hand. She gave him the stick. "I am at your command, madam."

She studied the table, clearly looking for the most difficult shot. She pointed to a red ball. "That ball in that corner pocket."

"That's a challenge." He moved around the table, studying the shot, then finally leaned down to position the stick. Long moved behind him, and he had the distinct impression she was looking at his form, not the shot. He glanced at her over his shoulder, but her eyes were on the table. Just his luck to want a woman who didn't want him back.

He drew back, hit the white ball, and sank the red ball she'd indicated.

"Good show," she said.

"Thank you." He handed her the stick. Now he had a decision to make. Be a gentleman and give her an easy shot or satisfy his curiosity and give her a difficult shot, so he could ask her one of the dozens of questions swirling about in his mind. Phin gave her an easy shot. No need to appear too eager.

Long gave him a patronizing look. She obviously understood what he was about. She sank the shot easily and handed him the stick then gave him a nearly impossible shot.

So they were to play that way, were they? He would not be so easy on her when it was her turn again.

Phin studied the shot for longer than he might have if his pride weren't at stake, then finally took it.

And missed. The chosen ball hit the side of the table and rolled back and away from the pocket. "Damn," he muttered. Then he looked at her, not attempting to conceal his curiosity. "You have a question for me?"

Without hesitation, she asked, "How old are you?"

Phin was slightly taken aback. He'd thought she would ask him something salacious. Why did she care about his age? That was no secret.

"Thirty-two."

She winced.

"That bad?" he asked.

"It's not as bad as it might have been. I had thought you closer to twenty-eight."

"Why does it matter?"

She took an indignant breath. "Your Grace, you made up the rules for this game. One would think you would follow them."

He laughed. "You're right. Strike the question. Your turn." He handed her the stick, but she didn't take it.

"You missed. You have to play until you sink the ball."

"That wasn't one of the rules."

"It wasn't *not* one of the rules."

He glared at her. "You cannot simply make up rules as we go along."

"I am merely clarifying a vague rule. Now will you continue to argue or take the next shot?"

Oh, he would take the next shot. And he would sink it too. And then he'd give her a question to rival all questions.

"That ball into the side pocket," she said.

Of course, it was the shot he would have given her. Phin pushed his anger away and narrowed his focus. He studied the balls and moved around the table to take up position. She was in his way. "Excuse me, Long. I'd hate to graze you with my stick."

"I'm sure you would." But she moved away.

Phin took his time and by the time he was ready, she had moved across the table from him. He ignored her, but just as he moved his arm to strike, she lifted a hand to toy with her bodice.

He missed the shot. God *damn* it! He glowered at her, but for the life of him, he couldn't tell if she'd done it on purpose or not.

"Another question then." She tapped her chin thoughtfully. "I can ask anything?"

"Anything." This ought to be interesting.

"What did you do in the war?" His face must have fallen because she looked concerned. "You said anything."

"I just didn't think you were one of those who wanted to hear tales from so-called war heroes." He'd known many women and men like that. They'd all invited him to dine when he'd first returned. They wanted stories of bravery and heroics and the numbers of all the French he'd killed. Phin didn't have those stories. He only had tales of losing friends and his own failings when a mission did not succeed.

"Not that I need explain myself," she said, "but I ask because I heard Draven's troop was highly skilled. I hope you might have a talent useful to helping me find my daughter."

And once again Phin felt like a toad. All he could think to ask were questions about her favorite sexual positions. Here she was asking him questions whose answers obviously meant something to her.

"My skill is in negotiations," he said. "I'm an expert in persuading people to tell me information or give me items they wouldn't necessarily want to part with. If you need a duke who can help you ferret out information from Waddlesworth, you probably could not have chosen better."

She gave him a faint smile then held out her hand for the stick. He frowned. "I thought I had to keep playing until I sank the ball."

"Change of rules. After two missed shots, play reverts to the other player."

Phin narrowed his eyes. "I don't agree to that rule. I'd rather make the shot."

"Suit yourself." She turned to look at the table.

"And don't give me an easy shot, either."

"I wouldn't dream of it. That ball in that side pocket."

Bloody hell. She hadn't given him an easy shot. He made his way around the table, but this time when she stood across from him, he kept his gaze focused on the ball. No one could say he was not a man of self-control.

The sound of the ball thudding into the pocket was like that of church bells at the end of a long sermon. He smiled and handed her the stick. She took it and waited for his direction. There was only one red ball left on the table, but he could direct where she had to sink it. Phin knew the shot he would give her. He'd been afraid she would notice it and give it to him. "Sink the ball in that pocket," he said.

She smiled. "I see you've decided to take me seriously." She moved past him, studying the shot. That heady mix of musk made his head turn to follow her. "And if I fail, what will you ask me? Whether I took your brother to bed?" She flicked a gaze at him then bent over the table. Phin tried not to notice the hint of her cleavage now visible. "No, that's too obvious," she said. "Perhaps how many lovers I've taken or my favorite position."

She glanced up at him and Phin made sure he was studying the table. "There's one way to find out."

"Yes."

He didn't know if she could make the shot. She had more skill than he'd anticipated, but he hadn't really challenged her either. She pulled back and hit the white ball. It sailed toward the final red ball but was too far to the right and barely knocked it. Phin had triumphed.

"Well?" she asked, straightening. "What do you want to know?" She wore a look that said she expected a salacious question. Phin almost wanted to ask one just to prove her right.

Instead, he said, "What is your Christian name?"

Five

"Annabel," she replied. His question wasn't what she'd been expecting. The color that had risen to his cheeks when she'd speculated as to what he might ask had been proof enough that he was wondering those very things. But he hadn't asked her. Instead, she felt as though he'd asked something even more personal.

He wanted her name. The name only her immediate family and close friends ever used. She'd told him, but that didn't give him license to use it. She couldn't help but wonder why she wished he would.

"Thank you," he said, not using her name. He pointed to the table. "I think I should give you the same shot."

She almost groaned. Her poor attempt a few moments before had left the red ball in an even more unfavorable position and made the shot more challenging. Her first obstacle was where to stand. The best angle was on the other side of the table, and though she was tall for a woman, she wasn't quite tall enough to hold the stick steady for such a reach.

She had little choice but to lean far over the table in what she was certain was a rather unladylike pose. Her bottom was sticking straight in the air, but a glance at Mayne showed he was intent upon the balls, not her. At least, he was making a good show of focusing on the table. She positioned the cue, shifted, and took the shot.

To her pleasure, the stick hit the white ball. Unfortunately, the white did not hit the red. She closed her eyes. She would have to answer another question, and she had no doubt this one would not be something so benign as her name.

She straightened and looked at Mayne expectantly. But the door opened, and she was saved by the appearance of the butler.

"Dinner is served, Your Grace."

Mayne moved around the table, plucked the stick from Annabel's hand, then after laying it on the billiard table, offered his arm. "Shall we, Long?"

"Of course." She looked up at him, pleased she did not have to crane her neck or look down. "What about your question?"

He shrugged. "I'll ask it some other time."

She frowned. "I'd rather you ask it now."

"I'm sure you would." He led her down to the dining room, which was set for two. The staff had placed her on his right, so conversation would be easy. She almost wished for a more formal arrangement, where she would be seated at the opposite end of the table. The duke waited until she was seated then took his own chair and flicked a hand for the service to begin. A footman poured wine and brought soup.

Annabel tasted the wine, and finding it very good, drank more. She'd already drank almost a full glass of brandy upstairs, and she knew she should eat the soup, but she'd been so nervous about what she had expected to happen that her belly was still tied in knots.

"So Wagglesworth," Mayne said after tasting his soup and nodding his approval at the footman, who went to stand against a wall. "Where can we find the good lady?"

Annabel looked at him a bit too long. He was so pleasing to look upon. She had the urge to smooth his hair away from his face. "At this time of year, I am sure Lady *Wavenwell* is at Ceald House, the Longstowe estate. She only comes to Town for the Season."

"And where is this estate?"

"Wiltshire."

"That's not as bad as I feared."

She dipped her spoon in the soup, more to give the appearance of eating than anything else. It smelled quite good. She could see chunks of vegetables floating in it, and she was always hungry for vegetables in the winter. "What do you mean?"

"We can be there in two days' time."

She dropped her spoon. "We?"

He eyed the spoon. "You don't care for the soup?"

"I don't care for your idea. I am not traveling to Wiltshire with you."

He leaned back in his chair and fixed those green eyes on her. She had to force herself not to look away. He really did have lovely eyes, and she could see herself acting like a schoolgirl and staring adoringly into them.

"Then I cannot help you," he said simply.

"You said you would," she argued now sounding like a schoolgirl as well. "You said you were a skilled negotiator. You never said I must travel anywhere with you."

"Then you expect me to walk up to the door of Castle Longstowe—"

"It's Ceald House."

"Fine. I am to knock on the door of Ceald House, introduce myself to Lady Wavenwell, and ask her for all the papers of her husband's late uncle."

Now Annabel sat back as well. "You do know her name."

Mayne stared at her for a long moment then began to laugh. He motioned with his hand and the footman moved to clear the soup away. As soon as they were alone, he leaned forward. "I want to help you, Annabel, but I need you with me."

She leaned forward so their foreheads were only a couple inches apart. "I didn't give you leave to use my Christian name."

"No, you didn't. Mine is Phineas, but my friends call me Phin. Now, will you come with me or no?"

How could she say no when he was all but mesmerizing her with those eyes? But how could she say yes? Her reputation would suffer, not that it mattered, but it didn't help. And she had avoided going to bed with him so far, but the chances of that diminished the longer they were together. She would not be able to fend him off once they were alone together in the middle of nowhere. "I don't know."

"We can leave tomorrow."

"Tomorrow?"

The door opened to admit the footman, and Annabel sat back, putting distance between Mayne and herself. He merely smiled and raised his brows as the footman placed the second course before them.

The reprieve from the duke's closeness gave Annabel a moment to gather her wits. "I do see your point and the necessity of traveling with you, but tomorrow is too soon to leave."

"I dare not wait much longer. My sister's husband John Clare has threatened to come to visit me in London, and I'd like to avoid him, if possible. He's sure to point out everything I do that I should not be doing as duke."

While she could understand the desire to avoid an annoying relative, that didn't change anything. She could not travel with him. "Tomorrow is just not possible."

"Why? Have your lady's maid pack what you need, and I'll collect you in the morning. I suppose you will want to bring your maid with you, and I should probably bring my valet. Perhaps I'll send him on ahead to secure lodgings for the first night."

Annabel speared a potato on her plate, desperate for an excuse now. "You see, that's where my problem lies. I don't have a lady's maid at present. She was given time at Christmas to visit her family, and she wrote saying her mother was ill. Mrs. Slightley has been seeing to my hair and clothing."

"Then bring Mrs. Slightley."

"Then who will manage my household? Crotchett is too old to do it himself."

She jumped when Mayne put his hand over hers. "You're scared," he said. "Anyone would be."

She pulled her hand away and drank more wine. "I'm not scared of traveling with you." Unfortunately, her voice trembled, making her sound unconvincing.

"You're scared to finally see your daughter after so many years." His voice was soft and quiet so it would not carry to the footman, but the words seemed to echo in Annabel's mind. "You worry she will hate you for abandoning her or, worse, remain indifferent. Perhaps she's been just fine without you all these years."

Annabel clutched the stem of the glass so tightly her fingers hurt. How did he know this? Could he see inside her?

"But you'll never know the answers to your questions if you don't take the first step."

He was right. She knew he was right. She'd come here today hoping that Mayne could help her, but she hadn't really considered what would happen if he agreed. What would it be like to see her daughter again? To hold her? Touch her?

Mayne rose and Annabel realized she had stood. "I should return home. It's late."

"Stay. Cook is famous for her desserts."

"I'm not feeling well," she said. It was true. She felt dizzy and too warm. The wine had gone to her head. That must be the problem.

"Then I'll show you out." He took her arm and led her from the dining room, holding up a staying hand when the butler stepped forward. She wasn't certain how she managed to don her pelisse, but a few minutes later, Mayne handed her into her carriage. He didn't close the door. She could feel the freezing air biting at her slipper-clad feet and knew he must be cold standing in the dark without a greatcoat, hat, or gloves.

"I'll remain in Town another day or so. If you make up your mind to come with me, send me word. After a few more days, if you don't need me, my solicitor has several estates he recommends I visit."

She nodded. He was a duke. She couldn't expect him to sit around waiting for her to gather her courage. "I shouldn't have asked for your help," she said. "Of course, you have more important matters to attend to."

"It just so happens one of the estates I need to look in on is in Wiltshire. I should travel there sooner rather than later, though. If you wish to come and introduce me to Lady Wavenwell, just send word. You know where to find me."

He closed the door to the carriage then knocked on the roof. She stared out the window, surprised he stood watching the carriage drive away.

***

Meg Slightley was used to navigating the town house in the dark. She'd been here ten years, and she knew the house better than almost anyone else. Crotchett, that old curmudgeon, might know it a bit better, but it was a near thing.

She'd slipped out of her warm bed only twenty minutes ago and was still yawning. She'd secured her long brown hair in a top knot, dressed in her livery, and stretched her forty-year-old bones until they ceased creaking. Her body wanted to climb back under her cozy blankets, but she had a job to do, and Meg was not one to shirk her duty. It would be dawn soon, and a day of work was ahead of her, but she didn't mind. She enjoyed working for Lady Longstowe. The countess was kind and even-tempered and didn't make ridiculous requests just to watch the servants scamper about doing her bidding.

Recently, Meg had been doing more scampering that she liked as Her Ladyship's maid was away, but Meg realized she actually liked caring for the countess's clothing and styling her hair. She wasn't half bad at it either. Who would have thought that a former circus attraction could run a household and dress a fine lady? How she wished R. L. Putnam, who had owned the traveling circus, could see her now. He'd told her she'd never be anything more than a curiosity. Well, she hadn't believed him then and she knew him as a liar now.

Carrying her basket of materials, Meg paused outside Lady Longstowe's bed chamber door. She set the basket down and opened the door silently. But all of her precautions were for naught. The lady sat on the edge of her bed, looking at something in the lamp light. Meg couldn't be certain, but she thought it might the locket with the picture of her daughter as a toddler. Her Ladyship never spoke of her daughter, but Meg knew this house and she knew all the secrets it held.

No one had told Meg that the Earl of Longstowe had been a sick, twisted man who tyrannized his wife. No one had told her Lady Longstowe had a baby who had disappeared. No one had told her the countess had not shed a tear when her husband had gone to his grave. These were things she'd absorbed over the ten years she'd lived and worked here. They were things everyone knew, but no one spoke of.

A Duke a Dozen | 85

Meg tried to back out of the room before Her Ladyship noticed her, but the countess looked up at her. "Mrs. Slightley."

"Oh, my lady! I didn't know you were awake. I came to light the fire." She lifted her basket in explanation.

"Why are you lighting the fire, Mrs. Slightley? Isn't that beneath your station?"

"Oh, I don't mind, my lady." Meg went to the hearth and began the chore. She hoped Lady Longstowe would allow the matter to pass.

"Meg, you have to stop coddling the house maids. If they don't do as they're bade, you let them go. Or I'll do it for you."

Meg turned from the hearth to give her a pleading look. "Not this time, my lady. Rosie had a bad night. Her man ran off with another, and she took it hard."

Her Ladyship frowned and pulled her knees to her chest. "Which means she drank herself into a stupor and you couldn't rouse her this morning."

Meg worked diligently at her task, neither confirming nor denying her mistress's supposition. Sometimes it was best not to say anything.

"How long have we known each other?" the countess asked.

"Oh, ten years now, my lady."

"And have I ever let anyone go without reason? You've given Rosie too many chances."

Meg sighed. "You're probably right, but I want to give her one more. You gave me a chance when you didn't need to." And Meg would be forever grateful for that chance.

"Is that what you think?" The countess straightened. "That I gave you a chance? I knew the moment I met you, you would make a wonderful housekeeper. Anyone who can manage a troupe of circus performers can manage a few servants."

Meg wiped her sooty hands on her apron. "You know what I mean, my lady."

"Very well. I suppose most countesses would not hire a housekeeper like you."

"An aberration of nature," Meg said as though reciting it by rote.

The countess rolled her eyes. "I did not care how tall or short you were. I cared that you could manage my household, and you do that admirably. Rosie is not doing anything but drinking until her insides are pickled."

"Give her one more day, my lady. If she makes another mistake, I'll push her out the door meself." And she would. Meg could be strict when the situation called for it.

Her Ladyship sighed. "Fine. I certainly know what it's like to have a bad day or a bad week or a bad year."

Meg considered saying more about that. Perhaps her mistress needed someone to confide in. But the countess was looking at the locket again. "Thank you, my lady. Do you want me to help you dress now?"

Her Ladyship looked up, considering. "Actually, I have been up most of the night thinking, and I have made a decision. I want you to help me pack. We're taking a trip."

Meg blinked. This was certainly unusual. She supposed she should act as though nothing ever surprised her, but that simply wasn't her personality. "Where to, if you don't mind me asking?"

"Wiltshire."

Meg made a face that matched her feelings. "Not Ceald House. That woman has no feelings. How many letters have you written her? How many times have you all but begged at her feet?"

"I won't be begging this time."

Meg raised a brow. This was more like it.

"We're not traveling alone. We're traveling with the Duke of Mayne."

Meg could barely contain a little squeak. "The handsome one who called here the other day? Oh, my lady! I wouldn't mind taking a bite of him."

"Meg!"

Meg laughed, not at all ashamed of herself. What was the harm in calling a man handsome if he was? "I knew he'd be good for you as soon as I saw him walk through the door. I said to myself, *That right there is just what my lady needs.* I do hope he apologized—for whatever he said or did."

Her Ladyship narrowed her eyes, and Meg smiled innocently. Of course, she knew every detail of the conversation in her drawing room, but she would never admit to it.

The countess rose. "I need you to pack my valise. While you do that, I'll write the duke a note. Ask one of the footmen to deliver it."

"When do we leave?" Meg asked, excited now.

"As soon as he's ready."

Meg nodded and all but skipped as she went about her work. An adventure!

***

While Meg packed, Annabel took a bath, read, and tried to rest, but she could not manage to settle. She lay on top of her bed, staring at the ceiling. She didn't know what distressed her more about her meeting with the duke—that Mayne had understood her so completely or that in that moment, she'd been tempted to tell him everything, to spill all of her secrets and lies and hidden longings like a river breaking through a dam. No one save Mary, who had been her friend since her debut, understood her. But even Mary had not guessed that behind the desperation to see her daughter again lay fear and guilt.

How could any child forgive a mother who abandoned her? Annabel hadn't done so willingly, and she had certainly paid for every small objection she made, but in the end, the result was the same. She had abandoned her child. Mary would tell her she'd had no other choice, but Annabel knew she could have fought harder.

But by then she had been married to the Earl of Longstowe almost a decade and she was well and truly broken. A part of her had wondered how she could protect a child when she couldn't even protect herself. For years she'd told herself Theadosia was better off where she was, but Annabel hadn't really known that.

And now there was nothing she could do. She couldn't go back and change the past. She'd wished for that more times than she could count. She lifted the locket she still held and stared at the painting of Theadosia as a rosy-cheeked child of eighteen months or so.

Now that she'd made the decision to travel with Mayne and hopefully find Theadosia, Annabel's fear receded. She knew it would be back, but for the moment she could push it aside and concentrate on preparations for departure. Crotchett was displeased, as she'd expected, but Mrs. Slightley reminded him that without his mistress in Town, he'd have very little to do. Annabel told him he could give whichever servants he wished a few days off if that would lighten his load.

A few hours after she'd sent word to Mayne, a knock sounded on the door and she rushed to answer it. Crotchett gave her a look filled with shock, and she sank back behind a wall where Mayne wouldn't be able to see her upon entering the town house. It had to be him. He'd come to collect her right away. She would have preferred a letter to announce he was coming, but she was almost ready to leave. Now that she'd decided to go, she did not want to wait a moment longer.

But instead of Mayne's baritone, she heard the soprano of Lady Buntlebury. There was no need to stand on ceremony now. She stepped out from behind the wall and smiled down at her friend, now being escorted up the stairs at a snail's pace by Crotchett.

"There you are. You were not here when I called yesterday, and I was worried to death."

Annabel felt her cheeks heat. In her agitated state, she had barely paid attention when Crotchett had informed her Lady Buntlebury had called. "I should have sent a note."

Mary smiled. "No need as I am here now, and you can tell me all of the delicious details in person."

Annabel didn't know why she hadn't thought to write or call on Mary herself. Surely it was folly to run off with the Duke of Mayne without telling someone where she was going and with whom.

Annabel led her friend to the drawing room where they talked of trivialities until after the servant who brought tea and biscuits withdrew. Mary leaned forward. "Tell me everything."

Annabel thought it best to start with the most salient point. "I did not go to bed with him."

Mary's eyes widened. "Is that good or bad?"

"It's good, of course. He offered to help me and seems to expect no payment."

Mary sipped her tea thoughtfully. "Why would he do that? It's very suspicious."

Annabel had been skeptical herself so she understood Mary's reasoning. "Surely there must still be good people in the world. Perhaps he is one of them."

"Oh, undoubtedly there are good people in the world, but none of those good people are part of the *ton*. One doesn't become rich and powerful by being *nice*. Besides, you know what people say about him."

"No. And if there are rumors about him, why did you not tell me of them before?"

"Truthfully, I just learned of them last night. I mentioned Mayne to Buntlebury and some of his rotten set, quite casually of course, and they were full of speculation about him. The chief piece of interest seems to be that he is suspected of orchestrating the death of his brothers so that he might inherit the dukedom."

"But didn't he have three or four brothers?"

"Four, I think." Mary sipped her tea again as though talk of fratricide was commonplace.

"He is only thirty-two and he fought in the war. He couldn't have been in England when every one of his brothers died."

"Annabel, no one is saying he killed his brothers. He had them killed."

Annabel thought of Mayne's green eyes and crooked smile. "I don't believe that of him. I spent at least two hours with him yesterday, and I don't think I can have misjudged him that badly."

Mary gave her a dubious look.

"Mary, I began to undress, offering him payment for helping me find Theadosia, and he actually told me if I continued to undress he would not help me."

"He wasn't attracted to you?"

"I think he was." She *knew* he was. "But he didn't want me if I was only offering because I felt I had to repay him. He is a gentleman."

"Then he will pay a call on Lady Wavenwell and find Theadosia for you?"

"Not exactly. He's insisting I travel with him."

Mary made a sound in her throat that translated to I-told-you-so.

"It makes sense, Mary. He cannot appear on the doorstep of Ceald House and demand documents."

"He can if he's persuasive enough."

"He made the point, and I agreed, that it would be much easier and quicker if I travel with him."

"Which means you'll be traveling with a murderer. Do you think that wise?"

Annabel gave a heavy sigh. "He is not a murderer. And anyway, I'll have Mrs. Slightley with me."

"He'll kill you both."

"Mary, you are judging him based on speculation, and I refuse to take part in it. I am the last person to believe rumors and innuendos."

Mary set her tea on the table and reached over to take Annabel's hand. "You are right, of course. It is idle speculation, and it's not fair to the duke. But you must admit that four of his brothers are dead. I want you to be safe."

"He hasn't even replied to my letter. Perhaps he changed his mind."

"If I had a few days I might be able to convince Buntlebury to go."

Annabel gave her friend a look rife with skepticism. Buntlebury rarely left London with its theaters and clubs and gaming hells. When he did leave it was to follow the Regent to Brighton so he might gamble and drink there.

"I know it's unlikely," Mary admitted. "But if I could, then Buntlebury would be there to protect you from Mayne."

"I don't need protection." And especially not from a drunken lout like Buntlebury. Annabel had not shed a single tear when the earl had died. She had hated being a wife and she was not interested in being under the thumb of a husband again, not even her dear friend's husband.

Crotchett entered then carrying a salver with a note on top. Annabel's heart began to pound as she watched him come closer and bend to offer the folded letter. "This just arrived, my lady."

She took the note. "Very good, Crotchett." She waited until he had closed the door again before she broke the seal. It was the duke's seal—an elaborate *M* set inside a circle.

"Is it from him?" Mary asked.

"Yes." She read the note twice to be certain she understood it. His writing was small and precise, quite neat and even. His words were difficult to mistake.

My dear Long,

I am in receipt of your request. I will collect you tomorrow at first light.

Sincerely yours,

Mayne

Annabel handed it to Mary who read it, her eyes going round as she reached the bottom. "Sincerely yours?"

"There is nothing wrong with being sincere."

"Are you certain you are comfortable traveling with him?"

"Mary, it is two days there and two days back. What could possibly go wrong?"

Six

Phin rode beside the carriage for the first few hours, giving the ladies the vehicle and privacy. He was no equestrian, and he would have to join them by midday or suffer for it. He didn't mind the cold as much as he had feared. They had the road to themselves, and he rather enjoyed the quiet. He was generally a social person. He preferred conversation to reading and his club to the solitude of his private chambers. But there were times when he found it productive to sit alone with his thoughts.

Today he ruminated on the question that had been plaguing him for the last twenty-four hours. What the hell was he doing traveling to Wiltshire with the Wanton Widow?

He should probably stop thinking of her as such. She was a widow, but as far as he could tell, she wasn't overtly wanton. Yes, she had tried to take her clothes off in his billiard room, but when he'd told her it wasn't necessary, she was quite content to keep that clothing on. He'd almost wished she'd argued more.

But he had to stop thinking along those lines. That was what had gotten him into this predicament. She was an alluring creature and he wanted her, and so instead of finding some other way to assist her—writing a letter or sending his solicitor—he had devised a way to spend more time with her.

It was only after they had driven through London this morning that Phin had thought about Long's concerns as to what the *ton* would have to say about this little venture. The *ton* had an opinion on everything, and that opinion would most certainly travel to the dowager duchess. When his mother found out about this, she would have plenty to say. And she would find out about it sooner rather than later. Phin had received a letter from his brother-in-law, John Clare, that he would be in Town and stop in at Mayne House in the next day or so. Phin had left a vaguely worded letter for John with Banks, but it wouldn't be long before John heard some rumor or other and passed it along. John was a pleasant enough fellow and seemed a good husband, but Phin had never been close to him, never really trusted him.

The first person John would inform of Phin's antics would be the duchess. His mother had told Phin he must plan to be in London for the Season and accept as many invitations as she directed. He was the duke now. He must find a wife to bear him sons. She even had a list of ladies she considered the most eligible. His mother and Phil had tried to draw him into that conversation, but after hearing his mother reject one of his sister's suggestions because, as his mother said, "Philomena, have you looked at her hips? Those are not childbearing hips," Phin opted out of the discussion.

He wasn't used to thinking of women as brood mares, and he wasn't used to thinking seriously about marriage. He had always assumed he would marry one day. He knew men who married. He had friends who had married, and that was all very well and good. But Phin was in no hurry. He had never been in love. He'd been fond of some women and lusted after others, but he had never looked at any woman as material for a wife. That was the privilege of a fifth son, a son not expected to marry. Honestly, no one had ever paid him all that much attention.

Until Richard, the Idiot, had gotten himself killed.

Now Phin would have to marry some chit with a titled father and childbearing hips—whatever those were—and his mother would harangue him constantly when he did anything other than produce sons, oversee his estates, and sit in the Lords.

This was why he hadn't wanted to be a duke. He couldn't even enjoy running off to Wiltshire with the Wanton

Widow without worrying what the *ton*, and thereafter his mother, would say.

The carriage window lowered and Long poked her head out. She wore a black pelisse and the hood framed her auburn hair and oval face. Her eyes were as blue as the sky on a summer day. "Are you not cold, Mayne?"

He considered. He couldn't feel his hands or his feet. "I'm quite cozy. Why do you ask?"

"We have a warm brick and blankets inside if you want to come in."

She was the one who looked cozy. Her cheeks were flushed a pretty shade of pink and he could smell the dark musky scent of her fragrance. He wouldn't mind climbing into the carriage and thence onto her lap and warming his hands and feet until they regained feeling.

"I'll ride a bit longer," he said. He could stand the cold until they stopped to change horses again. Once inside the carriage, he knew he would not wish to be outside her company again. But he had to remember he was doing her a favor. There was no place for seduction, no strings attached. The woman had a daughter she had not seen in years. She needed his help. He had to remember he was supposed to be acting nobly.

"How long until we stop for the night and a warm bed?" she asked.

It was an innocent question, but such questions did challenge his noble intentions. "I sent my valet on ahead this morning. He will secure lodgings and ride back to meet us. I am certain it will be before nightfall. He knows I prefer not to travel in the dark."

"That was very thoughtful of you. Thank you." She slid the window closed.

He appreciated her thanks, but the more grateful she seemed, the less he liked helping her. He didn't want her to feel grateful toward him. He wanted her to think he was amusing or clever or handsome. But no. She thought he was *kind*. She was *grateful* to him. He might as well be her brother.

He joined Long and Mrs. Slightley in the carriage later that day. The sun made intermittent appearances, which meant the temperatures weren't unbearable, but his legs were stiff and sore. He would have liked to close his eyes and sleep, but he did not think he could rest with Mrs. Slightley watching him so intently from across the carriage. Her feet did not reach the floor of the coach, and she kicked them like a child might. Nothing else about her was childlike, though, especially not the consideration in her dark brown eyes.

Beside her, Long had a book open and she seemed engrossed in whatever it was she read. The two ladies were wrapped in blankets and seemed comfortable with the silence.

Phin hated silence.

"What are you reading?" he asked Long.

She didn't look up. "A Gothic novel."

"Really? You look so engrossed I thought it must be something serious like a sermon or poetry."

She glanced up at him then back at the book. "I do read poetry from time to time, but I don't think it bears any more weight than a novel. The author must be just as creative to imagine all the misfortunes that have befallen this poor heroine."

Phin had read little outside the books his tutors and then his teachers at school had given him. Those were generally in Greek or Latin and the authors seemed inordinately interested in battles and mythical gods.

He leaned forward slightly. "What's befallen the heroine?"

She looked up again, this time meeting his gaze. "Would you really like to know?"

"I would. Wouldn't you, Mrs. Slightley?" He glanced at the housekeeper.

"I confess I am curious, though it seems wrong to be entertained by someone else's misfortunes."

"They're not real people, Mrs. Slightley," Long told her. "They're the invention of the author."

"Who is the author?" Phin asked.

Long glanced at the spine of the book. "A Mrs. Knightly."

Phin rolled his eyes.

"What was that for?" Long demanded.

"It's obviously a *nom de plume*."

"Knightly is a common name."

Phin waved a hand. "Who is the heroine?"

"Her name is Sarah, and she's recently lost her mother and father. She's traveled to the rocky coast of Cornwall to live with her uncle, but when she arrives she is appalled as his house is on a cliff that overlooks the sea, and it's been quite neglected over the years. Most of the rooms have been closed off and there are only a few servants and cobwebs everywhere."

"Ooh!" Mrs. Slightley shuddered. "I cannot stand spiders."

"Oh, there are worse things than spiders in the house, Meg." Long was obviously warming to her topic, and though Phin didn't really care much for the story—it sounded dark and he preferred comedy to tragedy—he liked watching her tell it.

"What could be worse than spiders?"

"Ghosts," Long informed her. "Spirits of the dead. The first night in the house, she looks out her window at midnight and sees what looks like a young girl walking out near the cliffs close to the water. She is worried for the girl and rushes outside to bring her in, but when she reaches that spot...*no one is there*."

"Did she fall in the water?"

"No," Long told Mrs. Slightley with more patience than Phin would have had. "She was a spirit trapped on the earth and doomed to walk along that cliff for eternity."

"Why?"

"Because her lover sailed off to make his fortune so he could return to marry her, and he died at sea. She learns this from her uncle when she tells him what she has seen."

"Her uncle should chastise her for walking along the cliffs at midnight," Phin said. "She could be hurt."

"She *is* hurt!" Long informed him. "The next night she goes out to seek the girl's spirit, thinking she can offer her some comfort, and she's surprised by a man in a black cape. She stumbles on the rocks and twists her ankle. He has to carry her back to the house."

"Oh, that sounds romantic." Mrs. Slightley put a hand to her heart.

Phin crossed his arms over his chest. "What is so romantic about a man in a black cape? I'd be wondering what he's doing out on the cliffs at midnight."

"No one knows because he disappears before she can ask him any questions."

"Convenient," Phin muttered.

"Of course, since her ankle is injured, Sarah must look for the spirit from her window, and she is doing that one night when, in the window's reflection, she sees flames behind her."

"The fires of hell!" Mrs. Slightley announced.

"No. But there is a fire in her chamber, and it's blocking the door. She's trapped inside with no way to escape except for a sheer drop to the rocks below."

"Does she jump?" Phin might consider reading the book if she jumped.

"No. The man in the black cape sweeps into her room and carries her to safety."

Mrs. Slightley sighed, and Phin sat back in disappointment.

"And that is all I have read thus far," Long told them. "But I am reminded that I had a question for you, Mayne."

He raised his brows at her.

"Will we be stopping at your estate on the way to Ceald House or on the return?"

He frowned. "My estate?"

"Yes, the one you wanted to look in on in Wiltshire."

"I don't have an estate in Wilt—" And then he remembered. He'd told her he had business in Wiltshire way so she would not feel quite so obligated to him. "Oh, *that* estate. I think we shall stop on the return."

But Lady Longstowe had set her book down and was looking at him sternly. "You don't have an estate in Wiltshire, do you?"

"Of course, I do. I'm a duke. I have estates all over the countryside."

"Very well." She crossed her arms. "What is it called?"

"It's called…ah…"

"You can't remember the name of your own estate."

"Too many to remember them all."

"Or it doesn't exist."

Mrs. Slightley shifted uncomfortably. "I think I had better get out and stretch my legs."

"And what if it doesn't exist?" he said in challenge.

"So you are admitting you lied to me?"

Mrs. Slightley rose to her knees and knocked on the roof of the carriage. "This looks like a good place to stop."

"I didn't want you to feel like I was going out of my way."

"But you are going out of your way."

"I am, but I don't mind it," he said, exasperated.

"I still don't understand why you would invent an estate!"

The carriage slowed, but Phin took little notice. "Because I didn't want any more of your gratitude," he hissed. "I'm happy to help, but I don't like people to feel as though they owe me something."

"And you thought I would feel that way?"

"Presumably that was why you were taking your dress off in my billiard room."

"I'll just get out now," Mrs. Slightley squeaked. She opened the door, letting in a burst of cold air.

Now they were alone, Long sat forward. "I didn't think you'd help me if I didn't offer you some sort of payment. We've already been through this."

"Yes, and I told you I don't want your body as payment."

"And I am supposed to believe you are helping me out of the goodness of your heart?"

"Is that so difficult to believe?"

"Yes! In my experience no one, especially not a man, does anything without expecting repayment."

Phin moved quickly, not giving her time to move away. He grasped her hand and held it until she looked into his eyes. "Hear me now, Annabel. I do not expect repayment. I will not accept repayment. You want to find your daughter, and if I can help you reunite, that is payment enough for me."

Her eyes narrowed. He could still see the doubt in the way her blue eyes clouded. Who had hurt her? Who had made it so difficult for her to trust?

"And you have no ulterior motive?" she asked.

Phin looked away. He did not want to lie to her, to allow her to believe he was all purity and light. "I didn't say that."

Annabel snatched her hand away. "I knew it!"

"I've made no secret that I'm attracted to you. It's hardly a crime to wish to spend time with a beautiful woman."

She looked at him as though he were a new species. "I am old enough to be your mother."

"You would have been a very young mother. Regardless, what difference does age make? I'm of age, and you would be beautiful at any age."

She inhaled sharply.

"Did I say something wrong?"

A Duke a Dozen | 109

"Why are you telling me this?"

"I suppose I was hoping you'd tell me how handsome I am and how you looked forward to this journey so you could spend more time with me."

She let out a bark of laughter, and though he had said the words partially in jest, it still annoyed him that she found them so amusing.

"I can't find you attractive. You're a child."

"A child?" Phin bristled, then decided he would rise to the challenge. He moved to the end of his seat so their knees brushed together. Just that slight touch was enough to make his body jolt alive. "I'm no child." He cupped her chin and moved slowly toward her. She had plenty of time to stop him, to draw back, to push him away. She did none of those things. Instead, she closed her eyes and allowed the kiss to happen.

Phin didn't know how much he'd wanted to kiss her until his lips brushed against hers. Hers were petal soft and plump, and he took his time learning the feel of them. With a sobriquet like the Wanton Widow, she must have been kissed many times. He wanted her to remember this kiss. He brushed his lips over hers until he had traced their curves and dipped into the hollows. He added slightly more pressure, moving his hand to cup the back of her neck as he parted her lips and finally tasted her. She tasted as sensual as the scent she wore. He felt as though he was falling into a bed of luxurious velvet when he rubbed his tongue along hers.

For several moments, she allowed the exploration, but as he deepened the kiss, she finally responded. The feel of her tongue twining with his, her lips pressed to his, her hands coming to rest on his arms tested his control. He wanted much more than a kiss from her. He wanted to devour her whole, touch and taste every inch of her. There was nothing sweet or tentative in the way she kissed him back. She took as much as she gave, and Phin knew in that moment he was ruined for any other woman.

Annabel, the Countess of Longstowe, was the woman he wanted. Now. Forever.

He broke the kiss first, pulling back out of a sense of self-preservation as much as from the shock of the realization that he wanted more than a few kisses or even a romp in the bedsheets. He barely knew this woman, and after one kiss he was already smitten. He wasn't used to these feelings and wasn't at all comfortable with them.

She blinked at him, seeming almost as disoriented as he. Had the kiss affected her as it had him or was it just one of many? Phin recalled their earlier conversation. "Do you still say I'm a child?"

She swallowed. "No. You're no child. But"—she held her hand up when he moved, almost instinctively, in to kiss her again—"that kiss is all there can be between us. I don't want a lover, and I won't be a mistress. That's all we could ever be to each other."

He didn't like her response, but he could acknowledge the truth of it. He would have to marry a woman who was young and could give him children. If they did allow this to continue, he would not want to give Annabel up, and yet she could be nothing more than a mistress to him. His mother would have plenty to say about that.

And yet, he would defy his mother if not for the uneasy feeling in his chest. The kiss he'd shared with Annabel had been dangerous. He'd felt…unseated—as though his horse had thrown him, and he was flying through the air and wondering just how much it would hurt when he landed. Better to stay off this horse, as it were. He did not relish falling.

And yet, he had never been one to shy away from a challenge.

Phin sat back. "Fair enough. We'll continue as friends," he said, his voice light and dismissive, though he wasn't at all certain he wanted to be nothing more than a friend of Lady Longstowe. "I need a breath of air, and then I'll instruct the coachman to drive on." He parted the curtains and looked out at the late afternoon sky. "It shouldn't be long now before my valet meets us and we can rest for the evening."

Though Phin doubted he would rest very easily with that kiss on his mind and the taste of her still on his lips.

***

Meg Slightley jumped down from the carriage and brushed her skirts off. The tension in the ducal coach had been so thick she could barely breathe. She was no stranger to lust, and the duke and her mistress radiated it like warmth from a hearth.

"What's wrong now?" the coachman called to her.

"My mistress needs a moment. The motion of the coach has made her ill." The lie came easily. Once upon a time she had been a performer, paid to lie nightly.

The outriders wandered off, ostensibly to relieve themselves and warm their hands and feet by moving a bit. The coachman grumbled to himself then gave her a toothy smile. "Why don't you come up here and keep me company?"

She tossed her head, knowing exactly what *keep me company* meant. "You have a hand for that, John Coachman," she replied saucily and walked away.

"You're only half a woman anyway!" he called after her.

She ignored him, moving to the back of the coach and leaning against the boot where he couldn't see her. She knew men like him. They wanted her because she was an oddity. They wanted to see if her breasts were real and if the rest of her worked like any other woman. She could have made good money in a brothel. Men paid well for something different, but she'd left the circus because she had tired of being gawked at. She had no desire to take her clothes off so men could gawk at her.

The sound of another coach approaching drew her from her thoughts, and she peered around the boot to see who else might have braved the cold to travel. But instead of passing them, the coach slowed and stopped. Their coachman exchanged friendly words with that coach's driver, and then the door opened and a thin, dark-haired man stepped down. He was dressed impeccably from his cravat to his polished boots, and he looked as though he had just stepped out of his dressing room rather than a cramped carriage.

He exchanged pleasantries with John Coachman, who called him Reynolds, and then moved toward the ducal coach. Meg realized all at once who he was and what he was about to do. She moved quickly, blocking him before he could grasp the door handle and open it to reveal—well, she didn't really want to know what was happening inside the coach at that moment.

Reynolds's brows shot up when she jumped in front of him, and he took a step back. His light brown eyes showed his surprise.

"You don't want to do that," she said, indicating the handle.

"How do you know what I want to do?" He didn't say it in a threatening tone. He sounded merely curious.

"You're the duke's valet."

"Yes. And who might you be?"

"I'm Lady Longstowe's maid. They need a moment alone to, er...discuss matters."

His brow arched in a way she found quite charming, and he nodded. "I see. Well, I must thank you for helping me avoid what might have been an embarrassing situation." He removed his hat, showing a full head of dark hair, almost black in color. "Would you like to walk for a moment? My legs have gone quite numb." He offered his arm and Meg stared at it as though it were something she had never seen before. Men did not usually treat her to such pleasantries.

Nevertheless, she reached up and took his arm, letting her fingers rest on his forearm as she'd seen ladies of quality do. He led her away, though not too far from the coach, and said, as they walked, "I think we must start over. I am the duke's valet, Barnaby Reynolds. I quite hate my Christian name. Barnaby sounds like the name of a hound, so I much prefer you call me Reynolds."

Meg stopped. "That's a lot of information for an introduction."

"I'm an impatient man, and this saves time. May I ask your name?"

"Margaret Slightley." She waited for him to chuckle. People always chuckled or remarked on her surname, given that she was short. But Reynolds didn't even smile.

"Pleased to meet you Miss Slightley. Or is it Missus?"

"The countess asked me to play lady's maid for her on this trip, but I'm actually the housekeeper and answer to Mrs. Slightley."

"And would it be too forward of me to ask if the Missus is merely a courtesy?"

"I'm not married, if that's what you're asking." And if that was what he was asking, how very interesting.

"Good."

"Good?"

His cheeks colored slightly, and didn't that slash of color make him all the more handsome? "I mean good that you don't have a husband missing you back in London right now." He cleared his throat. "But tell me about your mistress."

"She's the best sort. I couldn't ask for a better mistress." This was the sort of thing servants always discussed.

"And now long have you been with her?"

"Ten years."

"You seem young to be a housekeeper."

She pushed an unruly curl that had come loose in the wind back behind her ear. "Is that flattery, Reynolds?"

"I don't think so." He gave her a smile she wouldn't have minded seeing again and again.

"How long have you served the duke?" she asked.

"Thirteen years." He turned them so they started back toward the conveyances.

"And what sort of man is he?" This was not just an idle question on her part. One could tell a lot about a person based on their servants' opinions.

"The very best, though one does wish he would take a bit more care with his gloves."

She smiled. It was difficult not to smile when she looked at the valet. He was handsome and charming and fussy enough to be a valet but not so fussy that she wanted to hit him over the head with a blunt object.

"Mind if I ask you a personal question, Reynolds?"

"I am an open book, Mrs. Slightley."

"Is there a Mrs. Reynolds?"

He looked at her with brown eyes that seemed to light up with mischief. "There is, Mrs. Slightley."

She didn't know why she should feel disappointed.

"Mrs. Reynolds is my mother."

"Oh!" Her heart leapt, which was ridiculous. She was a servant for one household and he for another. Added to that she was a former circus performer and oddity. He was just being polite. He probably flirted with every woman he met. If their exchange could even be considered flirting. It had been so long since she'd flirted, she hardly remembered what it was like.

"Do you have any idea how long we might be stopped?" Reynolds asked. "If it's much longer the coachmen will want to walk the horses, and you and I should step inside." He indicated the other coach in which he'd arrived. "You should wait inside at any rate. I have tea and a basket with all sorts of treats from the cook at Mayne House."

Meg's stomach rumbled, but just as she was about to agree, the door of the ducal carriage opened and the duke emerged. He looked exactly as he had before she had left him, not at all like a man who had just tumbled a wench on the squabs.

"Ah, Reynolds. I thought I heard the carriage arrive. Tell me you have found us lodgings for the night. Lady Longstowe has had quite enough of the roads for one day."

"Your Grace." Reynolds gave a pretty bow. "I have indeed found us lodging at an inn called the Mucky Duck."

The duke's brows came together. "That does not sound promising, Reynolds."

"I assure you, Your Grace, the name is no reflection on the quality of the inn. I have reserved their two best bed chambers and a private room for supper."

Still looking skeptical, the duke nodded. "Very well. How much further?"

"A mere four miles, Your Grace."

"And they can accommodate the horses and two carriages?"

"I believe so, Your Grace."

"Tell John Coachman where to go then." He looked at Meg. "Mrs. Slightley, after you."

She caught a glimpse of Reynolds as she climbed up the steps to the ducal carriage, and she thought he mouthed the words, *I will save you an apple*. But why would he do that for her?

She settled beside her mistress. One quick glance told Meg her lady had not been ravished while she waited outside. Either that or Lady Longstowe had repaired herself quickly. Meg hoped for the latter. Her mistress could use a good ravishing. But then couldn't they all?

"Did the valet find an inn for the night?" she asked Meg.

"Yes, my lady. A place called the Mucky Duck."

"I suppose we must hope it rises above its name."

"Reynolds assured the duke it did."

"Reynolds? Is that the valet?" Lady Longstowe looked at her directly. "What did you think of him?"

Meg thought of the proffered arm and the offer to save her an apple. "He seems a very kind man, your lady."

She made a sound in the back of her throat, and Meg swore she muttered, "Just like his master."

Seven

Annabel was pleasantly surprised by the Mucky Duck, which was clean and had staff waiting to serve her. Her room was spacious enough for a tub, and when she requested a tub and hot water, the servants delivered it quickly. Meg unpacked her mistress's soap and a clean dress and put Annabel's hair up then went out to check on preparations for dinner, though Annabel suspected she left to give her mistress some time alone.

Annabel sank into the tub, which was much larger than she'd anticipated, and closed her eyes. He knees were pressed almost to her chest, but it was heaven to be able to recline in solitude. How she needed time alone. After that kiss, just being in Mayne's presence had been a trial. She'd tried to focus on her book, but she couldn't seem to stop her eyes from stealing glances at him.

Where had the man learned to kiss like that? She'd expected him to kiss like most other men she'd known—wet and with far too much tongue. They were overly eager and had no patience for seduction. But Mayne had kissed her slowly and deliciously, giving her a taste of how he might treat her were they in bed together.

At the memory, she felt a twinge of interest from between her legs, the same one she'd felt when he kissed her. It had been a long time since she'd been aroused. She didn't necessarily want to be aroused. It was easier to keep men, and the inevitable disappointment they brought, at bay when she didn't feel the pull of desire.

But she felt it now. She rubbed soap between her hands then slid them over her breasts. The nipples were hard and tender, and when she lingered, that tightness in her sex intensified. Her hands dipped under the water and down to the place where she ached. Slick with the soap, her hands moved easily, sliding between her legs and brushing over that little nub she knew could give her pleasure.

She bit her lip and slid two fingers over the nub lightly, feeling her body tense in response and a flood of heat shoot into her lower belly. She rubbed until her breath quickened and her nipples tightened. She closed her eyes, focusing on the sensation of her slick fingers on that sensitive flesh, but as soon as her eyes closed, she saw *his* face.

Not Mayne's face. *His face.* It was red with effort as he bent over her, and his gray hair hung about his cheeks like a mane. He thrust into her, hard and fast. Her head hit the bed's headboard, making her wince with each vicious thrust. "Is this what you want, little whore?" he growled, spittle flying from his lips. "You know you love when I fuck you."

Annabel's eyes opened, and her hands moved to grip the sides of the tub. How many years had he been dead, and she still couldn't forget him? Men and women talked of lovers who had ruined them for others. She'd been ruined but not in a way she could romanticize.

She climbed out of the tub, dried herself, and slipped on a clean chemise. Meg would help her to dress when she returned. In the meantime, she went to the first floor window and stared past the courtyard and out at the road leading toward Ceald House. It was surrounded by rolling hills and trees barren of leaves now but which would be green and full with leaves in a few months' time. She could picture Ceald House, stark gray stone against the slate-gray sky. The large park surrounding it would be dead and brown; the lake one had to pass as one approached the house would be black and cold.

Lady Wavenwell would not be pleased to see her. When her son had become the earl, she'd wasted no time evicting Annabel from all the Longstowe residences. She could not stop her from receiving the annuity that had been set aside for Annabel in the late earl's will, but there was no doubt Lady Wavenwell resented the payment. It had been years since Annabel had been to Ceald House, and she had no desire to return now. She would do it, though. If it meant she would finally see her daughter again, she would do anything.

Her eye was drawn to movement in the courtyard below, and she was surprised to see Mayne exiting the stable with one of the grooms. The young boy looked up at the duke with equal parts awe and fear clear on his face. As she watched, Mayne put his hand on the lad's shoulder and looked directly at the boy as he spoke. The lad nodded eagerly and when Mayne stepped back, he ran back to the stable, eager to complete whatever task Mayne had given him.

Annabel sighed. It was clear the duke was a kind man. He hadn't been haughty or impatient with the servant but patient and encouraging. She did not think most dukes would even take the time to ensure rented horses were fed and housed properly for the night. But the Duke of Mayne had seen to the task himself.

The man was making it difficult for her not to like him. He was not perfect, she reminded herself. He'd shown that the night he'd come to her town house. But he was thoughtful and considerate, and those were qualities that made it easy to forgive him. Mayne continued toward the inn, but at the last moment something caused him to look up. Annabel was too slow to move out of the window and he tipped his hat at her after favoring her with a teasing smile.

Annabel pulled the curtains shut and muttered, "That man."

"What man, my lady?" Meg asked, coming in the door with Annabel's boots, which she must have taken outside to clean.

"No one. Is it time to dress for dinner?"

"If you like. The innkeeper tells me it will be ready in about a half hour."

"I suppose we had better get started then."

A half hour later, Annabel made her way to the private dining room. The door was open, and she could see the duke standing near the hearth and staring into the flames. His blond hair was darker than usual, and she realized he must have washed it. When she cleared her throat after entering, he turned and she saw he had shaved as well. Had he made the effort for her or was it simply his custom?

He smiled at her. "You look lovely. Blue is my favorite color."

She glanced down at her blue silk dress. She'd chosen the fabric in this color because, after green, blue was her second favorite color.

He crossed to her, took her arm, and led her to a table. "You must be famished. I'll ring the bell for the first course."

"Thank you." She sat and smiled as a serving girl came in with wine and soup. When they were alone again, Mayne sat across from her and lifted his silverware. Annabel hadn't considered how awkward it might feel to be alone with him like this. She supposed she could have taken dinner in her room. Perhaps she would do that tomorrow night.

"How do you find the accommodations?" he asked, not seeming the least bit unnerved by their situation.

"Your valet made a good choice." She sipped her soup without tasting it. "Everything is satisfactory."

"Reynolds usually does make good choices. In general, I feel I have far too many servants, but I would not give Reynolds up for anything."

"He's been with you a long time then?" She tried to keep her gaze on the soup and not his face, especially his soft lips.

"Since I left Cambridge. He went to war with me, poor fellow. I was the only one of the troop to have his man with him, and I can promise you I was not allowed to forget it." He gave a rueful smile, as though remembering some past ribbing.

"But don't many of the peerage bring servants to war with them?"

"Yes, but I was in a special troop, and it was in our interest to put titles and privilege aside. We were something of a suicide troop."

Annabel set down her spoon. "A suicide troop? That sounds awful."

"By the time we were formed, it was looking more and more like Napoleon would win the war, and we thought it worth dying if we could keep England from falling under French rule." The way he said it, as though dying for one's country was simply an expected sacrifice, shocked her. Most men of their class did not speak like this.

"But you are the son of a duke," she said feebly.

"The fifth son, and that is why Reynolds went with me. Even on suicide missions, a duke's son must keep up appearances." He winked.

She laughed, surprised at how easy he was to talk to. Most men tended to be silent and taciturn, and dukes were known for their haughtiness. But if Mayne had pretensions, he did not show them often.

"It may have been a suicide troop, but you came home."

His smile faltered. "I did. Twelve of us came back, in fact. Eighteen we buried on the Continent."

"I'm sorry." She reached across the table and laid her hand on his. She rarely initiated contact with a man, with anyone, truth be told, but the sadness in his eyes made her want to comfort him.

"I suppose it's fortunate I did come home." His fingers closed on her hand so that he held it. She'd removed her gloves to eat, and the feel of his warm flesh on hers was arousing. She bit the inside of her cheek to stave off the feeling. It was a hand touching her hand. Nothing more. She was a widow and should stop acting like a virginal ingénue.

"Why is that?" she asked, her voice a bit huskier than she would have liked.

"Because someone must be the Duke of Mayne, and since all of my brothers were possessed of abysmal luck, it appears I am the lucky man."

She gently pulled her hand out of his on the pretense of lifting her napkin to her lips. "You do not sound as though you feel very fortunate."

"I don't feel fortunate," he said. "I didn't want to be the duke."

"I'm sure as a fifth son, you did not expect to ever gain the title." Most men would have been pleased as punch, but she already knew enough of Mayne to know he was not like most men. He wasn't necessarily interested in power and status.

"I didn't expect it, and I didn't want it," he said. "I was content as a soldier. I would be perfectly content to spend my days at my club or dining on war stories, but oh no. My brothers couldn't seem to take even a moment's care with their persons."

She raised her brows. "How did they—"

Before she could finish, the servant girl returned to clear the soup and bring the next course. When they were alone again, Annabel had reconsidered her wording. She had wondered about this, like everyone else, but she did not want to be like every other gossip-hungry person he met. "If it's not terribly tactless of me to ask, how did you become the duke?"

And so he told her. She watched his face as he explained about Phillip and George and Ernest and Richard. She saw genuine sorrow for the loss of his brothers and no trace of guilt or perfidy.

"You do know what people say?" she asked.

"That it's a doomed dukedom. All of my brothers died without issue."

"I am certain they do say that, but I meant about you."

He sat back. "Considering my good looks and amiable nature, I'm certain the praise must be effusive."

She snorted, which was quite unladylike, but she couldn't seem to help it. "And when has the *ton* ever praised anyone or anything effusively?"

"They do seem rather fickle. What do they say about me?"

"That you had your brothers killed so you could inherit the title."

She did not know what she expected, but it was certainly not uproarious laughter. Mayne laughed so hard that he banged the top of the table with his fist.

"I am pleased you find this amusing, but I assure you the speculation is very real."

He wiped his eyes. "I have no doubt, but if you knew me better you would see how ridiculous such a claim is."

"Why? Because you loved your brothers so?"

"God, no. My brothers were idiots, brutes, or dull as dirt. I much prefer the company of my sisters, who would tell you, as I am now, that the dukedom was the last thing I ever wanted. Do you know why I attended the Houghton ball that night I first saw you?" He looked at her expectantly, his eyes shining with mirth.

"Why does anyone attend a ball?"

"True enough, and I enjoy the company and dancing as much as the next man. Probably more than most men as I actually like to dance, but I would have much rather been at Southmead Cottage in the country with my family. I only attended because that idiot Richard insisted on making an appearance instead of traveling home."

"But you did travel home without him."

"I did, but that was only because I had been acting his shadow for weeks on end and could not stand another day of it. And do you know why I was following him about like a hungry puppy?"

She shook her head.

"Because I did not want him to come to an untimely end. Because, as anyone who knows me can tell you, I have never wanted to be a duke."

"But why not?"

"A better question is why." He rose from his chair and paced about the dining room. "It isn't a profession one can choose, like the clergy or the army. One has no choice in the matter." He held up a hand. "And do not say I can renounce the title. Even if it was legal, my family would be scandalized, not to mention the hardships that would befall our tenants. Now that I am the duke, I cannot escape it."

She rested her chin on her hand. "I always thought younger brothers craved the title and the power that went with it."

"Perhaps the second born does." Mayne continued pacing. "The title is just within reach for the second-born son. But I am a fifth-born son. The title should never have been within my reach, and I never wanted it. What interest do I have in managing the affairs of a duke? Do you know how many estates I am responsible for?"

She shook her head.

"Six. Two large estates and four smaller ones. Then there are the investments in shipping and minerals and whatnot. There are allowances and pensions to be paid and taxes to be collected and taxes to be paid. And let us not forget I am to sit in the Lords and keep up with political issues. It all makes my head spin. But I cannot ignore it. I cannot let it all fall to ruin. If I do, then what will I have to pass on to the tenth Duke of Mayne?"

She stiffened. "Your son, presumably."

"Oh, yes. There's the small matter of my son. The one I do not have, not to mention the wife I do not have. But I promise you as soon as the Season is upon us, my mother will waste no time trying to rectify that situation. I'll be forced to marry some empty-headed chit from an acceptable family. Then, whether I like it or not, I will have to bed her until she produces a son or three."

Annabel felt an odd prickling in her throat. Rather than acknowledge it, she resolved to be useful. "Then pick an intelligent girl. Surely, acceptable families produce a bluestocking or two."

"I don't want an intelligent girl."

She raised her brows, and he closed his eyes. "That came out wrong. I do value intelligence in a woman, but I don't want to be made to choose any bride from a proscribed list and marry her posthaste."

"Having been in your prospective bride's position, I doubt that is what she wants either."

Mayne stopped pacing and gave her a look of interest. She was sorry she had spoken those words. The last thing she wished to discuss was her courtship and marriage.

"You seem a reasonable woman," he said. She felt immediate relief at dodging the question of her marriage.

"I like to think so."

He sat across from her again just as the servant came in to clear away the second course and bring the third.

"How can I avoid this issue of marriage? Just for a year or two."

"Considering that your brothers all died without children, I don't think you can. Who inherits should you die?"

He thought for a moment. "My nephew, I suppose. My sister Anne has three girls and a boy. But they're children. My nephew is only nine…or eleven…or is it ten?"

"Well, that's not so bad. At least the heir isn't a third cousin living in America. Still, I think you might find a wife useful." She shook her head when she saw the way his mouth curved in a smile. "Not for that. But a duchess might take some of the weight off your shoulders. If she is reasonably intelligent, as you say you would like, she can manage estates and finances just as well as you. You'd have a partner."

"A partner." His voice held a note of incredulity as though he had never thought of a wife this way before.

He looked down at his plate and pushed his food around. She followed his example, the moment feeling awkward for some reason she could not explain. She was not very hungry, and the food was rather bland at any rate.

"May I ask you something?" he said. She looked up to find him watching her.

She nodded, though her every instinct told her she should say no. His eyes were large and very green, and when she looked into them, it was difficult to deny him anything.

"I have been thinking. I know I said we would be friends, and we are, but why can we not be something more? Why don't you want a lover? In the carriage, after I kissed you, you said you don't want a lover or to be a mistress. I wouldn't insult you by asking you to be my mistress, but if you wanted to take me as your lover, I would consider it."

She stared at him. He was hoping for her to ask him to be her lover? She was not used to being placed in the position where she had the power to do such a thing. She'd only ever had the power to say no, and that only since she'd become a widow.

"Oh, very well. I would agree and probably kiss your feet with thanks," he continued. "I have to admit that when I came to your town house, it was more because I wanted to see you than to find out information about my brother. I'd seen you at the Houghton ball, and I wanted to see you again."

"If you wanted to gain my favor, you went about it the wrong way."

"I won't argue. I don't know why I behaved like such a brute. I can only think that it's because I disliked Richard intensely, and it annoyed me to think of you with him. But that's really no excuse. I treated you poorly and made assumptions I should not have."

"They are the same assumptions everyone has made."

"Then let us start again. I'll push all my assumptions aside." He illustrated by pushing his plate and glass to one side, clearing a space before him on the table. "Here is what I know about you—and feel free to tell me if I am making any assumptions." He held up a finger. "You were married." He held up another. "Your husband is dead." He held up a third. "You have a daughter." He held up a fourth. "You are intelligent, beautiful, interesting, loyal, and I want you quite desperately. And, if truth be told, the fact that I want you so desperately terrifies me."

She blew out a breath. "That is quite a bit to say with only your fourth finger." She felt her cheeks heating. His words combined with the way he looked at her made him difficult to resist.

"I tired of counting. Since I am making no assumptions, do you want me at all or should I use my better judgement and stop imagining kissing you again?"

How on earth had they entered into this conversation? She liked frank speech, but she was not ready for this discussion with him because, truth be told, she wanted him very much. "I don't want a lover," she said.

"That's not an answer."

"I don't *have* to give an answer."

"Actually..." He sat back in his chair, and she remembered the game they'd played in the billiard room.

"I owe you an answer," she said. "And this is the question you want answered?"

"I can't think of a better one. Annabel, do you want me?" He narrowed his eyes. "The truth."

She met his gaze directly. "I want you, Mayne."

He shook his head. "Say that again, but call me Phin."

She laughed. "Like a fish?"

"It's short for Phineas. And now you are just avoiding having to say it again."

"I answered your question. That's all I owe you."

"True. I have another question."

She opened her mouth to object. He had only won a single question.

"You don't have to answer," he said, anticipating her. "Why won't you take me as your lover?"

She shook her head. "I don't want a lover."

"You want a husband then?"

"No!" No, she definitely did not ever want a husband.

"Then why?"

"I just don't." She rose and, because he was a gentleman, he did as well. But he didn't approach her as she walked about, trying to think how she could express herself best. "I like my independence. I don't want a man to tell me what I should or should not do. I've had a handful of lovers.

They were men who wooed me when I was a new widow. Each affair started out well, but soon I was being told I could not go to the theater on this night or wear that dress or dine with that friend. I don't like being controlled."

"I would never—"

"That is what you say now, but I think most men are used to owning women, and they find the practice difficult to give up."

"You have reservations. I have my own. You're a dangerous woman, Annabel. Dangerous to a man who does not want to become too attached to a lady. Is fearing I would seek to control you the only objection you have?"

It wasn't, but she would not tell him the other. It was too personal. She nodded her head. "The fact that you fear being under my control makes you more likely to try and control me." He jerked, obviously surprised at her statement. "Men control others because they fear control. Women too, I'm afraid."

"I am not like other men in that regard, and if I found myself behaving as such, I would give you up rather than continue in that vein."

She blew out a breath in exasperation. "It's a moot point because we will not be lovers."

He studied her for a long moment. "What if I can to prove to you that I do not want to control you?"

"And how will you manage that?" She crossed her arms in challenge.

"I don't know yet." He shrugged. "But I can't seem to give you up."

"You're wasting your time," she said, dropping back into her chair. In the public room just on the other side of the wall, she heard a crash and a holler. She could only assume someone had drunk too much or dropped a tankard of ale.

"No time I spend with you is wasted. You're worth it."

She stared at him. No man had ever spoken to her like this. What had she done to make him believe she was worthy of seduction? What would happen when he realized he'd been wrong about her?

The door burst open, and the innkeeper rushed in, his face red and his eyes wild. "Your Grace! Get out! Hurry before it's too late."

Mayne was already on his feet, and he moved quickly, taking Annabel's arm and pulling her beside him. "What it is?" he demanded. "What has happened?"

"There's a fire in the public room. Get out while you can!"

Eight

Phineas took Annabel's arm and pulled her to her feet. "Lead the way, man," he told the innkeeper. They followed the man out into the courtyard. From outside, he could see the flames through the windows of the public room. They were eating at the curtains and tablecloths and growing larger.

"Where did it start?" he asked.

"The public room," the man answered.

"Good, then we have time to get others out. Come on." He grabbed the man's arm. "We have to go back in and make sure all the guests and servants get out."

"What?" the innkeeper stared at him. "Go back into a burning building?"

"I'll go with you," Annabel offered. Of course, she would offer such a thing. She amazed him at every turn.

"I need you to organize these people into a fire brigade," he told her. "Find the well and make a line to pass buckets of water."

She nodded. "I can do that."

Phineas pointed at the innkeeper. "You and I are going back in." He put his hand on the back of the man's neck and pushed him back towards the building. Realizing he had little say in the matter, the innkeeper moved forward. When they had almost reached the door, Phin heard Annabel call him.

"Mayne! Be careful."

He saluted. And when he'd turned back to the burning inn, he smiled. She cared about him—at least a little. That was a start.

Inside the inn, Phineas could see at once that the fire was still contained in the public room. But he could hear the explosions as the flames reached the bottles of alcohol. The stairs leading to the bed chambers were close to the public room, and once the fire reached those, people would be trapped upstairs. He had to act quickly.

"Mr. Jackson. That is your name?"

"Yes, Your Grace!" he called over the roar of the flames.

"When we are upstairs, you go one way and I go the other. Knock on every door. If no one answers, force it open. You and I are the last ones out of here. Understand?"

"But Your Grace—"

"Mr. Jackson, I do not have time to argue with you. *Do you understand?*"

"Yes, Your Grace."

"Then let's go." He sprinted up the steps with Jackson right behind him. At the landing, he went to the left and motioned Jackson to the right. His throat began to burn as he pounded on the first door. The smoke was beginning to creep upstairs. No one opened the door, and he tried the latch. The door opened to a dark room. Phin called out but no one answered. He strode inside and called again, patted the bedding, and found nothing. Going to the window, he pushed the curtains aside and looked down into the courtyard. He remembered telling Annabel to organize a fire brigade, but he hadn't expected her to actually do so. But there she was, walking up and down a line of men and a few women, barking orders and gesturing with her hands as they passed a bucket full of water from hand to hand.

The woman was astonishing.

He heard Mr. Jackson banging on a door and went back to his work, leaving the first room and pounding on the door to the next. It opened and he looked down at a distraught Mrs. Slightley. "Your Grace!" she cried. "There's a fire, and I cannot carry all of Her Ladyship's belongings by myself."

"Leave them, Mrs. Slightley," Phin told her. "The important thing is that you get out. She can buy new dresses and petticoats."

"But Your Grace! I can't leave it. I'll never forgive myself if it burns to ashes." She ran to the bed and gathered an armful of dresses, stumbling over their skirts as she made her way back to the door. "You carry these." She shoved them into his arms. Phin looked down at the garments in bewilderment.

"Mrs. Slightley! I have them. You must get out."

"I'm coming." She lifted Annabel's valise and shuffled along, trying to carry it.

"I'll take that."

Phin turned to see Reynolds, carrying Phin's own valise, step into the doorway. He strode into the room and took Lady Longstowe's valise in his free hand.

"Reynolds, make sure she gets out."

"Yes, Your Grace." Reynolds stopped in the doorway. "Would you like me to take those, Your Grace?" He indicated the dresses. Phin tossed them over Reynolds's arm and watched as the valet directed Mrs. Slightley down the corridor to the stairs.

The smoke was thicker now, and he coughed to ease the burning in his throat. He had two more doors to check. "Mr. Jackson! How goes it?"

"There's no one up here, Your Grace!" Jackson appeared through the haze near the stairs. "I checked all the rooms."

"I have two more. Go down and make sure the servants are out and then see to the grooms and the horses. If the stable catches fire, it will go quickly."

"Yes, Your Grace." The innkeeper didn't hesitate to race down the steps.

Phin pounded on the next door, but it did not open. He stepped back and kicked it, shattering the frame. He burst inside and looked about. The room had a candle burning, but no one was visible. He blew out the candle, called out again, then went to the last room. Its door was open, and he recognized it as his own. There would be no one inside as Reynolds had already fled the building.

The door to the servants' stairs was at this end of the corridor, and he pushed it open. He would check the stairway and the servants' quarters and then go out and help Jackson or the fire brigade.

The servants' stairwell was black as pitch, and he wished he had taken the candle in the room beside his instead of blowing it out. He felt along the walls and made his way carefully down the steep stairwell. He had to turn halfway down and as he negotiated the maneuver, he thought he heard something above him. Phin paused. "Is anyone there? Do you need help?"

No one answered. He continued down another stair or two then something blunt and heavy hit him in the back of the head. He went down, losing his footing and pitching forward. He rolled down the last few steps and landed hard on the ground, crumpled against the servants' door.

He tried to get his bearings and rise to his feet, but in the darkness and with his head throbbing, he was disoriented. He felt as though he floundered for hours before the door he'd landed against opened and someone called, "Your Grace!"

Phin looked up, surprised he was lying on the floor. Mr. Jackson peered down at him, appearing equally surprised. "What happened? Your head!" He bent and Phin assumed he touched his head, but astonishingly, the innkeeper's hand came away red with blood.

Phin began to cough as the smoke on the ground floor was thick and acrid.

"Come with me, Your Grace." The innkeeper hoisted him up and put an arm under him.

"I can walk on my own," Phin protested, but he didn't complain when Jackson held on to him. He didn't feel at all steady.

As soon as they were out of the inn, Phin pushed away from the man, bent, and coughed as though he were trying to expel a lung. Blood ran into his eyes. It *had* been blood on Jackson's hands. Phin's blood.

"Oh, my God!" It was Annabel. Phin knew her voice. He looked up and into her white face. Her blue eyes were wide with shock and dismay. "You need to sit down."

He gestured to the inn. "I have to make sure—"

"The fire is almost out. The innkeeper will search one last time, but it seems everyone has been accounted for. You were the one we could not find." She put her arm about his waist, her form soft as it pushed against him. With gentle pressure, she led him to the stable, where several people were sitting on hay and coughing. She set him in an empty horse stall and called out. "I need water here and something to use as a bandage."

Phin closed his eyes. His head felt as though a horse had sat on him. Gingerly, he reached back and touched the epicenter of the pain and felt his own blood there. Had he slipped and hit his head? No. It had felt as though something had fallen on him.

Annabel returned and knelt before him. "Drink this." She handed him a metal spoon filled with warm water. He drank it and grimaced. It tasted smoky. "I'd rather some brandy," he said, his voice hoarse.

"Wouldn't we all?" she said. "Let me see your head."

He bowed it and she rose, bending over him to peer at it. He resisted the urge to lift his head and inspect whether her dress gaped at the bodice. The injury couldn't be too bad if he was still thinking about what she looked like naked.

"I can't see very well in here. It looks like a cut." She took a piece of linen and dabbed at his head.

"Bloody hell!" He grasped her wrist and held her hand still. "That hurts," he said between clenched teeth.

"I need to clean it."

"Then pour some brandy or gin over it."

"Fine." She disappeared a moment then returned with a jug. Before he was ready, cold water sloshed over his head and down his neck.

He half rose. "Woman! What the devil are you doing?" When his head swam, he plopped back down again.

"It needed to be cleaned, and I thought it better to be done with it." She reached forward with the linen, but he took it from her hand and wiped his eyes and his face. The blood was more pink than red, but now he'd begun to shiver as his coat and shirt were soaked through. "There was no alcohol, so this was the best I could do." She touched his arm. "You're freezing now. Let me see if I can find a blanket."

"Better yet, fetch my valet. Reynolds has my valise and can give me a dry shirt."

She nodded and left him. Phin moved to a dry area of the stall and impatiently tugged his own coat off. Once that was accomplished, he saw no reason to wait for Reynolds to assist with his shirt. He unfastened the cravat and the buttons but when he grasped the hem and lifted his hands to pull the garment over his head, he almost fell over.

So perhaps he would wait for Reynolds.

"I couldn't find him," Annabel said, walking back into the stall. "Oh." She stopped after taking only two steps and stared at him. "I should go look for a blanket."

"Help me take this shirt off first. Please." It felt as though someone was pounding his head with a hammer, and his teeth had begun to chatter, which only made the pounding worse. She hesitated, and he thought she might refuse. She probably ought to refuse. Now that he thought of it, his request was not at all proper.

"Very well." She moved forward, surprising him with her willingness. She took the hem in her hands and pulled it up. Then she looked more closely. "You haven't done your cuffs," she said. He had forgotten them. No wonder he'd had trouble before. She took one cold hand and unfastened the link at his wrist and then the other. Her hands were warm and soft. He imagined all of her was warm and soft.

"Now lift your hands." She grasped his hem again and dragged it up and over his head. His arms came free this time, and the cold, clingy garment was off him. He lowered his hands and stumbled from dizziness. She caught him, her hands on the sides of his bare abdomen. Her hands felt so good against his chilled skin. "You are freezing. Sit down before you fall. I'll be back with a blanket."

He sat, and when she moved away, he lay down, letting the hay cushion his head. It scratched his face, but he was too tired to sit any longer. He closed his eyes and the world seemed to spin. Fisting his hands, he demanded it stop, and as it slowed, he began to relax and drift into sleep.

***

"Reynolds!"

The valet turned at the sound of Lady Longstowe's voice. Her voice held authority without being shrill or demanding. The timbre of her voice was low and sounded calm, even in the pandemonium surrounding them now. She strode toward him, her auburn hair still neatly pinned back and her blue eyes blazing.

"Yes, my lady."

"I'm glad I found you. His Grace has been injured."

Reynolds's chest tightened. "Take me to him, my lady!"

"He's resting and is fine," she said. She waved to someone behind her, and he turned to see her housekeeper, Mrs. Slightley, approach. "I am fine, Mrs. Slightley. No need to look so worried."

The housekeeper did look worried. Her pretty face was scrunched in concern. Her lovely chestnut hair had come loose of its neat style and hung down, grazing her small waist. "I couldn't find you, my lady."

"No one can find anyone in this melee. I was just telling Mr. Reynolds that the duke was injured."

"Oh, no! What happened?"

"It looks as though he hit his head. The wound isn't deep, but it certainly stunned him. He is resting in a horse stall under a blanket. But I need you to fetch a doctor, a physician if available. If not, a surgeon."

The housekeeper nodded. "I'll ask the innkeeper where to find the closest doctor, my lady."

Reynolds frowned. He didn't like the idea of Mrs. Slightley wandering about the countryside alone in the dark.

"Reynolds," Lady Longstowe continued. "You go along and make sure the man comes. Promise to pay him whatever he asks. Bring him forcibly if need be."

"Yes, my lady." Reynolds liked her more and more. He would have taken such measures at any rate, but the fact that she also saw the need for them was commendable. "What about His Grace? Who will see to him while I am away?"

"I will, Reynolds. I will stay with him. Where are his things? I'll bring them to the stable in case he has need of them."

Reynolds took a moment to assess her. She was tall and looked strong and capable. Finally, he said, "I will fetch them, my lady."

She held up a hand. "Please. I am perfectly capable of carrying a valise. Go with Mrs. Slightley and bring a doctor."

He told her where he had stowed the duke's valise as well as his own belongings then followed Mrs. Slightley through the crowd of guests and servants milling about. For such a diminutive woman, the housekeeper had no problem making her way through the people and they found the innkeeper quickly. He told them where to find the surgeon and offered them a horse as the man lived almost a mile away. Mrs. Slightley refused and when they were far enough away from the inn that the sounds of the crowd had quieted, he turned to her.

"Why did you refuse the offer of a horse? We could have been there much more quickly."

She shook her head and snorted. "Those beasts are vicious. I stay far away from them when I can." She continued walking in the direction the innkeeper had indicated the doctor lived. Reynolds wished he had thought to bring a lamp as he could see it would be very dark once they were away from the inn.

"Those beasts, as you call them, are quite useful and docile in the right hands."

"Well, they don't like me. I've had more than one beast try to take a bite out of me. They must think I'm a large apple."

He smiled. "Don't be ridiculous. You look nothing like an apple. More likely, they sense your fear and it makes them nervous in turn."

"Well, you would be afraid of them too if you were as short as me." She gave him an indignant glare.

"Rubbish. Anyone could see that you're a strong, independent person. You weren't afraid of dying in a burning building, and I can't believe you would be afraid of an animal like a horse."

They had been talking as they walked, but now he realized he was walking alone. He looked over his shoulder and saw she had stopped on the side of the road. "What is it?" he asked.

She stared at him for a moment. "Nothing. I had a rock in my shoe." She joined him, not bothering to free the rock from her shoe. Reynolds could only assume he had said something wrong. Or perhaps he had said something right? He'd spent most of his life saying, "yes, my lord" and "no, my lord," and sometimes he felt inadequate when it came to carrying on a conversation, especially one with a beautiful woman like Mrs. Slightley. He was rarely in the company of beautiful women, and when there was a comely maid hired in the ducal household, as the valet, Reynolds did not have much interaction with her.

They walked in companionable silence for a few minutes, their steps slowing as the darkness enveloped them and required them to step more carefully. "Aren't you afraid of anything?" Mrs. Slightley asked.

What an odd question for her to ask. He liked that she surprised him. "Oh, a great many things," he told her. "I went to the Continent with His Grace when he was in the army. I was afraid constantly, even though I was rarely in the line of fire. Still, there were moments when I found myself in the midst of the fighting, and I thought my life was at an end."

"Why would the duke bring his valet into a war? Couldn't he dress himself for a year or so?" She sounded so offended.

"Oh, his mother insisted. She'd already lost one son, and she worried she would lose another. She asked me to go and keep him safe."

"You succeeded."

"I had very little to do with it," Reynolds said, and he was not being modest. "His Grace is remarkably nimble at avoiding being shot, and the few times we were faced with the prospect of capture, he talked his way out of it."

Mrs. Slightley looked up at him. Her face was in shadow, but he could imagine she had a crease between her brows. "How did he do that?"

"He has a gift for negotiation. When he is in a tricky situation, he has a knack for getting his way. And he can almost always get whatever he wants for the price he wants."

"And why is he taking my mistress to Wiltshire? What does he want now?"

Reynolds was silent. He had not heard the duke mention that he wanted anything other than to help Lady Longstowe, but he had his suspicions. "Perhaps he simply wants to help the lady. My understanding is she needs someone to mediate a dispute between herself and a relative at Ceald House."

Mrs. Slightley made a sound of disbelief. "I think he hopes to bed her."

Now Reynolds was the one who stopped short. He was not used to ladies speaking so frankly. Mrs. Slightley turned and looked back at him. "Well, go ahead and deny it, but I won't believe you."

Reynolds opened his mouth and then closed it, rather like he imagined a fish might. Finally, he said the only thing he could. "I cannot deny it, but I cannot confirm either. He has not said anything of the sort to me."

"That all sounds very proper, but I know men and I know what they want. You might as well tell him he won't get what he wants from Lady Longstowe. She may have a reputation as the Wanton Widow, but she's not free with her favors."

Reynolds cleared his throat. "I can promise you, Mrs. Slightley, I will say nothing of the sort to His Grace. It would insult him. I believe he has nothing but good intentions toward your mistress."

"You're loyal," she said finally, beginning to walk again. "I will give you that."

Reynolds could have said the same about her, and it was a quality he admired.

They spotted the doctor's house just around the next bend in the road. It was dark, indicating the man had already gone to bed for the night. But Mrs. Slightley didn't hesitate to walk straight to the door and knock loudly. When there was no response after a minute or two, she knocked again. "Doctor! Are you in? We need your help!"

"You will wake the dead," Reynolds hissed.

"I want to wake him in case he is dead asleep." She knocked again. "Doctor! There was a fire at the Mucky Duck. We need your help!"

"I don't think he's—"

"I'm coming! I'm coming!"

Reynolds glanced at Mrs. Slightley. "It appears he is home. Do you mind if I am the one who speaks with him?"

"Be my guest."

The door opened and a man of perhaps fifty stood in bare feet, a dressing gown, and a night cap. "What is it? What did you say? The Mucky Duck is afire?"

"Sir, I am Reynolds, valet to the Duke of Mayne. This is Mrs. Slightley, the Countess of Longstowe's housekeeper. We have been sent to collect you. There was indeed a fire at the Mucky Duck, and the duke and possibly other guests were injured. Would you be so good as to come with us and see to His Grace and the others?"

"I would, yes." But his eyes had fixed on Mrs. Slightley. "Come in while I change clothing. I could ready my gig, but it would be faster to simply walk."

Mrs. Slightley gave Reynolds a supercilious look. She really did not care for horses.

The doctor moved toward another room, presumably his bed chamber, then paused. He looked back at Mrs. Slightley. "Are you a dwarf?"

Mrs. Slightley's chin lifted sharply, and Reynolds felt offended for her. "What's it to you?"

"It's just I've never seen anything like you before. I've read about people like you, of course, but I've never seen one."

"Sir," Reynolds said, "His Grace has sustained an injury to the head, and we would be most appreciative if you could hurry and attend him."

"Of course." He went to his bed chamber and closed the door. When they were alone, Reynolds turned to Mrs. Slightley.

"I feel as though I should apologize for him."

"Why?" She had moved toward the window and didn't meet his eyes. "I *am* a dwarf, and I've been called far worse. It's not as though I'm not used to being gawked at."

"I'm sorry for that."

She gave him a look that said she didn't quite understand him then looked back out the window. Reynolds was still angry, and he wasn't sure why. She was obviously not offended by the doctor's words and the surgeon had spoken factually. But Reynolds didn't like the way he'd spoken to her—as though she were a thing, a specimen, not a person.

Finally, the door opened again, and the doctor emerged dressed in black from head to hat. He carried a black bag in one hand. "Shall we?" he said, indicating the door.

The small group then proceeded to walk back in the direction of the inn. The doctor asked questions about the fire and the duke's injury, and Reynolds began to relax and, if not like the man, feel that he was not as bad as he had first thought.

But Reynolds had forgiven the doctor too soon.

"Mrs. Slightley—that is your name, is it not?" he asked. Mrs. Slightley had said nothing on the return walk, allowing Reynolds to carry the conversation and impart the necessary information.

"Yes, sir," she answered.

"I wonder if after I examine the duke, you might allow me to examine you."

Reynolds opened his mouth to speak, but Mrs. Slightley was quicker. "I was not injured, sir."

"I realize that. But I'd like to examine you out of, shall we say, medical curiosity. You needn't take all your clothing off. You could keep your shift on."

Mrs. Slightley turned, hands on her hips. "I won't be taking anything off! I don't care if you are a doctor. You're just another man wanting to get a look at me tits."

"Well, I am interested in the sexual characteristics—"

Reynolds did something he had never done before. He reached out and grasped the doctor by the lapels of his coat. He then shook the man hard enough that the surgeon dropped his bag. Reynolds had never hit a person before, but he was sorely tempted. "Doctor," he said, his voice sounding like that of a stranger. "I think you had better stop talking to the lady now. She is not an insect to be examined and pinned on a board. She will not be taking her clothes off for you. In fact, if you dare speak to her again, I'll have to break your nose."

Reynolds released the man, and the doctor stepped back and brushed imaginary dirt from his coat.

"Stay away from me, both of you. One more word out of you, and I'll report you to the duke for verbally abusing a gentleman." He pointed to Reynolds. "Take your abomination and stay out of my sight."

Reynolds hit him. He knew he shouldn't do it. He knew he would be reprimanded later. But he didn't regret it at all.

He landed a solid punch to the man's jaw, managed to avoid wincing at the pain in his hand, and moved aside when the doctor stumbled and fell to the ground. Then he offered Mrs. Slightley his arm. She looked up at him, shock in her eyes. Then, slowly, she took his arm, and the two walked right past the sputtering idiot.

It might have been an instance of bad judgement, one of the first—if not the only—instance of such in Reynolds's life, but he didn't regret it. Not when he saw the smile on Mrs. Slightley's face.

Nine

Annabel closed her eyes and tried to keep the exhaustion at bay. She sat in the stable with Mayne's blond head cradled in her lap. His breathing was regular, but he hadn't stirred when she moved him. She knew it had not been more than half an hour since she had sent Reynolds and Mrs. Slightley to fetch the doctor, but she still wished they would hurry. She had read of men who hit their heads and never woke again. What if Mayne never woke?

No, she was being ridiculous. Of course, he would wake. Just look at him. Though she'd covered him with a horse blanket, she could see his bare shoulders and arms. They were strong and muscled. He was a healthy man in the prime of his life. He would be fine.

Still, she could see the lines of tension etched on his face. He was not sleeping peacefully. She imagined his head hurt him and that was what caused his features to contort in pain. He really was such a handsome man. She probably should not stare at him as she was. It was not proper, and it could serve no good purpose. When she looked at him, she wanted to touch him. She wanted to stroke his cheek or—God help her—move her hands down and over his broad shoulders and solid biceps.

But why tempt fate? Nothing could come of such familiarity. Nothing could come of a liaison with him. Even if it didn't cause a scandal, it would only open old wounds. She'd bandaged them years ago, and she did not want to yank her protection away. Not now. Not when she finally had a chance of seeing Theadosia again. For so long her daughter had been all she had thought about, all she had dreamed about. She wanted to see her daughter. She wanted to hold her daughter. And now the Duke of Mayne was distracting her, making her think there was more to life than going to bed alone and reading to pass the lonely hours.

She couldn't afford to think that way.

Mayne stirred, and Annabel put her hand on his shoulder to comfort him. "I'm right here," she murmured. In the dim light of the lamp, she could see his eyes open, the green color looking deep and verdant as he peered up at her.

"What happened?" He tried to rise, and she held her hand on his shoulder steady to dissuade him.

"There was a fire. You hit your head."

"I remember that. Why am I lying in a stable?"

"You fell asleep. I sent your valet to fetch a doctor."

He tried to sit again, but when she attempted to hold him still, he shrugged her hand off. He sat, giving her a view of his bare back.

God forgive her because she wanted to kiss every inch of it. He really was the most glorious male specimen. She had never seen anything like him.

"I don't need a doctor."

"I'm sure you don't. It's only a precaution." She knew how to deal with difficult men and added, "I'm only being silly and probably overreacting."

He turned to look back at her. "I can't think of a worse description of you. You're not silly, and I can't see you overreacting. My head must look bad if you sent for a sawbones."

"How does it feel?" she asked.

"Like I was hit with a brick." He moved to place his back against the wall where she sat. "I'm not so certain I wasn't."

"What do you mean? The ceiling fell in? Mr. Jackson said only the public room sustained significant damage. I thought you had gone back to search the guest chambers."

He told her about his search and his exit through the servants' stairwell, how dark it had been, and how he'd had no warning before being hit on the back of the head. "If it was debris falling from the ceiling, I didn't hear it crack or splinter. Of course, I shouldn't be surprised if accidents befall me."

She gave him a look of bemusement. "Because you are the Duke of Mayne."

"They do call it the Doomed Dukedom. Of course, your friends would probably say I hit my own head."

"They are not my friends, and that is possible. In the dark, you might have hit your head on a low beam."

"That would make sense if it was not the back of my head."

"Do you really think this is part of some sort of curse?"

He gave her a tired smile. "No. I think it bad luck. I should have asked earlier. Was anyone else hurt?"

She did not like the way her chest constricted at the question. It showed he cared about others, not just himself, and she did not want another reason to like him. "Not as badly as you. A few people were singed and others are having difficulty breathing."

"We'll make sure the doctor sees them."

She raised a finger. "Not until he sees you."

He cocked a brow then winced. "Remind me not to do that."

She probably wouldn't. He looked almost rakish when he made that expression.

"You know," he said, his look turning contemplative. She wasn't sure she liked that look as she'd seen it before, usually before he asked her a question she did not want to answer. "It almost sounds as though you care about me."

She felt her cheeks grow hot with embarrassment, which was ridiculous. She was a mature woman. Why should she blush like a school girl?

His finger grazed her cheek. "Imagine my brows raised right now," he said. "I think you must care for me if the question makes you blush."

She turned away from him and his dangerous touch. "Of course, I don't want you to be hurt. There's nothing more to it than that, I'm afraid." She kept her gaze focused away from him, so she didn't see whether he looked as though he believed her or not.

"Odd that I was the only one really injured."

"You should be more careful. And put some clothing on. Reynolds gave me your valise. I'll find a shirt for you."

She began to rise to do just that, but he caught her hand and that simple gesture caused her to freeze in place. They were not alone. The stable door was open, and people passed by every few minutes. Other guests and servants would be sleeping in the stable tonight as well, but none would have dared expect the Duke of Mayne to share a stall. And when they walked past, people kept their gazes fixed forward. Still, Annabel knew people could appear uninterested and still be watching closely for gossip they might later spread. She had given the public enough fodder by placing the duke's head on her lap and sitting beside him when he was half-dressed. And even if she didn't care much what people said about her, she did not want his family to be the subject of more speculation, especially concerning her.

"You should release my hand," she said.

"Then you'll move away. And I want you to stay beside me."

She didn't look back at him. "You need to dress."

"I'm warm enough with the blanket. Here. I'll wrap it about me if it makes you feel better." He released her hand. "See? I'm decent again."

She looked back at him, and he did indeed have the blanket over his shoulders and covering his chest.

"I'm sure you wish I had stayed asleep."

"No, actually. I was worried you wouldn't wake up."

His mouth quirked up in a grin. "You're certain you don't care for me? Not even a little?"

She really could not allow this to go on. She couldn't allow him to believe he would be able to seduce her. She did not want to jeopardize his help, but neither did she want him angry with her for leading him on.

"I don't like that look on your face," he said. "You look as though you want to tell me that I have no chance of wooing you."

"Wooing me? I think you mean seducing me."

"Oh, I may have my arrogant moments, but I'm not that presumptuous. My skills of seduction are paltry compared to yours. In fact, paltry might be giving me too much credit. *Meager* might be a better descriptor. To tell you the truth, I've never really had to seduce a woman."

One look at him and she could believe that. He probably just crooked his finger and women tossed up their skirts. "I am a challenge for you. Is that why you continue to give me compliments?"

"I give you compliments because you deserve them, and you're a woman, not a challenge. But I'd be lying if I said I didn't want you. You know I do."

She swallowed. She knew what was coming next. She'd thought he was different, but now that they were alone and far from London, he would make his demands. "And what about finding my daughter?"

He furrowed his brow then winced. "Remind me not to do that again too. What does your daughter have to do with my desire for you? One doesn't relate to the—wait a moment. You still think I won't help you if you don't spread your legs?"

"What am I supposed to think?" She felt tears sting her eyes, though she wasn't certain if it was from humiliation or fear at losing her chance to see her daughter.

"That I told you the truth back in London. I don't want you that way. I know you want me, Annabel—"

"Because you used your question to make me admit it." She wiped her eyes. "But look at you. Any woman would want you."

"Then why can't I have the one woman I want?"

She looked down then cleared her throat. "Because it's not that simple."

"I'm no rake, but I'm not a virgin. It's not like translating Latin, Annabel. I can give you pleasure."

And what would he think when he realized he couldn't? He'd hate her for making him feel inadequate. "Right now you can barely raise your eyebrows without flinching."

He laughed then held his head. "You're right." He closed his eyes. "The banging in my head has worn me out."

She sighed with relief, glad the conversation was at an end for now. "I'll go out and see if Reynolds is back with the doctor yet. I don't know what could be taking so long."

"Annabel." He didn't touch her this time, but the way he said her name was as strong as his hand holding hers. "Stay with me. I'm sure you're eager to be away, but could you stay until Reynolds returns?"

She grasped his hand and looked into his eyes. "I'll stay with you as long as you like. Just rest, Mayne."

"Phin. We're in a stable in the middle of the night. You might as well call me Phin."

"Rest, Phin. I'll be right here."

He closed his eyes again, and to her relief he relaxed but did not sleep. She was dozing herself when she heard Mrs. Slightley's voice. She'd slumped slightly so that her head was on Mayne's shoulder, but she sat up straight and attempted to look awake and alert just as Mrs. Slightley led Reynolds into the stall.

"My lady!" Meg rushed over to her. "I'm sorry we were gone so long. You look exhausted. I'll see if I can find some tea."

"That's not necessary, Mrs. Slightley." She kept her voice low so as not to disturb others in the stable who might be sleeping. Mayne had not opened his eyes, but she could tell he was listening. "Did you find the doctor?"

"We did," the valet offered. When he didn't say more, Annabel glanced at her housekeeper.

"Where is he?"

"There was a…misunderstanding, my lady." The valet looked down and rubbed a hand along the back of his neck. Annabel didn't know him at all, but he looked rather sheepish.

"What kind of misunderstanding?"

"I don't think the surgeon is coming, my lady." This from Meg who, strangely enough, also looked sheepish.

"Not coming?" Annabel began to rise, and the valet helped her to her feet. "That's unacceptable. Show me the way to his house. I will bring him back myself."

"Countess, that really is not necessary." Annabel looked at Mayne, whose eyes were red now and his face pale.

"Yes, it is." She didn't hesitate for a moment, and she wouldn't brook any argument. "Mrs. Slightley, find His Grace some tea to drink and then stay with him until I return. Reynolds, show me the way to this doctor's home."

"Yes, my lady." The two servants followed her out of the stable and then Reynolds cleared his throat.

"He's here, my lady."

She followed his outstretched hand to the figure of a man clad in black walking toward the inn yard. He had a splatter of red on his white shirt and a smear of it on his cheek.

"Reynolds," she said, without looking away from the doctor, "why does the doctor have a bloody nose?"

"I couldn't say, my lady."

She leveled the valet with a look, an easy trick as they were of a similar height. "You couldn't say, or you won't say?"

"He probably shouldn't say, my lady," Mrs. Slightley interjected.

Annabel squared her shoulders. "I will handle this." She started toward the doctor. Upon seeing her and correctly identifying her as a peer, the doctor slowed and bowed slightly.

"You must be the Countess of Longstowe."

"And you must be the doctor. What is your name, sir?"

"George Webb, my lady."

"And your credentials, Mr. Webb?"

He gave them, and though she was not familiar with his profession, they sounded acceptable. "If you will come this way, I will show you to the duke. I'm sure his valet told you he has sustained a head injury."

"Yes, my lady. I am eager to talk to the duke as I want to inform him that he should dismiss his valet immediately."

"Really? Why?" Annabel could guess, but she wanted to hear it from the doctor. She'd also noticed that the valet was nowhere to be seen, while Mrs. Slightley waited in the doorway of the stable.

"The man struck me in an unprovoked attack." Webb's face turned dark red.

"I am sure Reynolds would not do such a thing."

"He did, my lady. I assure you," he said, indignantly.

"Then you shall take it up with me after you examine the duke."

The doctor paused at the threshold to the stable, completely ignoring Mrs. Slightley who scowled up at him. "My lady, I am sure the conversation is not fit for a lady's ears."

She gave him a pale smile she often used when men tried to figuratively pat her on the head and shoo her away. "Be that as it may, I will not have the duke worried or upset right now. I assure you I am quite capable of dealing with any and all matters you might have to bring before the duke."

Mrs. Slightley blew out an indignant breath, and Annabel gave her housekeeper a look. Obviously, she disliked the doctor as much as Reynolds.

"Very well, my lady," the doctor said, acquiescing. She led him to the stall where Mayne rested then waited outside while he examined him. She wanted to give them privacy but also be close enough to intervene if the doctor brought up the matter of Reynolds despite her injunction.

Webb spoke of nothing but the duke's injury and when he emerged from the stable, she could barely give him time to breathe before she said, "Is it serious?"

"There is no need to worry, my lady. He should be fine in a day or two. His injury will heal on its own, and I prescribed rest and quiet for the inevitable headache. He may also suffer some dizziness or blurring of his vision. That too should pass. I gave him some medicine to ease the discomfort, but I will write down the dosage and instructions for use for you as well in case he does not remember or in case you need more and must see an apothecary." He withdrew a small pad of paper and a pencil and wrote for several minutes before tearing the paper off and handing it to her.

"Do you think his memory will suffer?" she asked.

"I think it unlikely, but if it does, I suggest you have him examined in—what is your destination?"

"Ceald House in Wiltshire."

"I am not familiar with it, but I am certain there is a physician who treats the family there. You should consult him. Now, if you would walk with me a moment, I wish to discuss the matter of the valet."

"Of course." She followed him out of the stable and at the entrance Mrs. Slightley, who was still standing there, fell in step behind her. It was quite dark now and probably past midnight, Annabel thought. The yard was full of activity and men who were tromping in and out of the inn, pulling wet and smoky furniture, rugs, and draperies out of the ruined public room. Others had found a spot to sit and smoke or lean their heads back and sleep. Annabel herself was beginning to tire, but she could not very well sleep in a stable and her room in the inn was out of the question. Perhaps she could have one of the grooms show her to the duke's coach. That would be comfortable enough.

"I would recommend to you, my lady, that you advise His Grace to release Mr. Reynolds from service as soon as possible."

"And why is that?"

The doctor had led them to the edge of the yard, and she followed him out of the hubbub and into the dark but quiet area beyond. "As I said, he struck me without provocation."

"And I said I do not think Reynolds would do such a thing." The doctor did not need to know she'd known Reynolds for all of a few hours and had no idea what he would or would not do.

"Well he did, and I insist the duke take some action or I will make the local magistrate aware of the fact that I was assaulted."

"I see." For the first time Annabel looked behind her, acknowledging Mrs. Slightley. "Have you met my housekeeper, Mr. Webb?"

Webb's eyes slid over Meg with obvious derision. "I have."

"She has been with me for over ten years, and I trust her implicitly. Meg, were you with Reynolds and the doctor when the altercation occurred?"

"I was, my lady."

"She has nothing to do with it," Webb objected.

Annabel raised a hand. "Then I will hear it from her, and I will thank you not to interrupt me, Mr. Webb. Mrs. Slightley, did Reynolds strike the doctor?"

"Yes, my lady."

"See, I told you," he burst out.

Annabel ignored him, keeping her gaze on Meg. "Mrs. Slightley, why did Reynolds strike the doctor?"

"He was defending me, my lady."

"Rubbish!" the doctor roared. "I did not touch that creature."

"But you wanted to," Meg shot back. "You wanted to examine me."

"That will be enough, Mrs. Slightley."

Meg crossed her arms and gave her mistress a mulish look.

Annabel looked at the doctor again. "Is this true, Mr. Webb? Did my housekeeper complain of an injury?"

"No, I simply wanted to examine her out of medical curiosity. She's abnormal, and I have never seen one of her kind before. I thought she might make for an interesting subject. I would still like to do so, with your permission of course, my lady."

"Mrs. Slightley," Annabel said. "Do you wish to be examined?"

"No."

Annabel looked at the doctor. "She says no, and that must be my answer too."

"But think of the scientific implications, my lady! I won't hurt her, I—"

"Mrs. Slightley," Annabel said, not raising her voice but speaking in what she liked to think of as her imperious countess tone. "Is this when Reynolds struck the doctor?"

"Yes, my lady."

"I see. Mr. Webb, I can only say that I am sorry Reynolds struck you."

"You should be."

She held up a hand. "I was not finished. I am sorry Reynolds struck you only once. He should have pummeled you into a bloody pulp." She was the same height as the doctor, but she managed to look down her nose at him. "Now get out of here or I may very well order him to do so." And with that, she turned on her heel and marched away, ignoring the doctor's sputters and protests.

When they were far enough away that the doctor would not hear, Meg looked up at her. "Do you think he really will send the magistrate?"

"No, but if he does, I will deal with him. Or the duke will."

"You think the duke will take my side?"

Annabel thought about it for a moment. "I do, yes." She raised her brows at Meg. "Reynolds obviously took your side, and he seemed quite forceful in his defense." It was dark in the yard, but Annabel did not think she was mistaken to see a blush on Meg's cheeks.

"He is a perfect gentleman, my lady."

"Is he?"

Meg sniffed at the teasing tone in Annabel's voice. "As well he should be."

"I think you like him, Meg."

"I like him as much as any man."

Annabel gave her a long look and Meg scuffed a toe on the ground, making a track in the dirt. Then she looked up. "I think you like the duke, my lady."

Now Annabel felt her own cheeks heat, which was ridiculous at her age. "I like him as well as any man," she said, parroting her housekeeper. She straightened, eager to change topics. "See if you can find where the duke's carriage is stowed. I need to find a place to sleep."

"Yes, my lady."

Annabel watched as her housekeeper walked away then looked back at the stable, trying to resist the pull of the man inside.

Ten

Phin woke with the same splitting headache he'd had before going to sleep. In fact, he was reasonably certain he'd had it while asleep. He did not feel rested at all, but sunlight streamed through the windows of the stall and people and animals were moving about. He might have laid there longer if the bed of straw had been even remotely comfortable, but it poked him in the back and tickled his nose.

Slowly, he sat and looked into a pair of eyes the color of the sky.

"You're awake," Annabel said, her voice low and smoky. Just the sound of it made his headache recede.

"What time is it?" he asked.

"A little after nine." She studied his face carefully, staring into his eyes as though examining him.

"I'm fine," he said, pushing to his feet. A wave of dizziness threatened to topple him, and she was instantly at his side, her arm around his waist to steady him. He rather liked the feel of her pressed against him and decided maybe he could use a little help.

"You should sit down."

"I couldn't sit another minute. I want to look around." If the dizziness ever receded.

"The doctor said you should rest."

"I've been resting." He started for the door to the stall, and she went with him, her arm still around him. "Where did you sleep?" *Please don't say in the stable*, he thought. He didn't want to have spent the night with her and not remember it.

"In the coach," she said. "There's really not much to see. Mr. Jackson is ordering everyone about and some of the people from the town have come to help him with repairs and rebuilding."

At the edge of the stable, she hesitated and waved at someone. Reynolds was beside him in a minute. Annabel slipped away, and Reynolds took her place, wrapping his arm about Phin's back. Phin wasted no time pushing his valet away.

"I'll see what I can find for you to eat," Annabel said, moving back into the stable, while Phin proceeded forward. He meandered about the yard, looked inside the inn, and saw to his personal needs before returning to the stable. He felt better for having walked in the crisp morning air, but his head still hurt like the devil himself was dancing on it.

In the stall, Annabel had set up a table of sorts and on it were two bowls of what looked like gruel. He eyed it with distaste. She gave him a smile of commiseration. "It's all I could find. I'm told it's porridge."

He grunted and lowered himself to the makeshift table. He spooned some porridge into his mouth, and when it didn't make him gag, he ate the rest of it. Annabel stared at him in wonder then handed her own bowl over.

"I can't eat yours."

"Neither can I. I don't want it to go to waste. After you eat, you should take this medicine the doctor left."

"It didn't help at all."

She gave him a stern look. "You won't be a difficult patient, will you, duke?"

He liked that tone in her voice. "What if I am?"

"Then I'll have to give you a very stern, motherly lecture."

"I think I might enjoy that, actually." He smiled.

She rolled her eyes. "Do you ever stop flirting?"

He considered. "Not when I'm with a beautiful woman, no. But I'll take the medicine if it makes you happy."

"It does."

"Then consider it done. We should make a start. We're leaving hours later than I wanted, but we might be able to make up some of the time."

She shook her head. "Absolutely not. You are in no condition to travel. We cannot possibly leave today."

"I can sit in the carriage as well as I can sit here, and I have no intention of sleeping in a stable again. I want a proper inn or Ceald House itself if we can press on."

She went very still, and he tried to think what he might have said to upset her. "What's wrong?"

"I didn't think we would stay at Ceald House. There's an inn just a mile away. I'd rather stay there."

"But you are the Countess of Longstowe, at least until the current earl marries. You have every right to stay there."

"I prefer not to." Her tone made it clear that was the end of the discussion, but Phin did not give up that easily.

"Why is that?"

"I don't get along with Lady Wavenwell."

"It's one night, and you won't be sleeping with her."

"If it's an issue of money—" she began.

He waved a hand. "It's not an issue of money. I'm simply curious as to why you dislike Ceald House so much."

She looked down then away. "I told you my husband sent me to the country with Theadosia when she was a baby."

"Yes."

"We stayed at Ceald House. My memories there are...bittersweet. I'd rather not be surrounded by them or reminded of those days any more than I have to be."

Phin could understand this reasoning, but something niggled at him. "What kind of husband was the late earl?" he asked. Colin had said he was a cruel man, but he wondered how Annabel would describe him.

She started, which was a curious response to a rather banal inquiry. "Why should you want to know that?" she asked.

"I told you. I'm curious."

"He was like any other husband, I suppose."

"So husbands are all the same then?"

She rose. "How should I know? I had one, and I don't plan to have another."

With that, she rose and strode out of the stall. Quite a reaction to a very reasonable question. She didn't want to talk about her husband. And now Phin wanted to know why.

***

They did not set out for Ceald House until almost noon. Mr. Jackson had busied almost all of the grooms with tasks related to the inn and the fire damage itself, and even a duke had difficulty persuading the innkeeper to allow him the use of a few men. In the end, the duke's own servants did much of the work to ready the horses, and he would have helped himself if Annabel had not admonished him time and again to sit down and rest. Finally, the team was harnessed and his coachman seated atop the box. Fortunately, none of his household had been injured in the fire, and everyone was eager to put the smoky ruin of the inn behind them.

Phin probably should have ridden in the first carriage with Reynolds and given the ladies their privacy, but he couldn't quite convince himself to part with Annabel. He'd grown used to the musky scent of her and her low, soothing voice. He sat across from her and tried not to wince as every bounce of the coach sent knives of pain through his head. For her part, Annabel read her book or watched him. She probably thought she was watching him covertly, but she would have made a terrible spy. She was obviously worried about him.

When they reached a posting house and Mrs. Slightley exited the carriage to walk about, Annabel moved to sit beside him. There was plenty of room. The ducal coach was large and lavish, the squabs outfitted in velvet and wide enough that even he might have lain down if he bent his knees. And still, he felt as though she were all but sitting on his lap. Being alone with her and feeling the heat of her body made him almost giddy.

"We should stop at the next inn. It's been a long day, and I'm quite fatigued."

Phin was not fooled. "You're perfectly fine. You worry I am not well."

"You don't look well," she said without argument. "You look pale and drawn."

"I've felt better, but I'm far from death's door. I can make it to Ceald House."

"I should never have asked you to come."

"I'm glad you did."

She gave him a look that said she thought the bump on his head had finally addled his brain.

"If you had asked another man—another duke—I wouldn't have come to know you as I do."

"There wasn't another duke I could ask."

She really did not realize how lovely she was or how much speculation swirled about her. "Oh, you could have asked anyone. You barely knew me, and what you knew was only that I'd insulted you. I have no doubt you have the courage to ask the prince regent if you thought it necessary."

She shook her head. "You have me mistaken. I have asked for help in the past, but either I was refused or the assistance came to nothing. You are the first person I've dared ask who can actually help me."

"That is yet to be seen, but I will do my best."

"I know. And I still don't understand why you agreed to help." She sounded genuinely confused.

"I told you. I wanted to spend time with you."

She stared at him. "Why? Surely you have friends you would rather spend time with than a stranger who makes you drive all the way to Wiltshire."

"Why?" He moved his bare hand to press a loose button at the sleeve of her pelisse between two fingers. "Because I like you. I'm intrigued by you." She didn't say anything, but she also did not tense as she usually did when he paid her a compliment or made his interest in her known. "I think you might be coming to like me as well."

"You are a difficult man not to like."

His hand slid from her button to the edge of her sleeve. "Is it my good looks?"

She looked down at his hand as he slid it under her sleeve, touching the edge of her gloves. "Those do not hurt, but I've known many handsome men who were cruel."

His finger brushed the bare skin just above her gloves and he heard her catch her breath. Her skin was so warm and soft. He slid higher up her forearm.

"Then it must be my sparkling conversation and wit."

"I think it's your kindness, actually." Her voice shook slightly. He might not have heard it if he hadn't been listening.

"That sounds like what someone says about a friend." He looked into her eyes. "I told you, I want to be more than your friend, Annabel."

"And I told you, I don't think that's a good idea."

"You did." He slid her sleeve up, revealing a swath of her bare arm. "You don't want to be controlled."

"Yes. I mean, no. I don't want a—oh!"

He bent to kiss the bared skin, brushing his mouth against it lightly. She smelled delicious. He kissed her again, moving his mouth up her arm. She shook but did not pull her arm away. "You say you don't want a lover," he murmured against her flesh. He darted his tongue out and tasted her. She gasped. "But I think you *do* want a lover, Annabel. I think you *need* a lover."

"It won't be like you think," she said, her voice hoarse and little more than a whisper.

That was an interesting statement. "How do you know what I think being with you would be like?" He moved his lips back down the path he'd traced, and she leaned closer to him. She wanted his touch, wanted affection. He did not understand why she refused to take what he offered.

"You think I am some seductress who will satisfy your every fantasy."

He looked up at her, feeling slightly annoyed. What had he done to deserve her low opinion? "That's where you are wrong, Annabel. My fantasy is not for you to satisfy me, but to spend the night satisfying you."

She pulled her hand away, and Phin felt loss like he'd not known before.

"Then I will surely disappoint you. I can't be satisfied, Mayne. Not like you think."

It seemed every cryptic statement she made was followed by another even more puzzling. He wanted to ask what she meant, but before he could Mrs. Slightley returned and Annabel slipped out of the coach. When she returned, she did not look at him but kept her gaze on her book. The rest of the journey was made in almost complete silence until the coachman called, "Ceald House!"

***

Annabel started at the announcement, and her hand shook as she parted the curtains. The drive was so familiar that she felt as though it had been only a few days since she had been here last, when in reality it had been many years. She'd come here after the earl's death. She'd wanted to collect her personal effects before Lady Wavenwell took up residence. But that was not the memory that stirred her now. It wasn't even the memory of arriving here with her baby girl in her arms.

It was the memory of coming here the day after her wedding. Her wedding had taken place on a cold, wet day in a dark church with only a few family members in attendance. She remembered looking down at her husband, as she was three or four inches taller than he, and noticing that, between the strands of his thinning white hair, his scalp was pink. She had been barely eighteen and he more than sixty. She was his third wife.

The first had died in childbirth and the child, a boy, had died as well. The second had given him only girls before she too passed away. She'd understood exactly why he wanted to marry her. She was young, and he needed a son. Her parents, gentry but not titled, had wanted her to make a good match. She'd been lovely at eighteen, and her parents had held out for a titled husband for her.

She hadn't wanted to marry the old man who came to court her, but she had not argued. The earl had praised her obedience and said it would serve her well. She had tried not to think of the wedding night and the long years ahead of her. She'd wanted to please her parents.

And she wanted to please her husband. She'd not been stubborn or willful then. She'd learned that later.

On the night of the wedding, her lady's maid had dressed her in a pretty garment, and she'd climbed into bed and waited. He'd come to her in the dark and, with very little preamble, deflowered her. He hadn't hurt her. He'd been, if not tender, gentle. But she'd shuddered at the way his bony fingers had caressed her hips and entered her sex. She'd not liked the sounds he'd made when he moved inside her. And she had not been disappointed when he'd left her to sleep in his own chamber.

The next morning they'd departed for Ceald House very early. He pushed his coachman hard and they'd not stopped to rest until they arrived. Annabel had been exhausted from the journey and from the effort of trying to behave perfectly in front of her new husband. She'd been shown to her bed chamber and fallen asleep almost instantly. She'd been awakened some time later by her husband, who was angry that she had not bathed and prepared for him. She tried to apologize, but he didn't want to hear it. He'd ordered a bath for her and embarrassed her by making her strip down in front of him and forcing her maid to wash her as he watched.

Then he'd taken her in the dark. That time he was not as gentle.

She'd come to hate Ceald House in the first few years of their marriage. When they were in Town for the Season, the earl was busy with social engagements, his club, and the Lords. It was when they were in the country that he had time to play his "games." That was what he'd called them. They took place in her chamber, often in the dark, and were meant to humiliate or hurt her. The more she cried or begged or screamed, the more pleasure he seemed to take.

She couldn't deny that he'd given her pleasure too. There had been times when he'd been kind to her, when he'd touched her in ways she enjoyed, when he'd done things to her that had caused her to climax. But the earl believed for every pleasure there should be equal pain. She'd learned not to allow her body to react to even his most skilled caresses or she would limp for weeks afterward.

He'd worried that a young woman like her would look elsewhere for fulfillment. He'd wanted to make sure that she associated pleasure with pain. And he'd succeeded. Even after his death, when she had gone to other men's beds or touched herself, she had not ever been able to feel pleasure again.

That was what Mayne did not understand. It did not matter how he touched her. She could not feel that sort of pleasure.

And it had all started here.

"Should we return tomorrow?" Mayne asked softly, causing her to look away from the window. They were almost to the main house. Even in the dark she knew the way.

"Do you think it too late to call?" she asked.

"I think you look like you just saw a ghost."

"Just memories," she said.

"Not good ones, I think. We can return tomorrow morning."

She shook her head. "We are here now, and I am family. We should get the preliminaries over with."

The coach stopped in front of the house, and a butler and two footmen stood on the drive. They must have heard the coach as they certainly couldn't have been expecting her.

One of Mayne's outriders opened the coach door, lowered the stairs, and announced first the duke and then, when he held out his hand and Annabel descended, the countess.

The butler, who had not been here when she had lived here, looked surprised, but quickly bowed and welcomed her.

"We've come to see Lady Wavenwell and the earl, if he is in residence," she said.

"The earl is away at school, my lady. But I will tell Her Ladyship you have arrived."

He escorted them inside, and Annabel was grateful for Mayne's steady presence beside her. His arm did not waver, and he was strong and solid. When she stepped inside and saw the foyer, she'd wanted to turn and run. There were the steps the earl had thrown her down and the slight discoloration of the marble where her blood had stained it when the earl had beaten her for trying to run away. And that was the chair where she'd held Theadosia and directed the servants to unpack the child's things. The memories of Theadosia hurt the most. Having them so fresh in her mind was like the turning of the knife that had pierced her heart all those years ago.

"I have you, Annabel," Mayne murmured so that only she could hear. "I'm right here."

"I shouldn't have come," she said. "I want to go."

"Too late," he said as a door opened, and the butler announced Lady Wavenwell. "Hold on to me, sweetheart."

The butler had finished announcing them, and Annabel watched as Lady Wavenwell's gaze flicked over Annabel but landed on Mayne with interest. She imagined he knew that look. He'd probably seen it a hundred times in ballrooms filled with matchmaking mothers.

"Your Grace and Lady Longstowe, to what do I owe the honor?"

Lady Wavenwell was of an age with Annabel, but she was small and thin and had a pinched face that made her seem older. Even when the earl had been alive and Annabel clearly outranked her, she'd felt like a silly girl next to Lady Wavenwell.

"The honor is all mine," Mayne said, releasing Annabel to make a sweeping bow. He moved forward and took the other woman's hand, bending low to kiss it. "I cannot believe we have never met before, my lady. For if we had, I would not have forgotten."

The pinched look seemed to leave the viscountess's face as Mayne bowed over her. Annabel wondered if she looked that way when he gazed at her. Was she as easily played?

He stepped back and took Annabel's arm again. "When my friend Lady Longstowe invited me to see Ceald House and meet you, I admit I said, *What can there be of interest to me in Wiltshire?* Clearly, I was very much mistaken." He paused and looked at Annabel, who realized belatedly it was her turn to greet the viscountess.

She nodded her head. "Clarissa, it is good to see you again."

"Annabel," she said, Lady Wavenwell's stiffness returning. "Why have you come? The earl is not here, and even if he was, I would not permit a woman like you see him."

Annabel stiffened, understanding exactly the implication the viscountess made. She was the Wanton Widow. She would not be allowed to corrupt a boy like the earl. "I haven't come to see the earl, I've come—"

Mayne waved a hand. "We shall discuss all of that tomorrow. It's too late tonight, and I haven't had dinner. We came tonight to ask if we might call on you tomorrow. Say 11 o'clock?"

"Why not say what you want tonight?" the viscountess asked.

"Because then I won't be able to see you again tomorrow," Mayne said. "And I do look forward to that." He bowed. "Until tomorrow, my lady."

Somehow Annabel made it back to the carriage. She didn't remember walking or even taking her leave of Lady Wavenwell. Once in the carriage, she could not quite seem to catch her breath. The tightness in her chest made it seem impossible to draw in air, and she began to gulp in as much as she could.

"My lady, what is the matter?" Mrs. Slightley asked, her face white with concern. The outriders had lit the carriage lamps while they were inside Ceald House, and the motion of the coach made the light shake eerily.

"I'm fine," she gasped. "I just need some air."

Mayne moved quickly, his voice commanding as he issued orders. "Open the window, Mrs. Slightley, then move aside so I can see to her ladyship."

Mrs. Slightley moved to the opposite side of the carriage and lowered the window, allowing the cold air inside. It felt good on Annabel's overly warm cheeks. Then Mayne took her hand. His was warm and gentle. It felt like a lifeline she could cling to.

"Lady Longstowe, sit back. Yes, like that. Now, close your eyes and concentrate on one thing only—taking a breath. Imagine the air coming into your lungs and then back out again. Slowly now. That's right."

She'd closed her eyes, and his voice was there in the darkness with her as she struggled to make her lungs do as she commanded them. They felt as though someone had squeezed them into a wrinkled compact sheet of parchment, and she could not seem to flatten and smooth the parchment out again.

"You are doing well. Are you imagining the air coming in? Yes, now let it out. Slowly."

She tightened her grip on his hand. Taking a breath did seem to be slightly easier. Finally, she was able to breathe without her chest hitching, and she opened her eyes. Mayne's face was before her. He gazed at her with concern but not pity. "Better now?"

She nodded.

"It was a mistake to come here tonight. I should have taken you to the inn and sent word."

"It's not your fault."

"It is. We are all exhausted from last night, and it's obvious Ceald House has bad associations for you. I'm inclined to take you straight back to London tomorrow."

"No!" She clenched the hand she still held tightly. "I don't want to go back to London. I am determined to see this through. I will be fine tomorrow. I just need rest."

He gave her a dubious look then glanced at Mrs. Slightley. "You will see that she rests tonight?"

"Yes, Your Grace. I will take excellent care of her."

"If you need anything, send for me or Reynolds and you shall have it."

"Yes, Your Grace."

Mayne looked at Annabel again. He gave her a searching look then released her hand and settled back. "I can already tell that Lady Wavenwell will prove difficult to deal with."

"No doubt you will have her in the palm of your hand in no time. Who knew you could be so charming?"

He smiled. "Sometimes I surprise even myself."

She wanted him to take her hand again. She needed to touch him. For the comfort, yes. But also because she liked his touch. He had said he thought she needed a lover. He might be right. Until she had spent time with him, she hadn't realized how much she craved touch and affection. Every time his arm brushed against her or his foot nudged hers or he took her hand in his, she wanted more.

It had been so long since she had been held by anyone. She had been so afraid to trust any man, but Mayne seemed different. What if she took the risk? What if she gave in, just this once, to her need for touch, for affection? She might not be able to feel the pleasure he wanted to give, but she could give him pleasure. And she would enjoy just being held. Perhaps that was what she needed to fortify her for the trials that tomorrow would bring.

And there was also the fact that she didn't want to be alone tonight. She did not want to be alone with her memories and nightmares. Could she trust him not to attempt to control her? She did not know, but in this moment when her thoughts were in a jumble and her feelings in turmoil, she couldn't think about that. She just knew she needed…him.

She needed Mayne and the comfort he could bring.

Finally, the coach reached the inn, and there was much activity as rooms were secured, the horses were unharnessed, and luggage was brought inside. Annabel took advantage of the hubbub to touch Mayne's arm. He gave her a distracted glance, and then, perhaps seeing something of what she intended in her gaze, turned fully toward her.

"What is it?"

"Come to my room tonight." He stared at her as though he hadn't heard. She didn't lower her gaze, didn't look away. "I'll send Mrs. Slightley away in an hour or so. Come to me then."

He still didn't speak and the two of them stared at each other for a long moment.

"Your Grace—" one of the servants called.

Mayne held his hand up, silencing the man. To Annabel, he said, "Are you saying what I think you are saying?"

Of course he would have to question her about it, and just now she did not want to think. She simply wanted to be held. "If you think I am asking you to come to my room, then yes."

"But I thought—"

"Do you really want to argue with me, Phineas?" Her voice was full of exasperation.

Her use of his Christian name seemed to snap him out of his confusion. "No, I don't. I'll knock twice, pause, then knock again."

She smiled. "A secret code?" He really was adorable. "Until later."

She spent the next hour washing, dining from a tray brought to her room, and then having Meg help her change into a nightrail. It felt good to be clean and comfortable. She really was quite tired, but the fluttering of anticipation in her belly would not allow her to rest.

What was she doing? This had seemed like such a good idea in the coach, but now she was not so sure. What if she was making a mistake? She laughed at the ridiculousness of that thought since it came far too late to be useful. Meg glanced over her shoulder to peer at her curiously. And why not? Annabel thought herself half-mad. Not only was she making herself vulnerable to a powerful man, asking such a man to come to her room was opening herself to scandal. Though her reputation was already in tatters. Besides, she was a widow and the duke was a bachelor, and they were traveling together. People would assume they were lovers even if they were not. As long as they did not flaunt their affair, Society would look the other way. That wouldn't stop them from talking about it, of course. Soon they would accuse her of having ten lovers, making her more wanton as the gossip was spread.

But Annabel had known that was the risk when she'd asked Mayne to help her. She'd been willing to face the consequences to get her daughter back. And she was willing to face them now if it meant a night in Mayne's arms.

"Meg," she said as the housekeeper finished folding the last of her traveling garments. "I'd prefer having the chamber to myself tonight. Is there somewhere for you to sleep or should I see about securing you a room?"

Meg's eyes went wide, but she recovered quickly. "The innkeeper did say he has a couple of empty beds in the maids' quarters, my lady. I can sleep there, but it's on the second floor. I won't be close if you need anything."

"Thank you, but I think I will be just fine."

"Yes, my lady." She hesitated for another minute. "I'll take my things and go then."

"Thank you. And Mrs. Slightley?" she said when Meg had gathered her satchel and reached the door. "You deserve a rest. Have a lie in if you want, yes?"

Meg nodded. "Yes, my lady. Are you feeling well?"

"Perfectly fine."

And she was, except for the thundering of her heart and the dryness in her throat. She sipped from her glass of wine, removed her robe, and waited for Mayne to come to her.

Eleven

"What are you doing up here?" Reynolds asked when Meg stepped onto the third-floor landing. She hadn't expected to see him there, though if she'd thought about it, she would have known he was probably sleeping with the other male servants in their quarters.

He held a tray, which she assumed had contained his dinner and which he was probably returning to the kitchen. Meg had eaten with Lady Longstowe, which was not exactly proper, but in private the countess didn't stand on ceremony.

"The same thing as you, I imagine," Meg answered saucily.

"I thought you would sleep with Her Ladyship."

Meg was not prudish by any stretch of the imagination. Working in the countess's household meant she didn't have as many opportunities to enjoy a good romp as she had when she'd been traveling with the circus, but these were the compromises one was prepared to make. And so when Lady

Longstowe sent her away, Meg knew why. She just wasn't certain what she ought to reveal to the duke's valet.

"She said she prefers to sleep alone tonight."

Reynolds raised a brow. "Interesting. His Grace also prefers to sleep alone."

Meg nodded. "The way they look at each other, it's no surprise they'd both want to—er, sleep alone tonight."

"You've noticed it too?" He leaned on the wall at the landing. He was still dressed in the clothing he'd worn when they traveled, and she could see from the shadows under his brown eyes that he was tired.

"I've noticed it," she said. "In fact, I had to share a carriage with them. There were several times I wished I had a fan just to cool the lust."

He laughed, a deep laugh that made him look so open and approachable. "Well, then I hope they both *sleep well* tonight."

"My lady is a good woman. She's not a loose woman as some like to say." Meg didn't know why she felt the need to defend Lady Longstowe. It wasn't as though Reynolds had maligned her.

"Are you implying His Grace is a rake or a scoundrel? He's not the sort of man who would ever hurt a woman. And your lady is not a debutante. Undoubtedly, she knows what she wants. She couldn't choose better than the duke." Obviously Reynolds felt the need to defend His Grace too.

Meg crossed her arms. "Is that so?"

"It is. I have served him for years. He can be quite generous with ladies."

She put her hands on her hips. "And you think you know what a lady would consider generous?"

"You don't?"

She looked him up and down. He was handsome enough and confident. She'd eyed him before when he wasn't looking, but now she made a point of looking her fill. Besides the almost black hair and brown eyes, he had long legs with well-formed calves, narrow hips, a slim waist and a pleasant smile. Her gaze went to his groin area. He looked to have all that was necessary there.

Reynolds barked out a laugh. "And I thought I was impudent. You just eyed me as though I were a thoroughbred at Tattersalls."

"You asked if I thought you knew what a lady liked. I had to determine whether you'd had any experience with the fairer sex yourself."

He leaned down to murmur, "Perhaps you'd like a demonstration of my knowledge."

Meg had been flirting with him. She often flirted as she enjoyed the give and take. She hadn't expected Reynolds to actually offer something beyond mere words. And she wasn't sure if she could trust him. She'd been treated as an oddity before, but Reynolds had hit that doctor. Maybe there was something different about the valet.

"I would like a demonstration, now that you mention it." There. She would see what he said to that!

He grinned, looked her up and down, then moved down a step to narrow the height difference between them. Taking her hand, he tugged her forward so she stood at the edge of the landing. Then he bent and kissed her.

From the first touch of his lips, Meg's insides went warm and melted. Ooh, but he was quite good at kissing. When he drew back, Meg frowned. "I think I need another demonstration," she said.

"Another?" He had a glint in his eye that said he knew exactly what she was about.

"Just to be certain."

"You don't want to rush to judgement."

"No, I—"

But he was already kissing her again, this time coaxing her lips open and slipping his tongue inside. She wrapped her arms about his neck and kissed him back. She could stand here all night kissing him. She didn't know how much longer they stood in that embrace, his mouth teasing hers and her hands fluttering through his hair as she tried to restrain the impulse to touch him elsewhere.

Finally, he pulled back. His eyes were darker than usual and his hair mussed. "I like you a great deal, Mrs. Slightley. But I'd rather not have to explain what we're doing to one of the inn's staff."

Meg nodded in agreement. If someone decided to inform the countess or the duke, Meg doubted His Grace or Her Ladyship would be pleased.

"Good night then," she said, running a finger along his cheek. She liked the feel of the rough stubble on her skin. He turned his head and kissed her palm.

"Until tomorrow. Sleep well." He retrieved his tray and continued down the servants' stairs, while she found the maids' chamber. She was alone, but it was easy to see which beds were not occupied. She placed her satchel on an unmade bed, but instead of shaking out the sheets and making it up, she sat on the edge.

Sleep well, he'd said. That was unlikely with the taste of him on her lips and the low throbbing between her thighs.

***

She couldn't possibly be suggesting what he thought she was suggesting. Phin had opened and closed his door half a dozen times. She said she wanted him to come to her. Why was he hesitating?

Because he'd seen the way she looked in the carriage and the foyer of Ceald House. She'd been, for lack of a better word, terrified. What the devil had happened to her there? It had to be more than having her child taken from her, though that was reason enough for her to experience discomfort. But was that really all?

And would he really stand here all night debating instead of going to the woman he had wanted since he'd first seen her? And yet, perhaps he should think this through. When he'd kissed her, he'd felt...he didn't know what he felt. If he kissed her again, if he took her to bed, then what? What if that wasn't enough?

Someone tapped on the door, and as he was standing right on the other side of it, Phin flung it open. His retort died on his lips as Annabel smiled at him. Phin didn't wait. He grasped her arm, pulled her inside, peered back out into the corridor, then shut and locked the door.

When he turned back, she'd removed her wrapper. He'd wanted to say something—to ask her something—but all thoughts fled from his mind at the sight of her in the thin, all but transparent garment. It bared her arms and a good portion of her bosom and ended just below her knees.

So much bare flesh, and Phin wanted to touch every single inch of it. If this was all he could have of her, at least he could remember this one night.

"You were taking too long," she said, her voice smooth and low. "I was impatient."

He swallowed. "I'm sorry." His voice was rusty as though from disuse.

"A gentleman should never keep a lady waiting." She moved toward him, slipping her arms about him. Before he knew what she was about, she was kissing him. Heat immediately flooded through him, and his cock rose to attention. She didn't force her mouth on his, but kissed him with slow, drugging kisses that even a stronger man would not have been able to refuse. Her mouth was so lush, so sweet, so soft. His hands went to her waist, and he felt the sweet curve of her hips.

She felt so good in his arms, so perfect. He dragged one hand up her back until he reached the coil of hair at the nape of her neck. His fingers plucked at the pins holding her hair in place until it tumbled in a soft auburn mass over his hands. Their kisses grew deeper and more fevered, and Phin wanted everything slower. He wanted this night to last. Sliding his hand along her jaw, he sought to slow the kiss and perhaps wrest some control of it from her. He moved his mouth, tracing her lips, her jaw, and then dragging his tongue lightly over the skin of her neck.

The scent of her was intoxicating and the feel of her skin was like a drug. But she didn't angle her head to give him more access nor did she make any moans or sounds of pleasure. He drew back to see her face, and her hands which had been resting on his chest dipped down to cup his erection.

Phin felt all of the blood drain from his head downward. With her hand on him one thought reigned supreme, and that was to take her fast and hard. He grappled with the urge, fought it, then grasped her arms and wrapped them around his waist. He pulled her into an embrace and rested his head on her shoulder, fighting to control his rapid breathing.

"Give me a moment."

She didn't object to his suggestion. Instead, she tightened her arms about him and laid her head in the crook of his neck. The warmth of her body seeped into him and Phin tried to quell his spinning thoughts. She'd walked into his chamber and overwhelmed him with the sight of her body and the way she'd plundered his mouth. Was she really so eager to bed him or did she just want it over?

As soon as he'd thought it, her hands moved down from his waist to squeeze his buttocks. Phin pulled back. "What is this?"

Confusion flickered over her face but was quickly replaced by a sultry expression. "Is there anything wrong with being eager?"

"Are you eager or do you just wish to be done with it?"

"What I wish is for you to take off some of your clothing. You're wearing too much."

"Where should I begin?"

"Your trousers." She ran her hands down his chest, over the bulge in his clothing, then sank to her knees before him. "You won't regret it."

Phin had no doubt she told the truth. She seemed to know exactly what she was about, and his body was responding as it never had to any woman before. He wanted her mouth on him. And the fact that she offered so freely was even more tantalizing. But quick release and then a farewell was not what he really wanted. He wanted to know her better, learn what she liked and didn't, explore every inch of her body.

And he wanted to give her pleasure before he took his own.

He pulled her back to her feet.

Now she did not bother to hide her confusion. "I don't understand. I thought you wanted me."

"I do want you. *You*. Not the Wanton Widow."

She shook her head. "I *am* the Wanton Widow."

He smoothed her hair back from her face. He could see a few strands of gray in it, and it only made her appear more vulnerable. He was beginning to understand she did not like to be vulnerable. He knew the feeling. "Not when you're alone with me. With me, you're Annabel. Not Lady Longstowe. Not the Countess of Longstowe. Not the Wanton Widow. Just Annabel. And I'm just Phin—not Mayne or duke or, God forbid, His Grace."

She stepped back then bent and picked up her wrapper. Phin thought it criminal to cover her beautiful body, but he didn't object.

"I don't think I can do what you're asking."

"Then we can sit and talk." He crossed the room and poured two glasses of the wine he'd drank with dinner. Handing one to her, he smiled and gestured to a chair at the small, round table flanked with two chairs. "Where were you born, Annabel?"

She looked at the wine and then the table. "You just want to talk to me?"

"No, I want to kiss every inch of you, kissing and licking my way over your breasts and between your legs until you're panting and screaming for more. But if that isn't possible, then I'm content to talk."

She sat heavily in the chair he'd offered. "I told you before, it won't be like that. I can't—I don't feel pleasure like that."

Phin sat in the seat across from her, taking his time in order to gather his thoughts. "Maybe you just haven't had the right lover."

"And you think you can succeed where others haven't? Of course, you do." She rolled her eyes.

"I'm a patient and eager student. I'll find what you like and show you how it can be."

He might have been mistaken, but he thought she shivered. She sipped her wine. "It's not—" She stopped and looked across the room to the fire blazing in the hearth.

"Go on," he said, trying to utilize that patience he'd just boasted of.

"I don't want to talk about it," she said, finally. "I just…can't be what you want." She began to rise, but he went to her, bending on one knee before her.

"You already are what I want."

"How can you say that? You hardly know me!"

"I know enough. I know you are compassionate, loyal, caring, a loving mother, a kind mistress, a clever woman, and I also know something happened in Ceald House that you don't like to think about. Something that still terrifies you."

Her face paled as she looked down at him.

"Whatever it was that happened, it won't make me want you less. I want you like I've never wanted another woman." God, that was the truth, and he was terrified to reveal it. What if she refused him now?

"This is foolish talk. It's infatuation. It won't last."

The dismissal hurt like the sting on one's cheek after a slap. But he did not think she'd meant to wound him, insult him. "And if this feeling does last?" he asked.

"Then you'll be forced to deny your feelings and marry a woman who can be your duchess. A woman who is young and a virgin and who will give you an heir."

Her words were like ominous thunderclouds on the horizon. They told of a storm coming he couldn't escape. But that storm wasn't here yet. *She* was here. "I can't think of anything I want less. I didn't want to be a duke, and I don't want to marry a girl barely out of the schoolroom."

"I can assure you that if you knew the truth about me, you wouldn't want me either."

"Then let's put it to the test. Tell me, and I'll prove you wrong."

She rose, and he was forced to stand and move out of her way. "This was a mistake," she said.

"Answer me one thing before you go." He was bargaining for time with her now. He could already see she wanted nothing more than to be away from him. He was surprised how much that knowledge hurt.

She looked at him, her expression impatient.

"Why did you invite me to your room tonight?" He held up a hand to forestall her quick reply. "The truth, Annabel. One truth tonight is all I'm asking."

She drew in a long, slow breath. Then she let it out, and her shoulders seemed to sag with it. "You were right," she said quietly. "I want affection. I want to be held and touched. It's been so long since anyone has touched me…the way you do."

Phin didn't dare move. He didn't dare breathe. He certainly didn't dare speak. Instead, he opened his arms and held them wide. It was an invitation with no expectations. If all she wanted was to be held, he would hold her. She looked at him for a long time, so long that his arms began to tire, and he began to think she would refuse him. He'd probably end up looking like a fool—again—but she was worth that.

Slowly, as though she were a frightened wild animal, she moved closer to him. He stood very still, not wanting to startle her. She moved closer then closer until she was safely inside the circle of his arms and he could close them around her.

He held her warm body cradled against his. He didn't know how long they stood there—a half hour? three-quarters of an hour?—before her body finally lost the tension she'd been holding.

He lifted a hand and stroked her hair. "I am not attempting to seduce you, but do you think we might continue this on the bed? My head is still aching from the injury."

"I should leave you to rest," she said, pulling away from him. He caught her hand lightly.

"I want you to stay. All I want to do is hold you. I just want to do it lying down."

She swallowed visibly then nodded and allowed him to tug her to the bed. He seated her on it then began to remove his coat. "This is only for the sake of comfort. I'll leave it on if you prefer."

"Of course you should take it off." She rose and helped him with the tight sleeves. Next came his cravat and the fastenings at his wrist. Then he sat and pulled off his boots. He would have liked to also remove his waistcoat, but he left it. "That's better." Because his head was pounding, he laid down gingerly and, as before, opened his arms to her.

This time she didn't hesitate. She crawled in beside him, surprising him by facing him and resting her head on his chest.

They lay like that for some time before she spoke. "I was born in Wiltshire," she said, answering his question from earlier. "Not this part of the county, but further east. That was how I met the earl. My father was a baronet and most of the gentry in the area knew each other. My father and the earl had quite a few friends in common."

Phin frowned, knowing Annabel couldn't see him. "Then your father and the earl were contemporaries." He'd had an idea of this from what Colin had told him, but he hadn't really considered the age difference until now.

"The earl was a few years my father's senior, actually."

"Ah." It wasn't uncommon for a girl to be wed to a man old enough to be her father or even her grandfather. But there was something about it that left a sour taste in his mouth. "It was not a love match then."

"No. Not at all." The tone in her voice told him exactly what he needed to know about the earl. He already hadn't liked the man for taking Annabel's child away, although, again, this was common practice when a child was mentally or physically aberrant. But to take the child without telling Annabel where she was or ever allowing her to see her daughter seemed particularly cruel.

She lifted her head and looked up at him. "Now you tell me something."

"What do you want to know?"

"Nothing in particular." She thought for a moment. "Are you really a war hero?"

"No. Nothing of the sort. Not unless you consider returning alive when most of your fellows are dead heroic."

"I don't know. Sometimes I think death might be easier than life. Is that a terribly unpatriotic thing to say about our fallen soldiers?"

Phin had to wonder if she was only referring to soldiers. "There are many things worse than death," he said. "Right after the war I used to dream of the men I killed. The troop I was with valued stealth, and we rarely killed with rifles or cannons. I remember men I shot as well, but I didn't dream about them like I did the ones I killed with a knife in my hand. Those whose blood I had to wash off my hands and face. I used to wake from those dreams and wish I was dead so I would not have to relive those moments over and over, night after night."

"But you chose to live."

He didn't know if she realized it, but her hand had begun to trace the floral pattern on his waistcoat. The light caress was soothing. "Every time I thought about death, I worried Hamlet might have a point."

"Hamlet?"

"What if we still dream when we're dead? What if death is one eternal nightmare?"

She rested her head on his chest again, her hand still caressing him. "I don't believe that."

"I'm in no rush to confirm."

"Do you still have nightmares?" she asked.

"Rarely. I think the nightmares mainly plague those who hold on to their guilt and their anger. I'm fortunate enough to see the men I served with often, and when I see what they have accomplished in their lives, I can hardly continue to feel guilt at having defended them or my country."

"Does it bother you to speak of it?"

"Not really. Why?"

"Your heart has sped up."

When he didn't respond right away, she looked up at him.

"That's because your touch excites me." He gazed pointedly at her hand, the fingers of which still slid up and down over his abdomen. "I'm not about to ravish you, but I'm not immune to your charms either."

"I've never known anyone like you," she said, her brow furrowed.

"That's what I keep trying to tell you, sweetheart."

She rolled her eyes again but didn't move away from him. He hoped that was a positive sign. She looked into his eyes for so long that he had to grip the bedclothes to keep from pulling her close for a kiss. Just when he thought he could no longer restrain himself, she said, "May I kiss you?"

"God, yes."

She lowered her mouth to his, her lips tender this time. He put his hands on both sides of her face, holding her gently and feeling the soft skin of her cheeks under his thumbs. She shifted more of her weight on him, her body warm where it touched his. She pulled back, looked into his eyes, then kissed him again, sliding her tongue between his lips.

When they broke apart, Phin groaned.

"That bad?"

"You're killing me," he admitted. "Please let me touch you."

She met his gaze, and he saw wariness and the beginnings of trust. "I'd like that."

Phin didn't hesitate. He slid out from under her and tucked her beneath him. The movement made him slightly dizzy, but he didn't care. He brushed the hair from her face then pressed a kiss to her eyes, her nose, her chin.

She laughed. "I think you missed my mouth."

"Don't rush me," he ordered. Next he kissed her forehead, her temple, and slid over to kiss that spot right below her ear. Her hands tightened on his back as he teased that spot with his tongue. "You like that?" he asked, pulling back.

"It makes me want to say all sorts of unladylike things."

Phin groaned again and lowered his head to her shoulder. Lust so sharp and hot lanced through him that he had to take several deep breaths before he had control of himself again.

He cleared his throat. "Who am I to censor you?"

She laughed again, and he kissed her throat, liking the feel of her laughter against his lips. He trailed kisses to her collarbone and her shoulder then down her arm. When he'd waited as long as he could, he shifted his mouth to the rise of her breast, kissing the linen covering it. Gently, he cupped it, feeling her nipple harden where his lips brushed over it. Her chest rose and fell rapidly, but he took his time, though he wanted to drag her chemise down and see the color of her nipples and take one into his mouth. Her breasts were as round and heavy as he'd expected, and he cupped the other then moved to kiss it.

"Stop." She shoved him hard, and in a haze of lust, he lifted his head. "Get off me," she ordered. Her eyes were large with desire, but the fear was quickly taking over. He sat and held his hands up, releasing her. She scrambled away from him, bending over and taking deep breaths. Phin wanted to go to her, but he knew better than to try and touch her now.

"What did I do wrong?"

"It's not you. I told you. I cannot do this." She reached for her wrapper and pulled it on.

"You don't have to leave. If you want to stop, I'll stop. But finish your wine. You look as though you need to sit down for a moment."

She looked back at him, her expression wild and also confused. "I have to go."

"I'll walk you to your room."

"You don't have to do that."

"I'm not sending you out into the corridor alone." He thrust a hand through his hair, attempting to tame it before opening the door and peering out. No one was in the corridor, and he motioned to her to come quickly. A moment later, they were before her door. She opened it and disappeared inside.

Phin stood on the other side, waiting to see if she would open it again and bid him goodnight. But all he heard was the lock snapped into place.

Twelve

She did not want to go down to breakfast. How could she face him after the way she'd behaved last night? She'd gone to his room, brazen and bold, then fled from him as though he were some sort of monster. She should have known it wouldn't go well. She should just accept she'd always be alone, that she was better off alone.

"Are you feeling well, my lady?" Mrs. Slightley asked as she pinned Annabel's hair into an elaborate coif. She'd returned to the room this morning, smiling and humming. Obviously, she had passed a much more enjoyable evening than Annabel had. Annabel was tempted to plead a headache. Mrs. Slightley had just given her the perfect excuse to avoid the duke. But she wasn't really that much of a coward.

Was she?

"I am just a little tired. I didn't sleep very well."

Mrs. Slightley made a neutral sound, but Annabel knew very well that her housekeeper thought she had spent the night with Phin. She should have spent the night with him.

She'd intended to. And she could have done it too, except that he hadn't wanted the façade she'd offered him. He'd wanted the real woman or no one, and she was not ready to give him her real self.

And then when they'd lain together on the bed, she'd begun to feel so safe and comforted in his arms. She wanted him, and that was no pretense. But without any of her usual protective armor, she had felt too much. She'd felt vulnerable. And when he'd touched her breast, she'd thought of *him*. In her mind, Phin's soft caresses became painful squeezes, and she just wanted to get away.

But Phin hadn't reacted as she'd expected. He hadn't been angry or insistent. He hadn't even seemed annoyed. He'd seemed concerned about her. She'd thought his offer of wine was a ploy to keep her in his room so he could convince her to go to bed with him. And then she'd thought he might try to come into her room and force her when he'd walked her back.

But he'd done none of those things, and she was ashamed she had thought him capable of them. She knew not every man was like the earl. Not every man expected to take his pleasure when and where he wanted, whether or not a woman agreed. But it was hard to trust a man again. It was hard to unlearn the old habits of flinching when touched and allowing her guard down for just a few moments of pleasure.

"There you are, my lady." Mrs. Slightley stepped in front of Annabel and admired her work. "I daresay you can hold your head high." She gave Annabel a hand mirror and Annabel nodded.

"It looks very good." She set the mirror down, not liking to look at her reflection too long. Every time she looked there were new wrinkles. "Is there anything you can't do, Meg?"

"I'm an awful cook, my lady. I can boil a potato but anything requiring more talent than that, and I'm hopeless."

"I'll keep that in mind." Annabel studied her housekeeper again. She'd known the woman for a decade, and she couldn't remember seeing her so…Annabel wasn't certain of the word. Happy? Certainly, Meg was not unhappy. She was no curmudgeon like Crotchett, but she didn't usually smile quite so much. "Where did you sleep last night, Mrs. Slightley?"

"In the servants' quarters. Why?"

"There's something…different about you this morning."

And then, to Annabel's amazement, Meg blushed. Annabel stared in amazement. "You're blushing."

"It's too warm in here. I should open a window."

"Don't you dare." It was freezing cold outside, and Annabel was only heated by the fire in the hearth because she had donned her warmest gown. "You needn't tell me why you are blushing, but don't give me frostbite trying to hide it."

Annabel rose, knowing she could not put breakfast off much longer.

"It's the valet," Meg said in a rush.

Annabel looked at her in surprise. "Which valet?"

"The Duke of Mayne's valet, Reynolds. He kissed me last night."

"He what?" Annabel's fists clenched. "I won't tolerate that sort of abuse."

"No, my lady." Meg waved her hands. "I wanted him to kiss me."

Annabel relaxed her hands. Of course, she had. That's why Meg was so giddy this morning—*that* was the word for it. She was giddy because she'd been kissed by a handsome man.

"I didn't know you liked him."

"Who wouldn't like him? He's handsome as the devil. All that dark hair and those light brown eyes."

"But he must be quite a few years younger than you."

Meg gave her a look.

Annabel looked away. "Not that age matters. Or so I have been told."

Meg straightened the brush and comb on the dressing table. "My lady, if you don't mind me saying, I thought *you* might smile a bit more this morning."

"Did you?" Annabel suddenly became very interested in a loose thread on the piping of her dress. "Well, I suppose that sort of happiness isn't possible for all of us. I had better go down to breakfast now."

"Yes, my lady." Meg dipped a curtsy, and Annabel avoided her eyes because she didn't want to see the sympathy.

Downstairs, the common room was bustling with activity. Annabel was shown to a private dining room, where the duke stood staring out a window. When she entered, he turned and smiled at her. She almost tripped at the force of that smile. It was so genuine, and he was so clearly happy to see her. Why was he not angry with her for running away from him the night before?

"I'm sorry I'm late," she said without smiling back at him.

"We don't leave for Ceald House for another hour, so there's plenty of time." He gestured to a table that had been laid with plate and a servant hastily poured two cups of tea then withdrew. Annabel sat and lifted the tea cup to warm her hands and to keep from fidgeting with them.

"I hope you slept well," the duke said, taking the seat across from her. It helped to think of him as the duke, not Phin. Not the man who had made her skin heat with his touches.

"Very well," she lied. "And you?"

"Not as well." He nodded as a servant entered carrying a tray with toast and jam, scones and cream, and an assortment of other typical breakfast items. When the servant withdrew, Phin—the duke—continued, "I was worried about you."

"You saw me safely to my room. There was no need to worry." Annabel busied herself spreading jam on a piece of toast.

"Annabel."

She looked up at the use of her name. His tone was firm but also slightly exasperated.

She set her knife on the plate. "I told you it wasn't a good idea. I knew something like that would happen."

"And yet you invited me to your room, and then came to my room unbidden."

"It was a mistake."

"Was it?"

He asked it so earnestly that the answer she had planned to give died on her lips. "Look how I mucked everything up."

He shrugged and gave her a look that said she was mad. "You didn't do anything wrong. I upset you, and I wanted to apologize."

She stared at him. "*You* are apologizing to *me*?"

"I'm trying."

The man was impossible. "I invited you to my room, then came to yours, took off my clothes, kissed you, got in bed with you, and then when you kissed me, I told you to stop and ran away. What exactly do you think you have to apologize for?"

"Whatever I did that made you want to leave."

She sighed. She didn't know what to do with this man. He'd told her from the beginning that despite his age, he was no boy. He was a man, and she was beginning to think that in some ways he was older than she. She couldn't avoid this conversation. She owed him some sort of explanation as she could believe he really had been kept awake, wondering what he'd done to make her flee.

"You didn't do anything wrong," she said. "When you touched me, it made me think of…the earl. He was not a gentle man. He was not…kind." If that wasn't the understatement of the decade.

"He was cruel," Phin said, seeming unsurprised.

She nodded. "I was so young when I married him, I didn't know any different. Only as I talked more frankly with other wives did I realize he was abusive. I didn't know how to fight back. It wasn't until I was older that I developed some armor, but somehow you manage to strip all that away. I suppose I felt vulnerable."

He nodded, and she could tell he was trying to think of the best way to ask whatever had come into his mind now.

"Just ask me," she said. "I don't see any reason to be coy at this point." She'd already told him far more than she'd told anyone about her marriage, save Lady Buntlebury.

To her surprise, Phin didn't ask anything but nodded as though he had all the information he needed. "It doesn't matter." He held out a hand, allowing her to choose whether to put hers into his or not. She wanted to touch him. She wanted to curl up beside him in the bed again and have him hold her close. She wanted him to kiss her again. But it was hardly fair to keep promising him one thing and then ripping it away.

Annabel put her hand into his, and his skin was warm and solid and he held her lightly.

"What matters is that I've come to care for you these past few days. You are a remarkable woman."

She shook her head. Why was he saying this to her? Why was he so understanding? She had never met anyone like him.

"Don't shake your head. You are remarkable. And I want to spend time with you on any terms. I hope you can believe I would never do anything you didn't want."

She did believe him. The problem was that her body wanted one thing and her mind another.

And because she was tempted to rise and go to him right that moment, she lifted her knife again and began spreading jam. "I trust you, Phin. I wouldn't be here in Wiltshire if I didn't."

"That's not what I mean—"

She interrupted because she couldn't risk continuing this conversation. She didn't trust herself. "We should discuss Lady Wavenwell and how we will persuade her to give us the earl's papers."

"Oh, that shouldn't be difficult. Leave it to me."

Annabel thought he seemed rather sure of himself. "I have been attempting to gain access to his papers for years. I don't think you realize how difficult it will be. I asked for your help because you are a duke, and she is a woman who respects power and wealth."

He sat back and crossed his arms. "She is a woman who wants power and wealth. All I need do is discover what she wants and begin negotiations. As I've said before, I am very good at negotiating."

She could well believe it. He had a way about him that made people want to do what he asked. "No doubt she'll want you to introduce her son to people, to take him under your wing."

Phin smiled. "Oh, she'll want more than that, I imagine."

Annabel's chest tightened with guilt. Why had she brought him here? Why had she asked him to do so much for her? "I don't want you to give her anything you don't want to. I don't know how I shall repay you as it is."

"You can find your daughter, and that's repayment enough." He sipped his tea. "Why are you looking at me like that?"

"Because this is either an elaborate scheme or you are simply too good to be true."

He grinned. "People do call me Perfect Phineas. It annoys me at times, but if you want to call me that, I won't object." He winked.

He really was too good. "I am not fond of arrogance, but I find I can tolerate it in you."

"It's not arrogance if it's true."

"Well," she said, rising from her chair, "you have certainly grown accustomed to being a duke."

His laughter followed her out of the room.

***

The house was as ugly and dreary as it had looked the day before. Perhaps it was lovely in the spring. Phin could see that it had potential. But as his coach approached, he couldn't help but think the edifice looked very much like an old, unhappy man. It seemed the windows sagged, and the roof wrinkled, and the arch of the door curved down like a frown.

But he would not be intimidated. Annabel was counting on him. He was determined not to disappoint her.

He'd suspected her husband had been cruel to her, but the fact that she'd confided it to him made him care for her even more. He wanted to protect her. To keep her from ever facing any more cruelty. That wasn't possible, of course, but he could attempt to give her one thing she wanted—her daughter.

Fortunately, his head was much better this morning. He still had a faint headache, but he could confine it to the back of his thoughts and concentrate on Lady Wavenwell.

And Lady Wavenwell was obviously expecting them. As the coach slowed in front of the house, the line of servants awaiting them straightened. The door of Ceald House opened, and the lady herself stepped out and came to the edge of the steps. They would have to go to her, that much was clear.

Phin looked at Annabel and extended a hand. She'd been tucked in the corner of the coach and silent for the drive. Now, as she moved forward, the light shining through the windows illuminated her pale skin and wide eyes. She looked more like a Roman slave being thrown to the lions in the Colosseum than a countess paying a call.

"I won't let her eat you," Phin said.

"What?" Annabel gave him a startled look.

"Lady Waddlesworth."

Annabel narrowed her eyes. "You know that is not her name."

"But I made you smile. Now keep that smile on your face. Here we go." The door opened and Phin stepped out, extending a hand to assist Annabel. He was proud of her. She kept her head high and her smile frozen in place as they approached. The viscountess held out her hand, and Phin released Annabel to bow and kiss that offered hand. The gesture was overdone, but it was something he had learned from his friend Rafe, who was a favorite of the ladies. It worked as Lady Wavenwell's cheeks colored slightly.

"How good to see you again, Your Grace. Please come in." As an afterthought she glanced at Annabel. "You too."

She led them through the foyer and into a drawing room. The house was not decorated in the latest styles, but everything was tasteful and well-maintained. He was offered a comfortable seat on a couch and Annabel was seated in a chair across from him. Phin thought about asking Annabel to sit beside him. She was still smiling, but her expression looked brittle. But Phin decided to see what Lady Wavenwell had in mind. He doubted she did anything without a reason.

She served them tea and when everyone had exchanged pleasantries, the viscountess cleared her throat. "How is it the two of you became *friends*?" She addressed the question to Annabel, but Phin hadn't missed the sneer in her voice on the word *friends*, and he jumped in.

"Lady Longstowe knew my brother Richard, and when he died, we bonded over our grief." Phin looked at Annabel whose smile had definitely faltered. He shrugged slightly. It was not untrue.

"How interesting. And he is the brother who hit his head on ice?"

This tedious conversation again. "No, that was Ernest," he drawled.

"Then he was involved in a duel?"

"No, that was George," Phin said. "But we could go on about my brothers' untimely deaths for hours. I was hoping we might speak about Lady Longstowe's daughter."

Lady Wavenwell reacted just a moment too late. Her feigned surprise did not fool Phineas in the least.

"You have a daughter, Annabel?"

Annabel narrowed her lovely blue eyes, and Phin wanted to shiver.

"You know I do," Annabel said sharply. "I've come to you before, asking to look through the earl's papers so that I might discern where she is."

"And how is it you lost her?" The viscountess's voice was sweet.

Annabel stiffened. "I did not lose her. She was taken from me."

"And now you wish to seek her out and undo the former earl's wishes? As I told you before, Annabel, the earl sent that child away for the good of the family. We can't have an aberration besmirching the family name."

"She was a child." Annabel rose. "Not an aberration!"

Lady Wavenwell turned her nose up. "Yes, well, you would say that considering the deviants you employ."

"How dare—"

"Ladies," Phin interrupted, seeing that the situation was quickly deteriorating. "Can we not discuss this calmly? Lady Longstowe, do sit."

Still breathing heavily, Annabel sat again.

"Lady Wavenwell," Phineas said with a smile. "I understand as well as anyone the importance of bloodlines. One does not want them tainted."

"Precisely."

Annabel stared daggers at him. He'd apologize later. Right now he'd get her what she wanted.

"But, as a mother yourself, you must also understand the force of a mother's love. Lady Longstowe wishes to see her daughter again. She does not want to flaunt her about Society. Surely, you can understand that and perhaps we might come to some sort of agreement. I would be happy to vouch for your son at White's and introduce him to some of my more powerful friends in exchange for you giving Lady Longstowe her late husband's papers." He glanced at Annabel, who was clearly holding her breath.

Lady Wavenwell sipped her tea and seemed to consider. "I will give Lady Longstowe access to the late earl's papers. She may have a few hours to look through them in the library."

"Excellent." Phin clapped his hands. "Where is it? I will assist her."

"But," Lady Wavenwell held up a finger. "I do not want your assistance with my son. He has connections aplenty."

Phin swallowed. He had known it was going too well. "What do you want?" he asked.

Lady Wavenwell lifted a bell and rang it. The drawing room doors opened, and a young woman was all but pushed inside by an older woman who Phin could only assume was her governess. The young woman was obviously Lady Wavenwell's daughter. She had the same dark hair and dark eyes and slim figure. She was, as far as Phin could tell, somewhere between the age of twelve and eighteen. Phin guessed closer to the latter as he realized what it was Lady Wavenwell wanted from him. Phin rose, as was polite.

"My daughter, Miss Bristol, will have her first Season this spring, Your Grace."

Phin's mind raced. First Season. So Miss Bristol was sixteen, possibly seventeen?

"I have been so occupied in overseeing the preparations for the trip to London that I fear I have neglected her. I thought you might amuse her for a few hours." She looked at Annabel. "While your friend searches for the information she needs."

Now Phin knew why Lady Wavenwell had not seated him beside Annabel. He could not tell, from across the room, what the countess was thinking. Her face was a mask of stone.

"Georgina, come have tea with us." Lady Wavenwell gestured to the empty place on the couch beside Phineas. And this was the other reason. She wanted her daughter beside a duke. But did she intend for him to marry her or merely to be able to say that Miss Bristol was acquainted with the duke, a status that would surely lend her cachet among other debutantes and could be embellished to say he had courted her?

Georgina shyly seated herself beside him and glanced at Annabel one last time before sitting. Did she object to the arrangement? He saw no harm in it. He could certainly chat with a young girl for a few hours. One look at the chit and he did not think her the sort to attempt to seduce him into ruining her. Not that he would have been tempted. She was younger even than his youngest sister and still seemed very much a child. Phin was not the sort of man attracted to innocence and virginity.

He listened with only half an ear as Lady Wavenwell detailed her daughter's accomplishments. Miss Bristol could play the pianoforte, embroider, draw, speak French, and dance beautifully. It was a list Phin was familiar with as every lady in the *ton* possessed a similar one.

Annabel said little during the exchange, but Miss Bristol seemed to warm to the attention and spoke softly and even managed to look Phin briefly in the eye. Finally, Lady Wavenwell rose and asked Annabel if she would be like to shown to the library. Annabel agreed.

Phin tried to catch her eye, to give her encouragement. He had thought he would search the late earl's papers with her. But he wanted her to know he felt she was perfectly capable of finding what she needed on her own.

Only Annabel did not look back at him. She walked away, head held high, behaving as though he was not even there.

Thirteen

"It won't work, you know," Annabel said as she paused outside the library waiting for Clarissa to unlock the door.

"I'm sure I don't know what you mean." Clarissa slid the key in the lock and pushed the library door open. It was dark and musty inside, but the familiar smell of *him* wafted out. After all these years, the earl's scent still lingered here. Annabel swallowed her nausea.

"I'm sure you do. And really I thought you had more pride than to thrust your daughter at a man simply because he is a duke."

"And I thought you had more sense than to seduce a man young enough to be your son. Shame, Annabel."

"You go too far."

"Do I? Consider this, Annabel. The man is a duke, and a duke needs an heir. You can't give him that. My daughter can. And if he doesn't choose her, he'll choose some other debutante. You can never be more to him than a bit on the side." She shoved Annabel into the dark library. "How the mighty have fallen." She shut the door on her words, thrusting Annabel into darkness.

Annabel wanted to panic. She didn't like this room and especially did not like it in the dark. But she kept her wits and felt her way to the heavy draperies. Once she had them parted, the weak winter light brightened the room and she was able to breathe again.

Ceald House was not much altered since she had last been here. Clarissa had refurnished it and changed out superficial pieces, but the look of it was still the same. Same marble floors, same chandeliers, same coldness about the place. Annabel had been able to pretend that she was in a different place in the drawing room. She'd focused on the chintz upholstery and the new lamps and unfamiliar paintings on the walls. But the library was another matter. It looked as though it had not been touched. Annabel's eyes roved over the bookshelves and the dark wood panels then finally settled on the desk. It had been *his* desk. She knew it well as she'd stood on this side of it many times while he berated her or ignored her, depending on how he was feeling that day.

She knew where he kept his papers too. They were in that cabinet behind the desk. She'd watched him unlock it to return or retrieve papers many times. She wondered if it was locked now.

Crossing to it, she knelt down, resisting the urge to look over her shoulder. Ridiculous. He was not alive. He would not walk in on her and beat her for snooping into his private affairs. She had permission to be here.

Still, her hand shook as she touched the knob and pulled. The door opened, revealing the stacks of files within. The many, many stacks of files. Clarissa really had not touched this room. Everything had been left just as it was. It would take hours to go through all of these files. Hours when Phin would be entertaining Miss Bristol.

No point in wasting her time. Annabel took the topmost two files on the left side and placed them on the desk. She sat in the large leather chair and tried not to think about the earl sitting here. But she could almost feel his presence here as she leafed through the contents of the files, looking for any reference to their daughter. It was almost as if the chair had soaked in all the rage and contempt of the man who had occupied it so often through the years.

She paused in her task and took a deep breath. Years ago she had decided to face her demons. For so long she had hidden her abuse out of shame and guilt. But when she and Lady Buntlebury had become friends, Annabel had confided much of what had happened to her friend, and Mary had not pitied her. Mary had told her that she was fortunate because she had another chance at life. The earl might have lived another twenty years, and she would have been trapped under his thumb and in his bed. But now she could do as she liked, live as she liked.

Annabel had lived as she liked for a time, but she'd found there were consequences to freedom too.

And that was another demon to face.

But right now she could not allow the ghost of her late husband to upset her. He could never hurt her again, and if he were here, she would not be the same wife he had known. She would fight back. She would challenge him. She would never allow him to take her child without a fight.

Annabel opened her eyes and glared at the room. Quietly, she said, "You are not here. You cannot hurt me. You are in hell, and I am still here. I'm alive. I will live my life."

She said it again and when the trembling left her body, she went back to the files.

Annabel hardly thought of the earl again while she worked. It was as though the documents he'd signed or written were the property of some long-lost stranger. Most of what she perused had little to do with her or the earl's home life. Listings of sales and purchases, accountings from other estates, correspondence with solicitors to send this information or that. It was all rather banal and typical.

Her mind wandered too often to the Duke of Mayne. What was he doing? Did he enjoy the company of Miss Bristol? Did he miss Annabel at all or was he happy to spend time with someone young and vibrant—not that Miss Bristol had seemed all that vibrant.

But Miss Bristol had not walked away from him last night. Annabel had been in his bed and she had left him to sleep alone. He'd made it clear he wanted her, and she'd done nothing but push him away. Even when she'd tried to seduce him, she had failed. He didn't want her to pretend with him, but Annabel didn't know how *not* to pretend with a man. It was the only way she had survived marriage. And then after her marriage, she had not really known her lovers very well. They'd seemed to expect something of her, and that was what she had given them. She'd hoped to find the pleasure they seemed to experience so easily, pleasure which had eluded her after the early months of her marriage. But now she wondered if the earl had left her permanently scarred.

But she did not like to think of the duke with Miss Bristol. She should have been happy he had another woman to lavish attention on. But Annabel had become accustomed to his attentions, and she did not want to share them. She still wanted him. Clarissa was right that he would never be hers, but even if she could not climax, would it not be a night well spent if she was in his arms, his hands on her body and her hands on his?

But if she dared be herself with Phin, could she keep the earl from invading her thoughts and ruining everything? She had pushed him away all afternoon. Perhaps she could push him away tonight.

She bent to retrieve another stack of files and straightened in time to see two figures pass the window. They were bundled up, but she knew the duke's form well. On his arm was the slender form of Miss Bristol. They were obviously going for a walk.

In the freezing cold.

Did they want to be alone that badly?

Hot jealousy lanced through Annabel, taking her by surprise. She had never been jealous before. In fact, she had prayed the earl would find a mistress and leave her in peace. But watching the way Miss Bristol's gloved hand wrapped around Phin's arm made Annabel want to tear the girl into bite-sized pieces.

When had this happened? When had she developed feelings for the duke? And what would she do when they returned to London and he went one way and she another?

What would she do when he married? She couldn't allow her feelings to deepen. She had to fight them.

With renewed intensity, she focused on the papers before her. She would find where her daughter had been taken. She would get Theadosia back and then she would have someone to take care of. Someone to keep her mind off the duke and all men.

Annabel leafed through page after page, gritting her teeth and forcing her thoughts to remain confined to what she was reading and the names she wanted to see. A few times she caught references to herself, but these were always made in passing and made her seem more of a thing than a person.

She turned another page over and then another page. A shot rang out in the distance and Annabel looked up at the intrusion. The house had been so quiet. It was probably hunters nearby—except who would be hunting in January?

That's when she heard the scream.

***

Phin had been relieved when the governess sat in a chair in the corner of the drawing room. It was awkward as hell attempting to have a conversation with a chaperone judging every word, but at least Lady Wavenwell wasn't trying to force him to be alone with the girl.

Once her mother was gone, Miss Bristol became somewhat more animated. She gained a trace of color in her cheeks and asked him dozens of questions about London and the Season. He was happy to answer them as they passed the time, but after an hour and a half he wondered how Annabel was getting on.

And then he wondered if he might be able to find a way to go to her.

"Mama has ordered me so many dresses, and I have received dolls dressed in miniature replicas of the dresses I shall wear. It is ever so entertaining to play with the dolls and pretend they are at a ball. I have even created tiny dance cards for them. I shall put your name on one of them."

He smiled at her indulgently. "Please do. If I see you at a ball, I shall be honored to dance with you."

She blushed. "Thank you."

"Excuse me for one moment," her governess said, breaking her long silence. "I will return shortly."

Phin watched the woman leave and took a step back from Miss Bristol. The governess had left the door open, and he had the urge to swing it wider. "Which is your favorite dance?" he asked, attempting to keep the conversation moving.

But to his astonishment, Miss Bristol leaped forward, grabbed his lapel, and spoke to him in a harsh whisper. "I need your help, Your Grace. Now, quick, before she returns."

"What are you talking about?" Indeed, her eyes looked rather frantic.

"I couldn't say anything in front of my mother or Miss Roman, but I need your help quite desperately."

"What is wrong? And can we not speak of it with more distance between us? Yes, that's better." He'd managed to move her back, more or less, to her original spot on the couch. He liked there to be three feet, at least, between them.

"There isn't time for me to explain, but I will once we are en route. Can you put on your coat? We need to go outside."

"Outside? It's freezing outside."

"I know. But it's the only way." She rose, and Phin was forced to do likewise. She ran lightly to the door, peered one way and then the other, then gestured for him to follow her out of the drawing room.

Phin looked to the heavens. "Why? *Why?*" With no answer forthcoming, he followed Miss Bristol into the foyer, where she thrust his greatcoat at him and quickly donned her own coat. He had one arm in his sleeve, and she already had the door open.

"Come on! Hurry!"

Like the fool he was, he followed her out into the bitter cold. The sun from earlier in the day had retreated behind clouds that very much looked like rain. It was not the sort of day anyone would choose for a stroll about the grounds. Perhaps he had relaxed too early. Perhaps she would try to force him into a marriage after all.

She began walking, and he gave her his arm, hoping it looked as though they were on a leisurely stroll. Just a casual stroll in the middle of winter. At least they kept close to the house. As long as they were visible to those inside, Phin felt confident he was safe from matrimony.

"What is this all about?" he asked.

"Twitchy," she replied.

"I beg your pardon."

"He's a rabbit."

Of course, he was. "And what does Twitchy have to do with me?"

"I need you to rescue him."

Of course, she did.

"I know I must sound a trifle daft."

"Not at all." She sounded *completely* daft. She directed him toward the rear of the house, where he spotted a cluster of buildings. Beside one of them, in a protected spot, was a rabbit hutch. Around the hutch was a fenced off area where the rabbits could come out to…hop around or whatever it was rabbits did. Being that the weather was miserably cold and rabbits were not as stupid as humans, they were inside the hutch.

Miss Bristol clutched his arm. "I should not have become attached to him. I knew his fate."

"His fate?"

"Rabbit stew."

"*Oh.*"

"It's horrible, isn't it? I begged Mama not to kill him last year, and she agreed, but she said she will not spare him this year. She said he's"—her voice hitched—"too plump and tasty looking. And it's all my fault."

God help him. She was weeping. He offered his handkerchief and she took it, wiping her eyes as they stood looking at the rabbit hutch.

"How is it your fault?"

"I spoiled him. I fed him special treats. If I had been a true friend, I would have starved him."

"That seems unnecessarily cruel."

"So is slaughter of an innocent rabbit. You will save him, won't you?"

How could he say no? Apparently, his lot in life was to help women and rabbits in need. "Which one is he?" At the moment he could only make out patches of white, brown, and black fur through the small openings in the hutch. The rabbits were obviously huddled together for warmth.

"He's the big brown one." She moved away from him and made a sound like an exaggerated kiss. And, indeed, one of the rabbits perked up his ears and looked out. Miss Bristol moved closer to the hutch and held out something green and apparently edible as the rabbit took a bite. He was a cute little fellow. Phin had always been partial to small, furry animals. But what was he to do with a rabbit? He could set the creature free, but presumably not until the weather warmed up a bit. So he would be responsible for the rabbit for at least another six to eight weeks. Did rabbits bite? Where did they sleep at night? What did they eat?

He crouched down to get a better look at Twitchy and felt the ball fly over his head. He must have heard the shot as well since he knew right away a rifle had fired. But it was the heat of the ball flying overhead that caught his attention and brought him back, for a moment, to the war. His training kicked in and he lunched forward and threw his body on top of Miss Bristol's. She screamed, but Phin covered her mouth and dragged her behind the building, offering them both cover from whomever had fired upon them.

"Are you hurt?" he asked, removing his hand from her mouth

She continued to scream, so he looked her over. He didn't see any blood. "Stay here." He inched along the back of the building and peered around the corner. In the distance there was a copse of trees. It was just the place to keep from being seen from the house. Phin watched for any movement, but whoever had stood there and fired was already gone.

Miss Bristol was still screaming and either that or the sound of a shot had drawn the servants. They came spilling from the house like ants from a disturbed anthill. What looked like the cook reached the young lady first, and as Miss Bristol was still incoherent, Phin supplied a quick explanation. Lady Wavenwell arrived next with the governess and then Annabel. Seeing Annabel outside made Phin suddenly nervous again. What if he'd been out here with her? What if she had been in the line of fire and been hit? He moved quickly to her side and pulled her into the shade of the building.

"Your Grace! I heard a shot and screams. What happened?"

"What happened, indeed?" Lady Wavenwell demanded, coming up beside them. "What on earth are you doing outside?"

"Why don't we go inside and talk?" Phin said, having difficulty not looking over his shoulder. "It's cold, and I cannot help but notice you do not have a coat." He said the last to Lady Wavenwell, though it was Annabel he was thinking of. She too must have coming running without stopping to don her outerwear.

The group returned inside, the governess taking Miss Bristol upstairs for a warm bath and a bit of brandy tea. Phin hoped they gave the poor girl more than a bit.

Back in the drawing room, he remained standing while Lady Wavenwell and Lady Longstowe sat. He was too worked up to sit.

"Miss Bristol wanted to show me the rabbits," Phin said before Lady Wavenwell could demand another explanation from him. "I agreed, knowing it would be a brief outing as the weather is quite chilly." And wasn't that an understatement? "We walked to the hutch and as she was near the structure, showing me the rabbits, a shot was fired in my direction. I assure you, Miss Bristol was never in any danger. She was beside the hutch and the shot went over my head."

"But who would be shooting so close to the house?" Annabel asked.

"I thought it might be one of your groundskeepers," he said to Lady Wavenwell, "but after I moved Miss Bristol and myself to cover, I looked out again and did not see anyone. Surely a groundskeeper would have revealed himself."

"Of course. And my groundskeepers have no reason to shoot right now."

"That leaves my other choice. Poachers. Have you had any trouble with them lately?" he asked Lady Wavenwell. "You have some wooded areas, and I suppose some deer. Do you have a lake nearby? Could someone be shooting water fowl?"

"Poachers?" Lady Wavenwell straightened. "We do not have poachers!"

"Then I am out of ideas." He exchanged a look with Annabel who opened her mouth then closed it again. He narrowed his eyes, but she shook her head subtly. Whatever she meant to say, she would say it later or not at all.

"This has all been quite upsetting," Lady Wavenwell said. "I must ask the two of you to leave."

"But I haven't found what I need yet!" Annabel protested.

"Perhaps we might return tomorrow," Phin said. "Everyone will be calmer by then, and I do want to make certain Miss Bristol is feeling better. I wouldn't want to leave without telling her goodbye."

The refusal Phin knew was on Lady Wavenwell's lips died away. "Of course. Yes, you should return tomorrow."

Phin and Annabel gathered their things and departed as soon as his coach was ready. It was only about a twenty-minute drive to the inn, so he didn't waste time. "What were you about to say in the drawing room?"

"It's nothing." She looked out the window, seeming more relaxed now that they were driving away from Ceald House. His heart had finally stopped pounding, though he still had pent-up energy. He remembered the feeling well from when he'd been on the Continent. "It was just a thought I had about who might have shot at you."

His attention jerked back to her. "I never said anyone shot *at* me."

"You didn't, and perhaps I'm wrong."

He leaned forward, staring at her hard across the coach. "Wrong about what?"

She looked away from the window and directly at him. "Phin, is it possible someone is trying to kill you?"

He sat back abruptly. "No."

She frowned, and he realized he had dismissed her rather quickly. She pressed her lips together then continued. "It seems farfetched, I know, but in three days the inn where you were staying was set on fire, you were hit over the head, and now you have been shot at."

When she put it all together like that, it did sound suspicious. *Was* someone trying to kill him? He spoke slowly, trying to convince himself as much as her. "There were others staying at that inn, and it might have been falling debris that hit me on the head."

"And the gun shot?"

He didn't have a ready explanation for that. He couldn't explain it away as he might the fire and the bump on the head. If he hadn't crouched down just when he had, he would have been hit in the head. He would most likely be dead right now.

"Do you think someone is following us and trying to kill you?" she asked.

"No." But her mad idea was making more sense to him now than he liked to admit. "Maybe?"

"Do you have any enemies?"

"No." That much was true. He was generally well-liked and friendly with everyone.

"There's no one you've made angry? Perhaps a jealous husband or a—"

"Jealous husband? I'm not the sort to run about Town cuckolding men. I can't think of any reason anyone would want to kill me." He raised his brows at her. "What about you? Do you have any enemies?"

"This isn't about me."

"Really? No one was trying to kill me before I traveled with you. That is if anyone *is* trying to kill me. I'm not so sure I believe it."

"But haven't you ever wondered about your brothers' deaths? It seems very strange that they all died so young and in curious accidents."

"Our family has bad luck." But the explanation sounded ridiculous. Was he really more willing to believe in a curse than foul play? And she had a point. All four of his brothers suffered untimely deaths. Was there really someone who had targeted the dukes of Mayne and now targeted him? It was difficult to believe.

But it was difficult to dismiss.

Annabel took a breath. "You're right. Poachers is a more logical assumption. I shouldn't have said anything. It's a foolish idea. I'm not thinking straight."

For a moment he saw how she had survived her husband. She'd placated him, apologized. Phin didn't want that from her. "It's not a foolish idea," he said. "It's as valid as any of the others." He waited until she looked directly at him so she could see he meant what he said. "You've given me something to think about."

"I hope I didn't upset you."

"No, the person who shot at me managed that nicely. But putting that aside for the moment, did you find anything in the documents you looked through?"

"Not yet. I wish I had been able to look through them more quickly. Now we shall have to return tomorrow."

"I don't mind."

"You wouldn't," she said under her breath.

"What does that mean?" The events of the day had made his temper short, and he couldn't seem to stop jumping to defend himself.

"It means I'm sure it's no hardship to have a pretty young girl fawning all over you." She crossed her arms over her chest and gave him a challenging look.

"Fawning all over me? I had to listen to a description of her dolls, and I assure you, madam, that *is* a hardship."

"Is that why you went outside with her?" Annabel pointed a finger at him, and Phin recoiled.

"I went outside with her because she wants me to rescue her rabbit."

"And I am supposed to believe that story?"

"Does it sound like something I would invent? Besides…" He paused and cocked his head. "Wait a moment." Some of his ire melted.

"What?" she asked, her tone annoyed.

"Are you jealous?"

"Of that girl?"

"You *are* jealous." Annoyance was now replaced by curiosity, and dare he acknowledge it, hope.

"No, I'm not."

"You *do* want me."

"No, I don't."

"Yes, you do. And you think I am interested in that child?"

"She's a much better match for you than I am. She could marry you and give you an heir. What are you doing?"

He'd crossed to sit beside her. He couldn't stay away from her now. He'd almost been killed, and now she had confirmed what he'd wanted since he'd first seen her. She wanted him. "I'm kissing you." He put his arms about her and pulled her to him.

"I didn't say you could kiss me," she said, her voice low and husky. She was most definitely a woman who wanted to be kissed. Even she couldn't have believed her lie.

"Then tell me to stop." He glanced at her eyes, waited a beat for her refusal, and then lowered his mouth to hers. For just a moment, he thought she would push him away or clamp her mouth shut or turn her head. She did none of those things. Her lips were soft as he took them, pliant and suddenly greedy.

She went from ice to fire in an instant. One moment she was cool and stiff in his arms and the next her arms were around him, one of her hands fisted in his hair, and she was kissing him like he had never been kissed before. Her tongue tangled with his, her body pressed against him, and she made small sounds of pleasure and desire. He leaned forward and kissed her deeper and was rewarded when her hand slid down his back and grasped his backside. She squeezed.

He pulled back and stared at her. "You don't like that?" she panted.

"Oh, I like it. I like everything about you." He cupped her face and kissed her again, and this time her hands slid up his thighs, making him tense and hot and so hard he could barely think straight. Before she could touch him where he really wanted, he pulled her onto his lap so that she straddled him.

She looked down at him, all lush red lips and hazy blue eyes, one lock of hair falling over her cheek. His hand went beneath her skirts and touched her knee. Her eyes closed, and Phin said a prayer. *Please let me touch you. Please.*

When he opened his eyes again, she was watching him with lowered lids. He nipped at her lips, kissed her chin, and put his other hand under her skirts. Both hands rested just above her knees.

"You are so soft." He kissed her again. "So warm." She lifted her neck and he kissed the throbbing pulse point at the base of her throat. His hands slid higher, and her breath hitched. "Do you know how much I've wanted to touch you, Annabel?"

"If it's half as much as I've wanted to touch you, I have an idea, yes." Her voice was low and husky and made him want to do all sorts of things that would make her call his name in that seductive tone. But she'd already run from him once. It was obvious that her husband's cruelty had left her scarred and any other men since then had left her unsatisfied. Phin could guess at what she'd like, but wouldn't it be better if she told him? Wouldn't it be better for her if she were to dominate, not be dominated?

"Tell me how you want me to touch you. I'll do whatever you want."

Her blue eyes sharpened slightly as her gaze met his. He knew his words would have shocked many women. Those women would have looked away coyly and told him they liked whatever he did. But Annabel's expression was one of interest.

"Anything?" she murmured.

God, what her voice did to him. He was half mad with lust.

"Test me."

"Move your hands higher on my legs. Like that. Spread your fingers."

"Your skin is so—"

"Don't talk."

He raised a brow but closed his mouth.

"A little higher. Mmmm. Move your fingers in circles and kiss me."

He took her mouth with his, rough and wild, while his fingers made small circles on her thighs, inching higher and higher. She wriggled on his lap and slid closer to his erection. He wanted her to grind against him, wanted the heat his fingers were near against his hard member.

But he was not in charge. And he continued making circles, moving the tiniest fraction closer to that heat.

She ended the kiss, breathing heavily. "Do you want to touch me between my legs?"

"Yes. Please."

"Please?" She smiled. "I like that. Touch me."

His fingers found her curls, slightly damp, and he threaded through them until he reached the center of that warmth. He slicked one finger over her opening and then slid up to brush over her tight nub.

"Again," she ordered.

He readily obeyed, this time lingering slightly longer on that tight bundle of nerves. She let out a moan and thrust her hips.

"Tell me what you want," he whispered.

"More of that."

He flicked his finger over her, circled, then dipped back for more moisture from her core.

"I want—" She broke off and opened her eyes.

He paused. "Say it. I'll do anything."

"I want you inside me."

He tried to contain the shiver of arousal that went through him. It took tremendous control not to come right there in his breeches. He focused on her face, on giving her pleasure. His fingers found her opening again and he dipped one inside. "Like this?"

She pushed down on his finger, taking him deeper. She was trying to kill him. "More," she said, her voice ragged.

He slipped another finger inside then curved upward and brushed his thumb back along her clitoris.

"Oh!" Her breath caught and she rocked against him. He could feel her muscles clenching and releasing. She strained for pleasure. He moved his fingers in and out of her, slowly, going deeper each time.

"Yes." She was practically incoherent and riding him with abandon. "More."

He paused and then carefully inserted another finger. She clenched hard around him. He watched her face. She was so beautiful. Phin wanted her naked. He wanted to see her breasts thrust upward as she arched her back.

Suddenly, she tensed and stilled. She looked down at him. "I can't," she said. "I know you're not him, but—"

Phin cupped the back of her neck with his free hand and brought her face down to his. "Look at me, Annabel. See only me."

She nodded, her eyes locked on his as he entered her again, allowing his thumb to move lazily over her small, hard bud.

"You are in control. Tell me to stop. Tell me you want more. Tell me anything, but say it to me. Look at me. Phin."

"Phin." Her voice was breathy as she moved her hips tentatively again. He could feel the carriage turning and slowing. He needed more time, goddamn it. But they would be back at the inn shortly.

He closed his eyes. "Annabel, we're almost to the inn."

She straightened and began to pull away. His hand slipped out of her, but he touched her leg lightly, staying her. "If you want me, come to my room later. It's your decision. You are in control. I have infinite patience, and I want nothing more than to touch you all night. But only if that's what you want."

He placed her gently on the squabs and moved back to his side of the coach, adjusting his breeches to ease the discomfort there. Annabel straightened her gown and pressed her hands to her pink cheeks.

"Will I—" She cleared her throat. "Will I see you at dinner?"

"I have some correspondence to see to, so I'll have a tray sent to my room. But if I don't see you tonight, then I will meet you at half past nine for breakfast in the private dining room."

The door opened, and there was nothing else they might say without the servants overhearing. Phin had made it clear he wanted her to come to him, but it was her choice. There would be no repercussions if she chose not to, and no awkwardness of dining with him—he wondering at her decision and she either not certain or deciding how to tell him.

She held all the power, and he only hoped she trusted him enough to give him her trust in return.

Fourteen

"Did you see how they looked when they stepped out of the carriage?" Meg asked Reynolds as they sat at the servants' table eating a quick bite before they were needed again. Reynolds had seen the duke and countess when they stepped out of the carriage, and he had a feeling he would not be needed again that night.

"It must have been warm in there," he murmured so the other servants wouldn't hear. Not that anyone was close enough to hear. The other servants gave Meg a wide berth. They were country people and had superstitions about those who might be different. If Meg minded, she didn't show it. For his part, Reynolds liked having her all to himself. They'd found ways to cross paths all day, and she always had a smile or some amusing tidbit to share before they had to part again.

"Very warm," she said with a wink. He swallowed down the urge to grasp her knee under the table and watch her own cheeks grow warm. He liked the way she winked and laughed and how she obviously cared about her mistress and wanted the best for her.

He wouldn't mind having a woman like that wanting the best for him, and he'd make sure she had the best of everything.

"Did the countess go down to dinner?" he asked.

"She had a tray sent to her room. What about the duke?" She broke off a piece of bread.

"The same. He said I was free the rest of the night."

"She'll send for me if she needs me."

He watched her take dainty bites from the bread, her unruly hair curling about her pretty face. "Do you think she'll need you?"

"Not if your duke knows what he is about."

"Then will you have a pint with me in the public room after dinner?"

"In the public room? You don't want to go somewhere more private?" she asked.

Oh, yes. Yes, he did. But he really liked Meg, and if all worked out as he hoped with Lady Longstowe and Mayne, he had the opportunity to turn this into more than one night of pleasure. "I'm a gentleman." He tipped his imaginary hat. "And I'd like to buy my lady a drink."

"Oh, go on with you!" She waved a hand, but she was smiling. "I'll see you there after dinner."

The conversation turned to other topics, but her cheeks remained pink and her eyes sparkled, and Reynolds could not take his gaze from her. He'd thought the duke was mad when he'd told Reynolds to pack for a few days in Wiltshire. Now he thanked his lucky stars he hadn't tried harder to foist the trip on one of the more experienced footmen.

Reynolds went to the duke's room one last time to be sure he was not needed before joining Meg in the public room. He found the duke had eaten little from his tray and though he'd said he had letters to write, he wasn't seated at the traveling desk Reynolds had brought him.

"Do you need anything else tonight, Your Grace?"

"A shred of sanity, Reynolds. Otherwise, no. I said you were free for the night."

"I will be in the public room if you need me, Your Grace."

"Good," the duke said, wandering to the window and flicking at the curtains. Then he looked over his shoulder. "The public room? Are you enjoying the company you find in Wiltshire?"

"I enjoy the company of Mrs. Slightley, who said she would join me if her mistress does not need her."

The duke looked a bit surprised but also pleased. "In that case, I hope you and Mrs. Slightley pass several enjoyable hours in the public room. She seems like a good woman."

"I think so. If you don't need me, Your Grace, I'll take my leave."

"Go." He waved his hand. "And don't come back tonight or I'll have to have a word with Mrs. Slightley."

"Yes, Your Grace."

He closed the door, smiling, then turned and almost ran into Lady Longstowe. He could see she was in the middle of turning around to go back to her room, but she hadn't had time to escape without being seen.

"Ah, my lady," Reynolds said with a bow. "His Grace is expecting you."

"Oh?"

"He has the, er, book you wanted to borrow."

"Oh? *Oh*. Yes. The book. Thank you, Reynolds.

"My pleasure, my lady." And as he trod down the steps in search of the public room and Meg, he was indeed feeling most exceptionally pleasant.

***

No point in turning back now, Annabel told herself. Reynolds would tell Phin he'd seen her outside his door. And Phin would ask why she hadn't come to him.

Of course, she could just say she hadn't wanted to. It was her choice, after all.

But if she was really making the choice, she knew there was nowhere else she'd rather be. She wanted to be in Phin's arms. She wanted his hands on her, his breath skating over her skin, his tongue teasing hers. There was pleasure in kisses and embraces and being held.

She tapped on the door to his room, and she heard Phin call. "I told you to go to the public room."

She frowned. "The public room doesn't interest me."

She heard a thump and then the door opened. Phin looked her up and down. "Thank God." He pulled her inside and closed the door, locking it. "I thought you were—Never mind. You're here."

"I'm here, and I won't play coy with you," she said, tugging off her gloves. He watched her like a starving street urchin watches an apple seller. "I want to begin where we left off."

He did not even blink. "Tell me where to start."

She liked the way he put her in control. She'd never been in control before, and she would not have thought she would have liked it. But she did like it. She liked that he cared what she wanted and was desperate to give it to her.

"Help me take off this gown."

He blew out a breath, and she knew how much effort it required to give his control to her. He wanted her, and he'd said it terrified him a bit. But he was willing to take the risk. Now she was as well. Because she wanted him. She just did not know if she could be everything he needed.

"Turn around," he said. She gave him her back and he began to unfasten the garment. Now that she wasn't facing him, it was easier to make a confession.

"After the earl died, I took several lovers," she said.

His hands did not pause as he continued opening her dress down the back. "There's hardly a widow who doesn't. And I imagine you were still young and"—now his hand paused—"curious."

She glanced over her shoulder at him. He was exactly right. She had been only a year above thirty when she'd been widowed. During her marriage, she'd lived so long in fear and without any kind of tenderness that she craved a man's loving touch.

"I did not find a lover immediately," she said as he continued undressing her, now untying strings and loosening tapes. "I mourned in public, and I healed in private. Lady Buntlebury was my confidante. I told her everything I had held in secret for so many years and those long talks helped me to heal and to realize that what had happened to me was not my fault.

"I had not been a bad wife. He had been a bad husband."

Phin lowered his lips to lightly kiss her now bare shoulder. "It pains me that you ever blamed yourself. You were little more than a child. He was a monster who terrorized you and stole your child."

Her heart clenched. She needed to hear those words more than she'd known. Of course, Mary had told her something similar, but Annabel could not hear it enough.

"I wish I'd known you back then. I would have thrashed him for you."

She laughed and turned into his arms. "Spoken like the rash lad you would have been at the time." She buried her face against his solid chest. "I am glad I did not know you then. I was not the woman I am now. I was rather lost and desperately searching for love. I was easy prey for the first man who treated me with an ounce of kindness."

"I don't like where this is going."

"He did not force me. I went willingly to his bed and to bed with those who followed, but I was not discreet. I did not choose men who were discreet." She pulled back and glanced up at him. "You see Society does not mind if widows indulge in bedsport, but they do mind if the lady is not coy about it. I did not go to the trouble to hide my affairs. My parents were dead, and I was young and finally free. In all I had four lovers over several years. I'm sure that is far fewer than many gentlemen of our acquaintance and fewer than many ladies as well. And yet I earned the sobriquet the Wanton Widow."

He slid his hand over her cheek, his skin cool against her heated flesh. "I did wonder how you acquired that. After our, er, first meeting, you did not strike me as wanton. Even then it was not until I made an ass of myself that you began to play the part."

She sighed. "Do you really want to hear this now?" Her gaze flicked to the bed behind him.

He gave her a wry smile. "I want to know you, and we have all night."

"Very well. A rumor began that I was…how should I put this…giving special favors to my footman. He was a handsome young man, and I believe he liked the attention. He confirmed the rumors, though there was no truth to them. Crotchett dismissed him, and that only added fuel to the flames."

"Let me guess. From then on it was assumed you'd bedded half the *ton*."

"I was the busiest woman in England, or I would have had to be to do half of what I was accused of. I was no longer invited into the best homes and ladies I had thought were friends shunned me, though I would never have done more than flirt with any of their husbands."

"And this was more than a decade ago? Ridiculous," he muttered.

"It is, but the *ton* does not forget a scandal, even one of their own invention."

"I'm sorry to say that you are still regarded as easy prey. That is why my brother went after you that night."

"I'm well aware of that."

"And I'm the idiot who barged in on you and accused you of sleeping with him." He looked rather sheepish, and she liked him all the more for it.

"I think we've punished you enough for that transgression. And since you mention your brother, I want to tell you something he did not know, something no one knows, I suppose. I haven't taken a lover in ten years."

Phin's eyes widened. "You mean you haven't—" He looked at the bed again.

"That's right."

"But why?" he sputtered. "If people believed the worst of you anyway then what did it matter what you did?"

"That wasn't why I didn't take a lover, but it is why I am telling you about my past. The earl—I fear he did something to me. He ruined me in some way."

Phin's brows came together. "That's ridiculous. You're perfect."

Now she touched his face and kissed him. "Will you let me finish?"

He frowned but kept quiet.

"The lovers I took were not boys. They were men who seemed, to me at least, to know what they were about. And yet despite their best efforts, I was never able to find satisfaction." Phin opened his mouth, but she placed a finger over his lips. "I know I can climax. I did with the earl, rather he demanded it. He would touch me until my body could no longer resist and then with the pleasure he would pair pain. Eventually, nothing he did, nothing any man did, could bring me to that point." She lowered her head, her cheeks burning. "Even I cannot bring myself to climax." Why had she told him any of this? She burned with embarrassment.

Phin didn't move away from her. Instead, he put a finger under her chin and lifted her head so he could look into her eyes. "He paired the pleasure with pain so you would avoid the one because you expected the other. Why would he do such a thing?"

She couldn't find her voice and had to whisper. "He knew he was old and unappealing to a young girl. He wanted to be certain I would not cuckold him. At least not until I gave him a child. After that he did not bother with me as much."

"Annabel." Phin kissed one cheek and then the other. "If he were not dead, I would kill him."

"But he is dead. And you and I are alive." She liked the feel of his mouth on her skin and wanted more. "And all I want is to be with you. I have no other expectations, and I'd rather you didn't stake your manhood on whether or not you can give me pleasure. I have pleasure in your arms and in your kisses. I just want to be with you, Phin."

"I'm yours," he said.

"Then take off my dress." It was already gaping at the bodice, and he reached up and slid it off her shoulder, holding her hand so she might step out of it and stand before him in chemise, stays, and petticoat.

"Do you want to know what I think?" he asked, turning her so he might untie her petticoat and slide it down her legs

"Certainly." She shivered at the feel of his fingertips as they brushed her skin. His fingers moved back up and paused at the knot of her lacings.

"I think you can climax, but I don't think I can make you come."

She shivered at his words as his hands began to unlace her stays.

"You have to take that power back for yourself."

"I told you. I've tried touching myself—"

He kissed the back of her neck. "Then tell me where to touch you, what to do to you, how to make you feel good."

Her stays were loose enough that she slid them off and stood in just her chemise. She turned to look at him. "You will want to take your pleasure as well."

He shrugged as though it were of no concern. "There's time for that later. If not tonight then another night."

"Another night?"

"I'll want you as long as you'll have me, Annabel. As many nights as you'll come to me." Then he stepped away from her. "Now, you said you wanted to begin where we left off in the carriage." He sat on the bed and patted his lap. "Come here then and let me kiss you."

Her heart began to pound as she crossed to him, well aware that with the fire behind her and only the thin linen on the chemise covering her, he could make out the outlines of her body quite clearly. And another thing was clear, though he was seated on the bed. He was quite aroused by what he saw. She liked that she could make him feel desire. She wanted to feel that desire inside of her. But he'd said he wanted her to take control, and she wasn't quite ready to tell him to undress.

Instead, she slid onto his lap, curving her hand around the back of his neck and bringing his mouth to hers. His mouth seared hers with heat, and she could feel how much he wanted her. He kissed her like a condemned man in his last hours. His mouth took hers so completely that she couldn't think of anything but the way the simple stroke of his tongue or nip of his teeth made her whole body hot and alive. She needed his touch.

"Put your hands on me," she murmured.

His hands slid up to her shoulders, surprising her as she'd thought he'd dive under her skirts. He brushed his hands over her collarbone and then down to the tie of her chemise. He pulled back slightly, waiting for her agreement before he pulled the tie loose, causing her chemise to gape and then fall to her waist.

His indrawn breath sent a throb of awareness through her. His hands slid down, his touch almost reverent as he cupped one breast and rubbed a nipple with his thumb. It peaked immediately, and he fondled it until was hard and aching. "May I put my mouth on you?"

She nodded, though part of her worried it would remind her of the earl and his bruising hands and lips. But Phin kept his green eyes locked with hers, and he took her nipple into his mouth. She couldn't think of anything but him when he looked at her like that. She was surprised by the moan that escaped her and the way her hips jerked forward, toward the heat of his cock. That gentle sucking tugged at her core, making her long for something to ease the tension there.

"Do you want me to touch you here?" He cupped her sex with his free hand, his breath tickling her breast.

"Yes."

"Tell me."

"Touch me between my legs."

His mouth moved to her other breast as his hand slid under her chemise and up her thighs to brush against the part of her aching for him. She wanted to arch back and close her eyes, but she kept her gaze on Phin. Kept her mind in the present. She moved against his fingers, demanding more from him, and he let her guide him. Let her show him where she needed his touch.

He skated his fingers over her nub, and when she whimpered, he went back, circling the tight button with his thumbs as he circled her nipple with his tongue. Her breath quickened.

"You're wet. May I put my finger inside you?"

"Please."

"I should be begging you. You're so warm, so soft." He eased a finger inside her, and she squeezed it with her inner muscles.

"More."

"Whatever you want." He inserted another finger.

She moved against his hand, taking him deeper then pulling away. All the while, his mouth teased her breast, flicking and laving and tantalizing. She watched his tongue on the hard bud of her nipple and her breath turned to pants.

"Tell me what you want."

"I like this."

"I can see you thinking about it, Annabel. Take control. I'll do whatever you ask."

"I can't ask you to—"

"Put my mouth between your legs? Would it help if I begged? Because I want that more than anything. I want to taste you there."

She closed her eyes. "It won't work. This is only prolonging the torture."

"Then tell me what you do want. My cock inside you? My fingers moving faster? My mouth sucking harder?"

Her body was so tense, so ready to explode. She did not want to dare to hope. "I want your mouth on me," she said, feeling suddenly powerful.

In a moment, he had reversed their positions, so she lay on the bed, her head propped on pillows. He quickly stripped off her chemise and spread her legs. For just a moment, a memory of the earl flickered, but then Phin was there, his touch gentle and his eyes on her as he skimmed his warm hands up her thighs.

"Watch me," he told her. "Don't think about anything but what I'm doing to you. Don't think about anyone but me."

He bent and kissed the inside of her thigh, his eyes flicking back up to hers. Then he bent his blond head again and licked her. Annabel threaded her hands through his hair, feeling him move beneath her touch, knowing she could pull him away or urge him on with the pressure of her fingers.

She met his gaze again before his mouth delved deeper, his tongue licking her and making her tremble. She knew what would happen. She would soar higher and higher never able to climax. Phin would grow weary of his fruitless efforts and take his own pleasure. But for the moment, she could not help but enjoy his ministrations.

His tongue flicked at her sensitive bud, and she arched suddenly. Her breasts felt heavy, her nipples tight and she reached for one. Phin lifted his head, his eyes dark as he nodded. She stroked the hard bud of her nipple as he stroked her sex with his tongue. He didn't rush, didn't try to urge her to climax. He simply teased and coaxed until she was writhing with need.

"You must be tired," she panted when all his efforts were still unsuccessful.

"I could do this all night." His lips brushed against her thigh. As if to prove his point, he spread her legs wider and slid two fingers between her swollen folds. His fingers entered her slowly as his tongue laved at her pulsing center.

"Please," she whispered, not certain if she was begging him or herself.

His fingers moved inside her, curving up and making her gasp with new pleasure. Just as she acclimated to that sensation, his tongue changed rhythm and she began to gasp in breaths. She ran her hands down her body and fisted her hands in his hair. He growled when she urged him deeper, and that growl said everything to her. He really did enjoy this. And he liked when she took control.

"There," she murmured. "Faster. Yes. Just like that."

Oh, he was an eager pupil, and he wanted to please her.

"Your fingers. Deeper." She gasped when he followed her direction. She breathed his name, and the sound of pleasure he made was the push she needed. She began to fall.

The orgasm cresting. She could still lose it. She'd been this close before.

"More," she cried. "More."

He obeyed, his control and his skills evident as he pleasured her. And then bright lights exploded behind her eyes and her body soared. She made incoherent sounds of ecstasy, not caring who heard. Not caring if she sounded exactly like her sobriquet. Her body clenched hard around his fingers and she rocked against his mouth and he grasped her hips with his free hand and pulled her closer to him.

After what seemed a decade, she went limp, her breath labored and her heart racing. She did not know if it had simply been a long time, but she did not think it had ever been like that. And for once, she was able to stay in the present, to stay with Phin, to let his hands and lips take her where she needed to go.

When she finally opened her eyes, Phin was beside her on the bed, lightly stroking her hair off her forehead. There would be no pain associated with this pleasure, only his handsome face and arrogant smile.

"You're beautiful when you orgasm," he said.

She said something that even she couldn't understand.

"You're beautiful now."

She closed her eyes, feeling beautiful and free and so very, very good.

"More?" he whispered close to her ear.

She laughed. There could not possibly be more. Her body could not take any more. But when she opened her eyes, he was looking down at her with a seriousness she could hardly believe.

"There's more?"

"If you'll let me touch you again. Now that I know what you like, I can make it even better."

"I don't think it can be better."

"We won't know unless we try." His hand flattened against her belly. "Do you want to try, Annabel?"

"Yes."

With a wicked grin he bent to kiss the valley between her breasts.

***

Sometime later, Phin watched the color rise to her cheeks as she neared orgasm again. She was indeed a wanton. She was wild and uninhibited and seemed to like to tell him what to do almost as much as he liked being told. He'd never been with a woman like her, such a mix of experience and innocence. She seemed to be learning as he did what she liked and what she needed. But she was not afraid to take what she wanted once she knew what it was.

His hand was between her legs and his mouth on her neck and ear as he teased her when her hand cupped him through his trousers. He stilled for a moment out of surprise. She hadn't touched him, besides kissing his lips or stroking his hair, and though he hadn't been able to completely ignore his needs, he had been able to suppress them.

But now his cock jumped at her stroke, and Phin had to grit his teeth to maintain control.

"Do you like that?" she asked, her hand on him, moving with bold and artful strokes.

"I think you can feel how much I like it."

"I want to see you, feel you."

"After I watch you come again," he murmured. He knew she was getting closer, and he wanted this night to be all she could have wanted and more.

She shook her head. "It's your turn."

"I don't need—"

She unfastened the placket of his trousers and his cock was free. Her hand gripped his bare flesh, stroking him from root to tip and making him groan. She pushed up to her knees, giving him a new view of her body. Her breasts were magnificent, as he'd known they would be. And the rest of her was all lush curves and sweet hollows. He wanted to lick every single one all over again.

She took hold of his shirt and slid it up his chest. He did the rest, unfastening it and pulling it over his head. Her eyes raked over him hungrily, making him even harder.

"You're the one who's beautiful," she said, her voice low and reverent. "Look at you."

Instead, he removed the rest of his clothing as she watched with avid interest. She didn't avert her eyes or show the least bit of shyness. Her lust was evident. He knelt before her on the bed, reaching out to lightly stroke one of her full breasts. She closed her eyes and arched into his touch then wrapped her arms about his neck and pressed herself against him.

The feel of her skin against his, her nipples pressing into his chest, was amazing. His hands roved her hips and her buttocks as his lips plundered her mouth. She licked into his mouth, and the urge to take her right then was so strong he bit down to crush it. "How do you want me?" he asked.

"I want you beneath me."

Phin yanked her onto his lap, so she straddled him. "Should I lay down?"

"I like you just like this." She took him in her hands again and guided him to her entrance. He could feel the heat of her, and he wanted to grip her tightly. He kept his hold light, let her take control. She rose up on her knees and took his tip inside.

He swore and groaned. He would not last long if she kept this up. And she was already well-pleasured. She'd need his stamina. She moved up then slid down again, this time rubbing his member against her folds and her clitoris. She shuddered along with him. His gaze met hers, and he kissed her as she took him inside her again. This time she took more of him, and though he wanted to push and drive himself in to the hilt, he resisted.

But it seemed as though she could no longer bear it either. She took him deep, and he growled with pleasure. She was hot and wet and he could feel the way she pulsed around him. He could bring her to climax and feel those muscles grip him like a glove.

"Shall I touch you, Annabel? Stroke you?"

"You'd better use your hands to hold on," she said as she rocked her hips. He was still deep inside her as she moved up and down, rolling her hips so she was tight against him. Phin slid his hands up her back as she took him and tried not to notice how seductive she looked, how she was making him feel. A fine sheen of perspiration slicked her skin when he closed his hand into a fist, desperately trying to hold back his climax.

"Almost there," she panted. He never wanted her to stop. He would have endured this torment all night to watch her ride him like this.

And then suddenly she stopped, her mouth opening. Her nails dug into his back as her hips bucked. Her inner muscles clenched him tightly, and Phin groaned out a release as he came hard. He struggled to hold onto her as the orgasm tore through him, and then he could not stop himself from thrusting into her.

"Yes," she cried, meeting his thrust. He drove hard and fast and she was with him until he finally toppled onto the bed and cushioned his weight above her. Her face was red, her hair tousled, and their bodies slick as they both drifted down.

When she opened her normally bright blue eyes, they were hazy with satisfaction. She lifted one limp hand and he kissed the palm when she put it to his cheek. "I didn't know it could be like that," she whispered.

"Me neither." It was the truth. He'd thought he could give her pleasure, but he'd never imagined she could give him all of it and more back.

She smiled weakly. "More?" she asked him.

He laughed. "Give me a quarter hour."

She blew out a breath. "Now I see the flaw in a young lover."

"What's that?" he asked, pleased she'd called him her lover. He gathered her into his arms and tucked them under the covers.

"You exhaust me."

He kissed her brow. "Then sleep and wake me when you're hungry again."

She did sleep, but in the end, he had to wake her bearing bad news.

Fifteen

Annabel considered Phin a wise man for serving her tea before attempting to speak with her. It was already light outside, and she should have been back in her room by now. There was no point in panicking about something she could not change. Especially before she had drunk her tea. She watched him from the bed. He sat at a small desk with his own cup of tea at his elbow. He wore trousers and a linen shirt, untucked at the waist and rolled to the elbows. His hair was disheveled, and gold stubble limned his jaw.

He looked good enough to eat. She could only imagine how she appeared after the night of debauchery they had shared. She set her empty tea cup on the bedside table, and Phin turned to look at her. His green eyes swept over her, and Annabel decided she must not look as bad as she'd feared. There was definitely interest in his gaze.

"Reynolds brought the tea tray and a letter." He held up a piece of paper. "Do you want to read it, or shall I tell you the contents?"

"Who sent it?"

"Lady Wigglewaggle."

She smiled despite herself. "Tell me the contents."

"Her servants have not been able to find any trace of poachers and her groundskeepers assure her they did not fire. Your theory about assassins after my head gains traction."

"It gives me no pleasure to hear that. What else does our friend say?"

"She implies she does not feel safe with us nearby. She's asked that our visit today be brief and our last."

"Clarissa always was ever so helpful."

Phin rose from the desk and went to the tea tray. "More tea?"

She nodded. "Thank you." He crossed to her and filled her cup.

"Shall we dress and go now? It's only nine, but country hours and all that. Besides, if we're to have our visit cut short, it might be best to start early."

"I suppose you are right." She stretched. "You should have roused me earlier."

He cocked a brow in question.

"Then we would have had more time for this." She rose on her knees and put her arms about his waist. He smiled down at her then returned her kiss with lips sweet from tea and sugar.

"I *should* have roused you earlier. But there's always tonight." His voice held a note of promise.

"Just stay indoors and safe at Ceald House."

He frowned and she drew back. "What is it?"

"I did promise Miss Bristol I would rescue that rabbit."

Annabel laughed, and when he didn't follow, she stared at him. "You cannot be serious."

"I'm very serious. I can't leave the rabbit to be turned into stew."

"And what do you intend to do with the creature?"

He shrugged. "There's room in the coach. Perhaps Twitchy can ride with Reynolds and the luggage."

"God help us."

An hour later she was praying for God to help her. Clarissa had been adamant they leave as soon as possible, and Annabel still had so many papers to look through. She'd hoped Phin might be able to join her, but Clarissa had wasted no time pairing him with her daughter again. This time Annabel did not suffer any pangs of jealousy. Phin had made it clear he wanted Annabel. And now that she had been reminded of the way he'd looked when he desired a woman, she knew Miss Bristol was nothing more than a chore to him.

She hoped he would not come to think of her the same way. She had dragged him across the countryside for several days and they would have more traveling ahead once she discovered Theadosia's whereabouts.

Annabel went back to looking through the papers, glancing out the window occasionally to be certain Phin did not take any chances outside. She did not want Twitchy to become anyone's dinner, but neither did she want Phin dead.

And she was still worried that the accidents that had befallen him of late might not be accidents.

She turned another page then stiffened and turned it back. There it was. Her name. Not *Annabel*, of course. The earl had never called her *Annabel*. It was always *my wife* or *my countess*. Here he had written about Lady Longstowe and child. Annabel put a hand to her mouth and turned the page, searching for more references. Two pages later she found a line indicating that she was in the country. He mentioned that she was in mourning for their child.

Glancing back up at the date, she realized the letter had been sent only a few weeks after their daughter's birth. Which meant he had never planned to allow her to keep Theadosia. He had seen she was different and had decided to be rid of her within days of her birth.

The question that remained was where had he sent the little girl? Annabel skimmed the pages quickly now, finding no more references to herself or their daughter. It was as though he had not given them another thought after making the decision to tell everyone the baby had died.

And then she came across a letter to his solicitor, perhaps a year after Theadosia's birth. In it, he mentioned bonuses for the servants at Ceald House. Annabel had no doubt those were intended to buy the servants' silence.

A clock chimed in the corridor and Annabel glanced at the time. Lady Wavenwell might return and ask her to leave at any moment. She still hadn't found where the earl had sent Theadosia. She turned pages more quickly, distracted when a figure passed by the window. She looked up briefly and saw it was not Phin then looked down.

Then back up again.

Was that *Reynolds*? Why was Reynolds—

Annabel blew out a breath. Of course. Phin had sent his valet to free the rabbit. Thankfully, if someone was looking to take another shot at Phin, no one would mistake the dark-haired valet for his master. And she was impressed that Phin had actually taken precautions. He might not be certain he was in danger, but he had listened to her.

She had to be careful there. She liked him too much already, and after what they had done last night, what he had made her feel, she had to keep her feelings close. She couldn't afford to fall in love with him. She did not relish having her heart broken when he married another woman. He would have no choice. A duke must have an heir, and she could not give him an heir. Even if she could, a widowed countess fifteen years his senior would not be an acceptable duchess in his family's eyes or Society's.

Annabel looked back at the papers before her, hoping Reynolds did not draw any attention and convince Lady Wavenwell to throw them out sooner than she already planned. She turned a page and then another and let out a frustrated sigh when she saw she was almost at the end of this file. Now she would have to open a new one and start—

> *--arrangements to send the child to Brookwood Place, where it will be well cared for.*

That was it. Annabel had no doubt. What other child would he send away? Brookwood Place must be a sanitarium, one of those places the wealthy sent the family members they wanted to forget about. But a place where they could console themselves that their father, mother, or daughter was taken care of.

So where was Brookwood Place? She couldn't very well ask Phin to drive around the entire country asking after sanitariums named Brookwood Place. She should probably not ask him to do any more for her at all. They could return to London, and she could go on her own. But she had to know where to go.

She heard a commotion outside, shouts and calls for help. Reynolds had caused some sort of tumult, and now the clock was definitely ticking. Should she open a new file? Should she review the previous files and see if she perhaps missed any references to Brookwood Place before? She would try looking back first. Hurriedly, she flipped through the documents, slowing as she came to the letter to the solicitor referring to the extra pay for servants. There was a reference to Brookwood Place as well. Annabel snatched the paper out of the file and held it close. The address where payments were to be sent was also listed, and it was in Berkshire, on the way back to London.

"What is the meaning of this uproar?" Lady Wavenwell cried from somewhere inside the house. Annabel folded the paper and stuffed it into her bodice. Then she quickly closed the file and stuffed it back in the cabinet, stacking others on top of it.

Now other servants were speaking, and she heard the word *rabbit* over and over. She stood just as Phin opened the door to the study.

"Darling, I hate to rush you, but we might wish to take our leave before we're thrown out."

"I'm ready." She came around the desk. Lowering her voice, she said, "I have it."

His eyes widened, but he didn't speak.

Lady Wavenwell was behind them. "I do not know what is happening, but I know you are somehow behind it."

Phin turned. "Me? Why, I have been playing cards with Miss Bristol. I heard all the hubbub and came to ensure Lady Longstowe was well."

"Lady Longstowe." Clarissa's eyes narrowed. "I think it's time you took your leave."

"I think you are correct." She stepped out of the library, without looking back. The earl was behind her now. She knew his last secret, and she needn't ever think of him again. "No need to worry that I will be back. If I never see this house again, it will be too soon."

"How dare you!"

"Good day, Clarissa. Give your son my best. I do hope he is nothing at all like his great-uncle."

She swept out, head held high. Phin was right behind her.

"How long have you been thinking of that send off?" he murmured.

"Years," she said with a smile.

"Well done."

The butler opened the door, and Annabel spotted the duke's carriage already waiting for them. A footman opened the door, and Annabel stepped inside followed by Phin. He rapped on the roof and they were gone. As soon as the carriage was in motion, she leaped across the coach to sit beside him. "I found it!" she said, reaching into her bodice for the paper she'd secreted.

Phin's eyes followed her movements then widened when she produced the paper. "What's this then?"

"Payments made to servants. Bonuses for silence about my daughter. Do you see this payment to Brookwood Place?" He took the paper and examined it. "I found a line in a letter he wrote to his solicitor mentioning sending the child there. That's it, Phin. She's at Brookwood Place."

"And this is it? The Brookwood Place in Berkshire?"

"I think so, yes."

"Well, we know our next destination then."

Annabel shook her head. "Phin, no. I can't ask that of you. You take me back to London, and I will hire a carriage to take me to the sanitarium."

"And what hope do you think you have of gaining entrance? I'd better go with you. In any case, there's nothing of interest for me in London and I can't stay here. I'll soon be a wanted man."

Her brow furrowed. "Wanted for what?"

"Theft." He tapped his walking stick on the roof of the carriage, and it began to slow.

"What are you doing?"

"Freeing my valet and Twitchy." Phin rose, crossed the carriage, and when it had stopped, lifted the seat cushions across from him off the wooden base."

"What are you doing?" She gasped when he loosed a latch and the top of the seat was lifted. "Is that a secret compartment—Reynolds!"

"Yes, my lady. I'm here."

She couldn't think how he had managed to fit in that cramped space. He must have been bent in double. With Phin's assistance, he began to climb out, handing the duke a small brown bundle first. Phin immediately handed it to her then helped pull Reynolds free.

Annabel looked down at the soft, warm creature in her arms. The rabbit peered up at her with large brown eyes. His nose twitched. "Is this Miss Bristol's rabbit?"

"Yes, why?" Phin asked as he heaved Reynolds free.

"You stole him?" She directed the accusation at Phin, not Reynolds, who would have been acting on the duke's orders.

Phin scowled at her. "Well, I couldn't leave him to become stew, could I? Besides, I made a promise to the lady.

Annabel blew out a breath. "What will happen when Lady Wavenwell discovers the rabbit missing?"

"Oh, we should be in Berkshire by then. We'll leave first thing in the morning."

Reynolds cleared his throat. Phin raised a brow. "Is that hemming supposed to mean something, Reynolds?"

"I'm afraid so, Your Grace."

"Well, what is it?"

"I fear Lady Wavenwell will discover the rabbit's absence before the morning."

"Why is that?" Phin crossed his arms over his chest.

"I might have set the lot of the rabbits free. The whole, er, herd, Your Grace."

"How many were there?" Annabel asked.

"Oh, about a dozen, my lady. I didn't mean to, but there were several brown ones, and I had to examine them to see which had the white patch. I might have left the door to the hutch open, but I could hardly set one free and leave the others to their fate."

"You have a soft heart, Reynolds."

Annabel laughed. "Says the man who just instructed his valet to steal a rabbit."

Reynolds had the seat put back to rights now, and Phin took his place beside Annabel. She handed him the rabbit, while Reynolds sat across from them. Phin tapped the roof of the coach. "I hardly think Lady Wavenwell will come after us tonight, but I suppose we'd better not chance it. Reynolds, can you have my things packed and ready to go in an hour?"

"Of course, Your Grace."

"It will take Mrs. Slightley closer to two," Annabel said. "That should give Reynolds time to make traveling arrangements."

"Very good, my lady. Shall I inform Mrs. Slightley that we are leaving when we return?"

Annabel didn't answer right away. Clearly there was something between Reynolds and her housekeeper. Mrs. Slightley was her own woman and at forty plenty mature enough to make her own decisions, but Annabel still felt somewhat protective of her. After all, she had brought Meg along and she would not have met the duke's valet if she had not been here. "What are your intentions toward my housekeeper, Mr. Reynolds?"

Phin burst out laughing. "Forgive me, but you sound like a father or two who have pulled me aside after I made the mistake of dancing with their daughter too often."

"I am only looking out for my housekeeper."

"She can look after herself, I'm sure."

"Your Grace, if you don't mind, I would like to answer," Reynolds said.

"Go ahead, man."

Annabel nodded. "Please."

"My intentions are honorable, my lady. I find Mrs. Slightley's company pleasing. She's witty and I enjoy conversing with her."

"And that's all you've done, Reynolds? Conversed?"

Phin laughed again, but Annabel ignored him.

Reynolds turned a shade of pink she'd only seen on carnations. "I've kissed her, my lady. I promise it was a welcome gesture. If you think I mean her some harm because she is different—"

"There are others who have tried to exploit her, who have exploited her over the years. Did she tell you about her time in the circus?"

"She has mentioned it to me, my lady. But I assure you, her size doesn't matter to me except to tell me she must be a remarkable woman, else she would never have been elevated to the status of housekeeper in your household, my lady."

"That's true enough. You may inform Mrs. Slightley we are leaving, Reynolds. And if you are an intelligent man, which I think you may well be, you might ask her to assist you in making the travel arrangements. I promise you she is ruthlessly efficient and quite shrewd when it comes to bargaining."

"Thank you, my lady. I will."

Annabel looked over at Phin, who grinned at her with amusement and obvious fondness. Her belly did a little flip at the look in his eyes. It reminded her of the way he'd looked at her right before he'd kissed her senseless. She cleared her throat. "As for you, Your Grace."

His eyes darkened, obviously liking the chastising tone of her voice.

"You have been very naughty. What do you propose we do with this rabbit?"

"I propose we let the capable Mrs. Slightley deal with the rabbit." He leaned forward and handed her the bunny, whispering in her ear as he did so. "You can deal with me when we're alone."

***

"And I'm to arrange all of this in two hours?" Meg asked, her eyes wide as she stared up at Reynolds, who was holding a rabbit in his arms.

"Too much for you?" he asked.

She bristled. "Go on with you. But I just hung laundry out to dry, and now I have to collect it and pack it damp. And I was planning to repair the hem of her ladyship's day dress, and now I'll have to do it in the carriage, and my sewing is not as straight with all that bouncing and jouncing and whatnot." She began to fold the dress in her lap and put her sewing materials into the small basket at her elbow. He'd found her in the common room the servants used next to the kitchen. She would have rather been alone and away from the curious eyes of the inn's servants, but she could not see well enough to sew in the gloomy servants' quarters.

"I'll leave you to it then," Reynolds said, taking a step back. Seeing that he was leaving, Meg dropped the dress and stood.

"Wait just a moment." She looked about to see if anyone else was within ear shot. They were more or less alone. The other servants about were in the kitchen, and all the banging and clanging of pots and pans made it all but impossible for them to be overheard by the cook and scullery maid. "You saw His Grace and Her Ladyship together."

"I rode back with them in the coach."

"So?" She raised her brows suggestively.

"So?"

She gave him a light whack with the back of her hand. "Don't play coy with me, Reynolds. You know I'm not after gossip."

Now it was the valet's turn to look about. Then he leaned down and spoke softly. "They did seem rather more friendly than before. I can't say for certain whether they spent the night together, but if I was a gambling man—which I am not—I would bet on it."

She latched on to his lapels, keeping his face close to hers. "You know what this means then?"

"I can't imagine."

She scowled at him then yanked him close and kissed him quick and hard on the lips. "More of this when we return to London. The more *they're* together, the more *we're* together."

"Then I'm all for the two of them seeing each other as much as possible." He tried to kiss her again, but she pushed him away.

"None of that now. People will talk."

He smiled, and she loved how his eyes lit up when he smiled. "Then I'll take my leave. I have some arranging of my own to do," he said, which reminded her of all the work set before her.

"You said you wanted me help with the travel arrangements."

"And I haven't changed my mind. We'll need an inn in Berkshire, and a good one as I assume we will stop there for several days. But I have the coaches to see to. If I arrange things just so, there might be room for three in the luggage coach."

"Three?" She raised her brows.

"One." He pointed to himself. "Two." He pointed to her. "And three." He gestured to the rabbit, cradled in his arms.

"I don't think Lady Longstowe will travel alone in a closed carriage with the duke."

He shrugged. "We'll see."

Meg watched him go, hand over her pounding heart. She wouldn't mind some time in a closed carriage with him. No, she wouldn't mind a'tall.

Sixteen

The coaches were packed and ready by late afternoon, and Phin praised the efficiency of his valet and Mrs. Slightley. Either Lady Wavenwell hadn't yet noticed the escape of her rabbits or hadn't thought to blame their freedom on him, and now he would be gone before she had the opportunity to chastise him in person.

He had no doubt she would write him a strongly worded letter. That was fine. He didn't receive enough entertaining letters. He'd received a letter from Rafe from America, and that had been quite entertaining, but otherwise his mail was comprised mainly of accounts due, advice from his mother, and treatises on the state of his various properties about the country.

Annabel emerged from the inn, tugging her gloves onto her hands and looking very pretty in a pale green dress that made her blue eyes look slightly green but no less vibrant. "Apparently, Mrs. Slightley has grown quite attached to Twitchy," she said, looking up at him.

"Oh?" He hadn't thought Mrs. Slightley overly sentimental.

"She's asked if she can ride in the luggage carriage with him to make certain he is comfortable during the trip."

Phin glanced over at Reynolds, who was speaking with the coachman perched on the box of the luggage carriage. "You don't say."

"I think it is a ploy so she might be alone with your valet."

"Surely not."

She tapped his forearm with her fan, which was surely an unnecessary accoutrement in this cold weather. "You didn't have anything to do with this, did you?"

"No, though I have no objection if you do not."

"It means we would be alone in a closed carriage."

He raised his brows. "Afraid I'll ruin your reputation?"

"I think it's too late for that."

He offered her his arm. "Then come into my lair."

"You are incorrigible." But he didn't fail to notice that her cheeks blushed pink. Before following her into the coach, he spared one last look at Reynolds and saluted the man. His valet deserved a raise.

They were soon well underway, but one glance across the carriage at Annabel showed him she sat straight and stiff and with her hands tightly clasped.

"Nervous?" he asked.

"Why would I be nervous?"

"You haven't seen your daughter in eighteen years, and now there is every likelihood you will see her again tomorrow. I can imagine that would make anyone nervous."

She let out a shaky breath. "What if she hates me, Phin?"

"She won't hate you."

"She might." Her eyes looked slightly wild. "What if I arrive at the sanitarium and she won't see me?"

"Then you go back again the next day and the next until she consents to see you."

"And then she might only consent so she can tell me how she despises me. I left her all alone in the world. And what if Brookside Place is awful? What if she's been kept in deplorable conditions all these years?" Tears brimmed on her lashes, and he had the urge to comfort her.

"I suppose it's possible but based on the amount the earl was sending for her upkeep, I think it rather unlikely."

She nodded, but she was not relieved. Her teeth worried her lower lip.

"Annabel, have you considered that she might not harbor any feelings, positive or negative, toward you?" He did not want to upset her, but neither did he wish for her to have unrealistic expectations. "You said she was slow to develop mentally. Perhaps she won't have an understanding of what a mother is or that she was even abandoned."

"I don't know whether I should hope for that or dread it. I just know I want to take her home with me."

"And I will do everything in my power to see that your wishes are granted."

Now she looked at him sharply. "I still don't understand why you agreed to help me. Is it lust or guilt for the way you behaved when we first met?"

He considered, then spoke honestly. "It was both of those initially, and I suppose there was an element of ennui as well. I never wanted to be a duke, and it seemed vastly more interesting to venture off to Wiltshire with you as opposed to sitting in my solicitor's chambers for hours on end or trying to find some amusement to entertain my brother-in-law when he came to Town. Both the solicitor and Anne's husband, Mr. Clare, will be waiting when I return to London."

"You cannot escape your destiny forever." What an ominous statement that was.

"Being with you makes that destiny easier for me to bear."

She rolled her eyes. "You and your sweet words. It's no wonder you were such a good negotiator in the army. You always know what to say."

"Yes, but I'm not playing a part with you, Annabel." He crossed to sit beside her on the squabs. "I told you. I've never met a woman like you. I can't help but be intrigued by you."

"And what happens when you've tired of me?"

"I daresay you'll tire of me long before I tire of you." He drew her bonnet from her head and brushed a hand over her sleek auburn hair.

"Well, I certainly won't share you," she said, surprising him.

His brows shot together. "You think me so inconstant?"

"I think you are a duke, and you must marry." He waved a hand, but she grasped it and held on. "You dismiss the notion so easily, but I can promise you the rest of Society will not. Your family will not. Long after the earl tired of tormenting me night after night with his vicious games, he would seek me out because he needed an heir. Even after five years, six years without conceiving, he would not give up. He could have had many women, but none of them could give him what he needed—an heir. Why else marry a girl young enough to be his daughter?"

Phin had to unclench his jaw to speak. Any mention of the earl made him angry. "Not all men are the same, and I promise you that the earl and I have *nothing* in common."

"I know it seems that way." She cupped his cheek. "But in one way you are very much alike. You are both titled gentlemen. And if he, who was only an earl, felt compelled to produce an heir, how much greater will the pressure be on you, a duke?"

Phin did not argue. He had already felt the pressure of his position, and he'd only gained the title a few weeks ago. She was correct in that the pressure for him to marry and father not only an heir but a spare or two would mount as time passed. He was only thirty-two, but even a young duke was expected to do his duty and marry an acceptable young girl who could give him children.

But Phin was also not afraid to flaunt convention. He was in a carriage with the Wanton Widow, wasn't he? He'd stolen a rabbit from a viscountess, hadn't he? Why shouldn't he enjoy himself with Annabel as long as he and she liked? When it ended, he could look about the marriage mart. And if it didn't end…well, he would not think of that now.

"Do you know what I like about you?" he asked.

Her expression turned confused as his response bore no relation to her question. "I have a few ideas," she said.

"Other than that." He winked. "I like how you think ahead and so logically too. I've found foresight and logic valuable qualities."

"As have I," she said slowly, warily.

"But sometimes they can cause one to overthink a situation and worry too much."

"Are you suggesting I worry too much?"

He had best be careful here. "Far be it from me to criticize a lady, but since I am here and since you *might* have a tendency to fret about things out of your control, perhaps I can help."

"Because you can order the universe?"

"Not exactly. But I might be able to help you forget. For a little while." He slid off the seat to kneel on the floor of the coach.

"What are you doing?"

"Giving you something else to think about." He moved before her and slid his hands up her legs and over the soft material of her dress. Her blue-green eyes followed the progress of his hands, and the higher they moved the darker her eyes grew. He retraced his path back down to her ankles, and this time when he molded his hands to her legs, he took her skirts along.

"You are certain this is not why Mrs. Slightley rides in the other carriage?" she asked, her voice low and husky.

"I had nothing to do with that, but I'm not one to waste an opportunity." He bent to kiss her knee, covered by a fine white stocking. He moved her skirts higher, almost revealing her to his gaze. "Do you want me to continue?"

"You'll stop if I say so?"

"I'll sit on my side and behave like a perfect gentleman." He kissed her other knee. "Or I can sit here and behave like a perfect scoundrel."

"I like the scoundrel."

"At your service." His mouth moved from her knee to her thigh and finally to the bare skin above her garter. It was soft and smooth, and he relished the feel of it on his lips. He brushed his mouth over it again and again until she shivered and opened her legs a bit wider.

"Higher," she said.

"That's right," he murmured, moving higher. "Tell me what you want." She needed to feel in control to fully enjoy this. She needed to know that her body was hers to give or take away. And for his part, Phin didn't mind being ordered about in the bedroom—or the carriage. He rather liked not being in control for once.

He rubbed his cheek on the silky skin of her inner thigh then licked a trail toward her core. He could smell her, a heady mixture of desire and woman. Her legs trembled as he lifted one to his shoulder and then the other. Her skirts fell back, revealing her pink sex. He couldn't take his gaze from her.

"Where should I kiss you?"

"Lick me," she ordered. "Here." Her finger slid over her folds, parting them so her small clitoris came into view. She kept her hands in place as he leaned forward and licked the tight nub. She sighed and nudged her hips toward him. He licked again.

"I love how you taste," he said.

"Don't talk."

He was hard now, uncomfortably hard as he stroked and flicked and suckled her. She moaned, her hips rolling toward him, and her legs tightening about his shoulders. He teased and tantalized until, with a broken voice, she ordered, "Inside me."

He slid his tongue down to spear inside her. She gasped, and when he caught her gaze, her eyes were wide and shocked. "Your fingers," she whispered. "But not quite yet."

His tongue thrust in and out and her head fell back. When his fingers replaced his tongue, her muscles tightened around him. His tongue found that now swollen nub, and he teased as his fingers slid slowly in and out, moving deeper and curving upward to stroke her as he did. Her gasps were fevered now, fast enough that her chest rose and fell in quick pants.

He was so hot from watching her, he hoped he did not explode himself when she came.

"Deeper," she said on a sob. He went deeper. "Your tongue. Faster."

Phin obeyed, his cock straining for the warm wetness coating his fingers. With an anguished cry of pleasure, her hips bucked, and her muscles tightened around him. Her legs opened wider as she climaxed hard. His tongue did not relent, and her head whipped back and forth on the back of the seat. He watched, entranced by her beauty until her eyes opened. They were the purest blue.

"Your cock," she croaked. "Inside me. Now."

Phin didn't argue. One handed, he opened his fall, slid her off the seat and onto the floor with him. He let her ride him, still in the throes of climax as he moved inside her.

"Yes. *Yes.*" Her words were all but sobs as she took her pleasure. When she was sated, she opened her eyes and looked down at him.

"God, you're magnificent," he said.

"You're still unsatisfied," she murmured.

"I'm distracting you. I think my mission is accomplished." He could have spent hours buried inside her, but today was not about him. Her fingers tightened on his shoulders and she rolled her hips.

"Distract me more. Lay me down and take me on the carriage floor like a common wench."

"You could never be common." He shifted until she was under him, and with his hand beneath her head, he laid her down. He kept his hand under her head and locked his other hand with hers, lacing their fingers. His gaze met hers, and when he began to move inside her, she looked away. He wanted her to look at him, but he wouldn't ask, wouldn't demand that much intimacy from her yet. She sighed as he moved, slowly and deliberately.

"That feels so good."

He could only grunt in agreement. He'd wanted her to come again, but he wasn't certain he had the control. Her hand wrapped around his neck and tugged at his hair just enough to sting. "Let go," she said. Their eyes met for an instant, and he let her see his passion and his need for her. And then he was over the edge, pulling her close, burying his head in her neck.

She held him afterward, as though he were the one who needed comforting. As though he were the one about to meet a long-lost child. And yet, he put his head on her shoulder and welcomed her caresses. He feared the closer they came to finding Theadosia, the closer he was to losing Annabel.

***

Annabel's body still felt warm and sated when she was helped out of the carriage a few hours later. They'd arrived in Berkshire, but it was too late to make a call at Brookside Place. The innkeeper and his wife were very accommodating. They had gone out of their way to make the duke's party comfortable, but it was a small inn and Annabel would have to share her room with Meg. She would have liked to spend another night with Phin, but propriety certainly prevented it. Lying in bed, Meg sleeping beside her, Annabel thought how different being with Phin was than any other man. The lovers she'd had after her marriage were decent enough men, but she had not wanted to spend more than a couple of hours with them. She certainly had not wanted to share a bed with them all night.

But last night she had slept in Phin's arms. And she'd slept well. Of course, she'd been exhausted from his lovemaking. She didn't know how he was able to bring her pleasure again, but his patience and willingness to let her be in control had finally given back that part of her she had thought gone forever.

And as she lay in the inn, she wished he could come to her. How different from when she'd been married to the earl and dreaded the possibility that he would want her. She'd often lay awake, unable to sleep for fear.

She turned onto her side and tried to fall asleep now, but Phin had been correct that she'd needed distraction. Tomorrow she would see Theadosia again. Tomorrow she would hold her child, look upon her face, say all the things she had wanted to say for so many years.

And she would finally bring Theadosia home.

"Shall I fetch you some tea with brandy to help you sleep?" Meg murmured.

"I'm sorry. My tossing and turning must be keeping you awake."

"I don't mind. You've been looking for the child ever since I've known you. Of course, you can't sleep."

"I don't want you to get up, Meg," Annabel said in the darkness. "At least one of us should sleep."

After a long silence, Annabel thought perhaps her housekeeper had gone back to sleep. But then Meg spoke quietly. "I hope you are ready to see her, my lady."

"I've been ready for years."

"Yes, but sometimes our longings and our memories do us a disservice."

Annabel sat. "I don't understand."

Meg looked up at her. "The earl sent her away because she was not like other children."

"He called her mentally deficient. She was two!" Annabel clenched the sheets in her hands.

"And he may very well have been wrong about her, but what if he wasn't?"

"Then I will love her just the same!" Her voice came out more harshly than she'd intended.

"Of course, you will, my lady."

Annabel took a deep breath. "Meg, I understand what you are saying. Your own past cannot have been easy."

"My parents gave me away to the circus, my lady. They didn't want anything to do with me once they realized what I was." There was pain in her voice, a pain Annabel could only imagine.

"I hope you know me well enough now to believe I would never willingly abandon my child."

A Duke a Dozen | 329

"I do, my lady. I only spoke—and perhaps it was not my place—but I spoke because I…I hope your expectations are not too high."

"Thank you, Meg." Annabel lay back again. "I know your intentions are good."

And even though she hadn't said it, her advice was good as well. Annabel had years to create a play in her mind of how her reunion would transpire. But it was based on nothing but fancy and memories of a toddler. She must be prepared for anything tomorrow. She must realize that her daughter would most likely not know her, have no memory of her.

And that was the possibility that scared Annabel the most.

***

"Are you not hungry?" Phin asked her the next morning as they broke their fast in the dining room. The inn did not have a private room as it was too small, but none of the other guests were dining. Annabel suspected the innkeeper had their breakfasts delivered to their chambers so the duke and countess would have privacy.

"Not really," she said. "I'm too anxious to eat."

"Well, then it's a good thing we have an appointment in less than an hour at Brookside Place."

Annabel blinked at him. "An appointment? But we just arrived last night."

"And I sent Reynolds with a letter requesting an audience with the physician overseeing the sanitarium. I received a reply late last night from a Dr. Poppinbock—"

She laughed. "That is not his name."

"Oh, I assure you it is." His eyes glittered with amusement. "And Dr. Poppinbock agreed to see us this morning."

"How did you manage it?"

"I am a duke, my love. I thought that was why you brought me along."

She nodded, her throat tight and suddenly dry at his use of the endearment, *my love*. Had he meant that, or had it been one of those things men say to women without really thinking? Had he lain awake last night wishing she were beside him? She rather doubted it. He had probably spent the evening in a much more productive manner—writing letters and issuing commands to physicians and who knew what else.

"Do you intend to eat that cinnamon bun?" he asked.

She looked down at her plate. She hadn't even touched her food. "No."

"May I have it?"

"Please." She rose, and he hastily followed. "Excuse me. I should gather my shawl and bonnet if we're to leave soon."

"I'll wait for you in here."

She was almost through the door when he spoke again. "Annabel."

She looked back over her shoulder.

"Everything will be fine."

Seventeen

"It looks pleasant enough," Annabel said as she and Phin gained their first view of Brookside Place.

"Very pretty."

The building was large and white with grand old beech trees dotting the lawn. In the spring and summer, she imagined the lawn was green and the beeches full of leaves. It would be a pretty prospect and a lovely spot for the residents to picnic or walk. Her hands twisted in her lap, and Phin reached over and took one. He'd moved to sit beside her as soon as the carriage had left the inn.

She was glad of his comforting touch. "Do you know what I am afraid of?" she asked.

"Spiders?"

Sometimes she did not know whether to laugh or smack him. "No."

He looked at her. "You aren't afraid of spiders? I confess I scream like a girl when I see one."

She gave in and laughed. "I see what you are doing."

"Is it working?"

"Yes." She was distracted, but only for a moment. "Do you know what I truly fear? That the outside is lovely, and the inside is a prison. What if it's terrible? What if my child has been living a nightmare these past years?"

"Then we'll take her away and spend the rest of our lives making it up to her." He squeezed her hand, and her throat closed again in that peculiar way it had this morning when he'd called her *my love*. He had made himself her partner, if only in his statement. She had never had a partner before, and the thought both thrilled and terrified her. How could he make such a statement when their time together could not but be fleeting?

The coach stopped, and the doors of Brookside Place opened. A man with a large chest and thin legs who was dressed all in black stepped outside followed by two women in white. Annabel assumed the people must be Dr. Poppinbock and two nurses.

Once out of the coach, Phin greeted them and introduced her, and they were all shown inside. Much to Annabel's relief, the foyer was bright and clean as was the parlor they were shown to. But she'd lived years of her life in a marriage that had looked ideal from the outside and had been nothing short of torment on the inside. Annabel did not trust easily.

When they'd been seated and served tea Annabel did not want, Dr. Poppinbock addressed her directly. "Lady Longstowe, I understand you wish to see one of our residents, Lady Theadosia."

"Yes. She is my daughter."

"I know." He sipped his tea. Annabel could not help but think his name suited him. His legs really were very thin and bird-like while his chest was large and puffed up like a peacock's.

"When your husband—"

"My late husband," she interrupted.

"Of course. My condolences."

Annabel merely nodded.

"When the late earl brought her here, he said you did not ever wish to see her again. In fact, he gave strict orders for you to be turned away should you ever make an appearance. I was young and quite new here when he came, but I remember his words to my predecessor clearly."

"I trust those directives are null and void now that the man who gave them is dead," Phin said.

"Not exactly," Poppinbock said. "His wishes were in writing, and he was her legal guardian."

"And now I am her guardian," Annabel said, "and I wish to see my daughter."

"And we will accommodate you, but if you desire to remove her or do more than visit her, I am afraid we will have to take the matter up with the courts. It is only His Grace's"—he cleared his throat—"persuasive missives that have swayed me today."

Annabel gave Phin a sidelong look. Missives? He had not mentioned that he had written multiple letters or that he'd had to be persuasive.

"Thank you, Dr. Poppinbock," Phin said. "If you could bring us to the lady."

"We will bring her here." He lifted a finger, which must have been a sign to one of the nurses because she gave a quick bow and retreated. The other nurse cleared her throat.

"My lady, if I may speak?" the nurse said, her voice low and soothing.

"Of course."

"I have been caring for Lady Theadosia for the last three years. She has a very sweet disposition, and she is almost childlike in her understanding. She does not speak much. Her hearing is not good. But she quite enjoys looking at books with pictures, so I have brought some of her favorite books to the parlor in case you would like to look at them with her." She gestured to a small table with perhaps half a dozen books stacked on top. Annabel looked through them. All of them had colorful illustrations of plants or animals and some were stories of mythology.

"She doesn't read herself?"

"I'm afraid not, my lady. As I said, she has a very childlike understanding. I hope you will understand, as well, that she will arrive with her very good friend Miss Oliver. Miss Oliver fell from a horse when she was sixteen and her brain was damaged. She is…more advanced than Lady Theadosia, but she cannot function in society. The two are very good friends. One might say they are inseparable."

"I see."

"We have fostered the friendship, my lady," Dr. Poppinbock said. "It seems to be good for both of them."

Annabel nodded, trying very hard not to focus on the disorienting feeling swirling about her. How odd that all of these strangers knew her own daughter better than she.

"I will withdraw," Dr. Poppinbock said, standing. "Men seem to make Lady Theadosia anxious. Your Grace, would you care to withdraw as well?"

Phin looked at Annabel, and she wasn't certain what message to convey to him. She wanted Theadosia to be at ease, but she also needed the comfort of Phin at her side.

A man in a servant's livery entered and whispered in Poppinbock's ear. The doctor nodded then looked at Phin. "If you do not mind joining me in my study, it would seem we are overrun with guests today. Your Grace has a guest waiting to speak with him."

Annabel glanced at the duke in surprise.

He rose abruptly. "*I* have a guest? Surely you must be mistaken."

"Not at all, Your Grace. He's been here waiting for you for the past hour, and he has become quite insistent that he see you."

Phin looked at her then back at Poppinbock. Annabel rose and placed a hand on his arm. "Go ahead, Your Grace. I shall be fine."

"Are you certain?"

"Yes. If, as Dr. Poppinbock says, men make Theadosia anxious, perhaps I should meet her alone."

He nodded, still seeming stunned that he had a guest waiting for him. "I'll return as soon as I finish and wait outside the door. If you need me, you have but to call."

"Thank you." She squeezed his arm with her hand before he withdrew.

Now was the time for her to be strong and brave. She'd always imagined having to do this by herself. She didn't need Phin at her side, but she wanted him. How strange, after all these years of avoiding men and feeling uncomfortable in their presence, she now wanted a man with her at one of the most trying moments of her life.

She sat on the couch again and lifted her tea, trying to steady the cup enough to sip from it. The nurse pretended not to notice. The sound of the clock on the mantle seemed intolerably loud as did the crackle of the fire in the hearth. Finally, she heard the sound of a woman speaking low. Annabel rose, clutching her skirts in her hands, and stared at the door as it opened, admitting a short, dark-haired woman.

***

Phin followed Poppinbock to his study, but when they reached the door, the man gestured to it and withdrew. "I shall give you your privacy, Your Grace."

Phin thought he should at least see who was in the study first. He might not want privacy. "Thank you," he said and put his hand on the latch. Half a dozen ideas as to the man waiting for him had occurred to him on the short walk to the study. It was Draven, his former senior commander, come to give him another mission. It was Jasper, another Survivor, who needed help tracking some criminal in the rookeries. It was Ewan, the big burly Survivor, and he needed Phin to negotiate a good price on a new space for his boxing studio. Or perhaps Neil. Neil might want help with a new building for the orphanage his wife ran. Rafe was in America. Surely,

Rafe couldn't be behind the door. But he didn't dare put anything past Rafe…

What about Colin? He was secretive enough to show up, unexpected, in a place like this. Duncan? No, he was wild and a certifiable lunatic. Secrecy was not his style. Stratford? Nash? Nicholas?

Oh, God. It was Aidan. Aidan had always had a penchant for thievery. He was in trouble and needed Phin to get him out of it.

Phin opened the door, prepared to chastise Aidan before helping him in whatever capacity he could. But it wasn't Aidan at all.

"John?" Phin said, stopping in the doorway in shock. No wonder Poppinbock had not seen a problem with leading Phin to meet the stranger. John Clare was married to Phin's sister Anne. "Is something wrong with Anne? Has something happened to the children?"

John rose, tall and handsome with dark blond hair and small brown eyes. "Anne and the children are all well."

"Then my mother—"

"She is also in good health, but I will admit she is the reason I am here. Will you sit with me, Your Grace?"

Phin waved a hand. "Don't you start calling me by honorifics. You've known me since I was a boy at Eton."

Phin closed the door to the study behind him and took the seat next to John.

"I've known you for years, that's true. And I always knew you would become the duke."

Phin blew out a breath. "Well, you're the only one. I'd hoped to avoid it, especially when Ernest took on the mantle."

"He wasn't as careful as he should have been," John said.

No." Phin gave his brother-in-law a long look. He was not certain whether he should comment on the odd phrasing. "You said something about my mother?"

"Yes, she sent me."

Odd again. "My mother sent you to find me?"

"It seems she's quite disturbed by some rumors that have reached Southmeade."

Phin felt the first ripples of annoyance. "What rumors are those?" he asked, though he already suspected.

John reached into his coat, a fashionable garment most likely made by Schweitzer or Meyer on Savile Row, and withdrew a sheet torn from a newspaper. Phin took it and scanned the headlines.

Doomed Duke elopes with Wanton Widow

"Don't tell me my mother believes this rot," Phin said without reading any further. "I haven't eloped with anyone."

"But you have run away with Richard's former lover, Lady Longstowe."

Richard's former lover. Those rumors about his brother, like these, were also not true. "No, I haven't run away with her. Not that she is any of your business."

"And if you haven't run away with her, what exactly were you doing with her in Wiltshire?"

Phin opened his mouth to reiterate that it was not John's business—or his mother's for that matter—but he reconsidered. He had a few questions of his own. "How did you know I was in Wiltshire? How did you know I was here, come to think of it?"

John shifted in his seat. "It's not as though you were traveling under an assumed name. You have the ducal coach and a retinue—"

"I'd hardly call it a retinue."

"—and that is relatively easy to track. I only tracked you down because your mother asked me to."

"Because she read this rag?" Phin waved the paper.

"Because she is concerned that you are still thinking like a younger son, not a duke."

Phin rose, crumpled the paper, and threw it to the floor. "Why don't we stop speaking in circles, John? Out with it. What is the real reason you are here?"

"Your mother wants you to give up Lady Longstowe, come home to Southmeade, and agree to marry an acceptable woman. I'm to bring you home today."

***

The girl who entered the parlor was not familiar to Annabel as a whole, but there were features in her she recognized. There were the blue eyes, so bright and vivid, much like her own. There was the tawny brown hair, that was the same color as her father's in his youth. And she remembered other things that had differentiated the girl as a baby. She had a somewhat flat nose and a short neck. Her eyes were rather slanted, and she was quite short. Annabel felt she towered over her.

But Theadosia was clean and dressed simply in a white dress with a brown shawl. Her hair was short but neat, and she smiled shyly at Annabel. The short, plump girl with her whose hair was blond and close-cropped smiled as well. Annabel assumed she was Miss Oliver. The nurse tapped Theadosia's arm, and she looked at Annabel.

"This is Lady Longstowe," the nurse said slowly and clearly. Annabel noticed how Theadosia watched the nurse's lips carefully. Then Theadosia nodded briskly and dropped an awkward curtsy. Miss Oliver did the same.

Something about the gesture caused a lump to rise in Annabel's throat.

Theadosia watched Annabel, and her brow creased. She shook her head and said, "No."

The nurse looked at Annabel. "She's afraid she has not done the right thing." She patted Theadosia's arm. "Yes. Good."

Theadosia looked at Annabel again. Annabel nodded, trying very hard to hold back tears. "Yes," she said with a forced smile. "Very good."

How had she not realized her child would no longer be a child? Of course, she had known that in the back of her mind. She knew Theadosia was twenty. But she had still expected the toddler to come through the door. The woman standing before her was no longer that toddler, and Annabel wished the earl were still alive so that she might slap him for depriving her of all those years with her only child. Theadosia did not even know her. That much was clear.

"Shall we sit?" Annabel asked. She gestured to the couch, and then Theadosia's eyes fell on the books. She clapped her hands, and Miss Oliver gave a delighted gasp. After a glance at the nurse, who gave an approving nod, the ladies ran to the books. Theadosia pulled one from the stack and opened it. She sat on the couch, turning pages, and now it was Annabel's turn to look to the nurse.

"Does she know—I'm sorry, what is your name?"

"Penny, my lady."

"Penny, does Lady Theadosia know who I am?"

"We told her you were coming. I told her you are her mother, but I don't know if she understands what that is. She's never had a mother."

Annabel felt her lip tremble. "No, I suppose she hasn't. May I sit with her?"

"Oh, yes, my lady!"

Annabel sat beside Theadosia, who continued turning pages in the book. Miss Oliver had chosen her own book and seemed quite absorbed. Annabel had imagined countless conversations with her daughter. There were so many things she wanted to ask her. Now she had to let all of that go. She could see those conversations would be impossible.

Theadosia pointed to a picture of an owl and made a hooting sound. Annabel smiled. "Yes, that is the sound an owl makes." She moved closer and looked at where Theadosia's finger rested on the page. The artist had drawn a brown owl with his wings outstretched. He was flying, obviously looking for prey.

Annabel looked at the text underneath. "It says here that owls hunt for mice, rabbits, and other small mammals."

Theadosia watched her lips carefully. It was an odd sensation, being the object of such close scrutiny, but she understood that with limited hearing, it was the way she could understand what was said. Her daughter went back to the book and turned several pages until she found what she wanted. It was a picture of a large brown and white hare. Annabel nodded. "That is what owls eat." An idea occurred to her. "Do you know, I have a rabbit?"

Theadosia frowned, looking from the picture to Annabel.

"You?" she asked, her voice slightly muted.

"Yes. His name is Twitchy. Shall I bring him when I come to visit again?"

"Yes! Want. Want!" Theadosia all but bounced off the couch in her excitement.

"Oh, please do!" Miss Oliver said, looking up from her book.

"Then I will bring him for you to meet tomorrow."

Theadosia turned to her and gave her a huge hug. Taken off guard, it was a moment before Annabel wrapped her arms around her daughter, but once she did, she wanted to hold tightly. Her baby was in her arms again. Theadosia was finally with her again. They had survived the earl, and holding her daughter again was the best revenge she could think of. He'd tried to separate them, but in the end, love had won.

Theadosia pulled back, and though Annabel wanted to go on holding her, she let go. "What is it?" she asked, looking down into her own eyes in Theadosia's face.

"Yes!" Theadosia said, smiling broadly. It was the sort of smile that would have brought sunshine to any room, and it warmed Annabel's heart.

"Yes." She brushed the hair off Theadosia's forehead, while her daughter grabbed her book again and began to page through it. When she'd shown her mother all of her favorite pictures, she opened another. Annabel looked at every page and read the captions aloud. She kept one hand on her daughter's arm or stroking her hair or patting her back. Touching her seemed to make her real. Now that she had her daughter again, she did not want to lose her.

Finally, Penny, who had been sitting across the room quietly all this time and only interjecting when Theadosia looked to her for an answer or confirmation, rose. Miss Oliver went to the nurse and Theadosia immediately put her book down and went to stand beside Miss Oliver. It was clear to Annabel that though Theadosia might be comfortable with her, she wanted to stay with her friend.

"I hope you don't mind, my lady, but Lady Theadosia tires easily. It's almost time for her nap."

Annabel rose. "But it's not even been an hour."

"I'm sorry, my lady. Perhaps you might return tomorrow."

"Of course. I'll bring Twitchy, the rabbit."

Theadosia clapped her hands. "Yes!"

Annabel crossed the room and looked down at Theadosia. "I will come back. I'll see you tomorrow, darling."

Her daughter smiled brightly and gave her a quick hug before following Penny and Miss Oliver out of the room. Annabel watched her, feeling as though she were losing her daughter all over again. She reached back, took hold of a chair and lowered herself into it. She would not cry. Her daughter was happy and well-cared for. That was what mattered.

But it hurt that she did not know her mother. It hurt that she seemed to have no memory of her. It didn't matter that no child separated from her mother, and especially not a child like Theadosia, would remember anything from such a young age. Annabel's chest ached as she thought of all the years and all the milestones she had missed. When had the little girl learned to walk? To say her first word? To learn to love books?

The door to the parlor opened wider, and Annabel looked up, expecting to see Phin.

But it was Dr. Poppinbock. He smiled rather sadly when he saw her face. "She will never be able to live on her own," he said. "But she is happy here."

Annabel cleared her throat. "And her, er, tuition is still being paid?"

"Every month without fail. I promise you, Lady Theadosia wants for nothing. But in truth, she wants very little. Just her friend and her books."

"I had hoped to bring her home to London with me."

Poppinbock shook his head. "I am afraid I would advise against that. Brookside is her home. To take her away from all she knows would unnecessarily traumatize her."

"I'm beginning to see that." She had not wanted to admit it, but the best place for Theadosia was not with her.

"And there is another consideration." Poppinbock gestured to a chair. "May I?"

"Please."

He sat and took a breath. "Lady Theadosia was never a robust child. She was often ill and tires easily. I examined her and then sent to London for a renowned associate of mine to examine her and give a second opinion. We agreed that Lady Theadosia has a weak heart."

"I see," Annabel said, her voice sounding a thousand miles away.

"I sent a letter to the earl informing him. I assume you never saw it. I received no reply."

Annabel shook her head.

"I was frank in my letter, Lady Longstowe. May I be frank now?"

Annabel clenched the arms of the chair and wished, again, for Phin. She hadn't known how much she would need someone—a friend—to see her through this. Somehow she found words in the swirling maelstrom of her mind. "Yes, do be frank, Dr. Poppinbock."

"We did not expect Lady Theadosia to live this long. She has been doing rather well these past few months, but the stretches of time when she is ill have grown longer and longer. I do not think she can withstand many more."

"You are saying my time with her is short?"

"I am, my lady."

Annabel felt bile rise in her throat, but she swallowed to keep it down. How could life be so cruel? How was it she could find her child only to be told she would lose her again so soon?

"You might have another year, perhaps two. I cannot say, but I do not think it will be much more than that."

"Thank you, Dr. Poppinbock."

His brows furrowed as the tears she'd been struggling to keep from falling trickled down her cheek. She hated crying in front of people.

"Is there anything I can do for you, Lady Longstowe?"

"You can fetch the duke, please. Tell him I'd like to go back to the inn now."

"Yes, my lady. He is still in my study, but I will knock on the door."

Annabel blinked back the tears. "Who has come to see him?"

"I believe it is his brother-in-law, my lady. With a summons from the duchess, his mother."

***

"Mr. Clare," Phin said, using John's surname. "I don't suppose you or my mother stopped to consider that I am a grown man, capable of making my own decisions."

"No one is arguing otherwise, Phin." John spread his hands in a disarming gesture.

"And yet my mother has sent you to fetch me home. I am not some errant child who needs to be called home and taken to task. Nor do I need my mother to find me a bride. I am perfectly capable of finding a wife all on my own."

"Are you? You've spent the last week gallivanting about the country with the nation's most scandalous woman."

Phin wondered when John had become so sanctimonious. Had he lectured all the dukes of Mayne or just decided Phin needed his guidance?

"The nation's most scandalous woman?" Phin said, not bothering to temper his tone. "She is hardly that. She took a lover after her husband died. What is the harm in that? Even if she'd taken ten or twenty? What does it matter? Her only crime is being found out. It's nothing half the peerage hasn't done, and most of them don't have the decency to wait until their spouse is dead first."

John stared at him. "Your mother was right to be concerned." Phin waved a hand, dismissing him. "She was. You're enamored of the woman."

"Enamored?" It was the sort of word one might use to describe the feeling a schoolboy had for the first girl he danced with. It was not at all the way Phin felt about Annabel. And he didn't really care whether his mother or his brother-in-law or the King of bloody England understood that.

"You're smitten with her, but you're a duke now. You have to think about more than…carnal pleasures."

"You think this is about my cock?"

"What else? You can't think to marry the woman."

A tap sounded on the door and a man cleared his throat. "Your Grace, Lady Longstowe has asked for you."

Phin jumped up, glancing at his pocket watch. "It's been a bloody hour," he muttered. Then louder, "I'm coming."

"She snaps her fingers and off you go," John murmured.

"Shut up, John. If you had any idea why she is here—"

"To see her idiot child? I know all about it. I might not be a war hero, but I'm capable of gathering information."

"Go home, John. Go home to your wife and children. Tell my mother that I'll see her when I'm good and ready. And if she wants to play matchmaker, she would do better to spend her efforts on Philomena. I need no assistance." Phin went to the door, opened it, and left his brother-in-law in the study.

In the parlor, Annabel stood looking out the window. Her back was rigid, and her face looked pale and beautiful in the weak light of the winter day.

"Annabel," he murmured, moving inside the parlor. She turned abruptly, and her face was drawn and tight. "I'm so sorry I was not here. My sister's bloody husband came to—"

She crossed the room in three steps and threw herself into his arms. "Just hold me, Phin." She wrapped her arms around him. "Please."

He held her, easing her onto the couch and enveloping her in his arms. He murmured soothing words and stroked her hair as she spoke through broken sobs about seeing her daughter.

"I should have been at your side," he said.

"You're here now. Take me back to the inn. Please."

He had to leave her for a few moments to order the coach. When he returned, she'd dried her tears and gave him a shaky smile. A few minutes later, the coach was out front and he escorted her inside. As he sat back and looked out the window, he thought he saw John standing in the dark foyer of Brookside Place, watching them go.

"I don't care what that innkeeper says," Phin told Annabel. "When we get back, I'm not leaving you. Not now, and not tonight."

"Dr. Poppinbock said your mother wants you to come home. She's obviously heard some rumor about us—although can it really be a rumor if it's true?—and wants you to find a proper wife."

"I'll handle my mother." He moved across the coach to sit beside her. "My only concern right now is you. If we're to stay in Berkshire we will want to lease a property. We can send for our servants from London and…"

But she was shaking her head. Annabel closed her eyes and pressed her fingers to the bridge of her nose. "Are you listening to yourself? You and I cannot lease a house together."

"Then we'll lease two for propriety's sake."

"And then what? You'll live in Berkshire for the next year or two? You are the Duke of Mayne. You have tenants and farmers and hundreds of people relying on you to oversee your estates and take care of them. You can't twiddle your thumbs in Berkshire, and honestly, I don't understand why you would want to."

Phin stared at her. Did she really not know? Perhaps he had not been plain enough with her. "Because I want to be with you. In Berkshire or Brighton or bloody Borehamwood."

Phin did not know what he expected her to say but it was not the next words out of her mouth.

"Duke, your mother is right."

He frowned and pulled back from her. "My mother is right? What does that mean?"

"It means you should go home. You should marry. Have children. Live your life. Even if I wanted you to, you can't waste your time sitting about in Berkshire."

Even if I wanted you to...

The words were clear. Her meaning was clear, but he couldn't seem to wrap his head around them. He winced, anticipating the punch, but he would have her speak plainly. "What are you saying, Annabel?"

She looked him directly in the face, her bright blue eyes clear and steadfast. "I'm saying goodbye."

Eighteen

As soon as she was alone in her chamber, Annabel threw herself on the bed and wept. She wept for her lost youth and her lost daughter, and she wept because the look on Phin's face had broken her heart.

She'd hurt him. She, who had been so afraid of being hurt, so afraid of opening herself up to any emotion, had done nothing short of slapping him across the face. He'd looked stunned and wounded at her dismissal.

He'd recovered quickly. He'd said he was an expert negotiator, and she could see why. He was able to mask his pain almost instantly. But then he probably never thought she would cause him pain.

She had not wanted to. She'd hated the coldness that settled like ice in the coach after she'd spoken. He moved rigidly back across the coach and sat, not looking at her, staring out the window, his eyes seeing nothing.

She had wanted to go to him. She had wanted to throw herself into his arms again and tell him she hadn't meant it.

But it had been a mistake to do that in the parlor. It had been her own weakness and unfair to Phin.

"My lady?" came a quiet voice. Meg stood just inside the door, looking uncertain. "Are you unwell?"

"Yes, Meg. I just need"—she hiccupped—"need to be left alone."

"Did something happen with your daughter, my lady?"

She hesitated. "Yes."

"And His Grace? His face looks like a storm cloud."

"The duke and I are parting company."

Meg gasped. "But why, my lady? I know it's not my place to ask—"

"Then get back in your place," she barked.

Meg blinked at her. "Yes, my lady."

"No!" Annabel sat. "I didn't mean that, Meg. I'm so sorry." She wiped the tears from her face.

"You don't need to apologize to me, my lady."

"I do. I feel as though I need to apologize to everyone. I don't want to part with Phineas—His Grace. But can't you see, can't *he* see, it's for the best? He is a duke, and he has a responsibility to sire heirs and oversee his dukedom."

Meg came closer and reached out a hand. Annabel took it.

"I realized today that my daughter can't come to London with me. I can't take her away from all she's ever known. And she's not"—Annabel's throat threatened to close and the tears stung her eyes—"she's not well. Her heart is not strong. She may not have many years left. I have to spend as much time in Berkshire as possible."

Meg squeezed her hand. "We'll find a house here, my lady."

Annabel smiled weakly. "That's what he said. Of course, he did. He is such a good man."

"If you'll forgive me for being so bold, my lady, I do think you love him."

Annabel started to shake her head, to deny it, and then she stared at Meg. "I do!" she cried. She'd fallen in love with him during that first game of billiards when he'd teased her about wanting to disrobe and insisted on calling Clarissa Lady Waddlesworth. "I do love him, Meg. I love him so very much."

"But you don't believe he loves you? Forgive me, my lady, but from everything I've seen, you are far more than an infatuation to the man. He cares about you. Deeply."

"I don't know. We haven't even known each other for a month."

"Sometimes it doesn't take even a day. Sometimes you just know."

Annabel gave her a long look. How had she not seen what was so glaringly obvious before now? Meg was in love too, and judging by the way she squared her shoulders and hummed as she worked, Reynolds felt the same.

But Annabel wasn't a housekeeper, and Phin wasn't a valet. It wasn't so simple for them. Although, perhaps it was not so simple for Meg and her Reynolds either.

"I do love him, Meg. I do. And that's why he has to go his own way, and I have to go mine. I can't ask him to stay in Berkshire. I can't ask him to forgo his duty to his tenants and his title by staying with me. I can't ask him to bring scandal on his family by continuing to associate with a known fallen woman. He can't marry me, and the one thing a duke must do is produce an heir. I can't give him that, or at least, it's unlikely that I will. It's better that we part now."

Meg looked down, pain etched on her features.

"And if you want to leave my service, I understand. You were hired to manage a town house in London, not whatever I might find here. And I sense that your loyalties may have shifted."

Meg gave her a startled look. "I will always be loyal to you, my lady!"

"I know that well, but far be it for me to stand in the way of your happiness."

Meg looked down, and when she looked up again, her brown eyes were set and her chin was high. "My place is with you, my lady."

"Meg—"

"There's nowhere else I'd rather be." She released Annabel's hand. "And if we are to stay in Berkshire then I should begin preparing to move somewhere more permanent. I will speak with the innkeeper's wife and see if she knows of a cottage we might let. And I'll write to Town and have Crotchett send Cook and several maids. Please tell me we don't need Crotchett himself. Let's leave him in London to make the populace miserable."

Despite the tears that still threatened to spill over, Annabel laughed. "Poor Crotchett. We'll discuss how to arrange everything later."

"Then I'll leave you to rest, my lady. It's been a trying morning, and you look as though your head is pounding."

"It is, Meg—Mrs. Slightley. Thank you."

"I'll come back in an hour or so with tea, my lady."

When she was gone, Annabel lay back and closed her burning eyes. She didn't allow the tears to fall. She had no right to cry. For years, all she had wanted was to see her daughter again. She'd cried herself to sleep many, many nights out of fear and worry and anguish for her daughter. It was too much to expect that she would find Theadosia again without having to pay some price.

And that price was Phin. She had no illusions she would ever find another man to compare to him. He was charming and witty, kind and thoughtful, handsome and…skilled.

But she wasn't really letting him go because he'd never been hers to begin with.

***

The duke had returned and instructed him to pack. Then he'd stared out the window for ten minutes and turned on Reynolds, asking him what the hell he was doing.

"Packing, Your Grace," Reynolds had replied.

"The hell you are. I'm not leaving." And he'd marched out of the chamber.

That had been a half hour ago, and Reynolds had been at a loss ever since. He'd spent far too much time polishing His Grace's boots. They did not need polishing, but he found the repetitive actions calming. If indeed they were leaving, he had to find Meg. But if they were staying, he could speak to her later. No doubt she was with her mistress, and he had no good excuse for fetching her. Perhaps he could say that he needed her to help him feed the rabbit.

Reynolds winced. Even a child would see through that paper-thin pretext.

A knock sounded at the door, and Reynolds set the boot he'd been polishing these last ten minutes down and went to answer it. He knew it wasn't the duke. He wouldn't knock on the door of his own chamber. He didn't dare to hope it was Meg, except that his heart apparently did dare because it galloped in his chest.

When he opened the door, his heart sputtered to a stop. It was her, and her expression told him everything. "That's it then?" he asked.

She looked over her shoulder. "Can I come in? I saw His Grace in the public room, and I sneaked up here to—" She looked down.

"To say good-bye?"

She looked up at him, tears making her eyes look large and dark.

"Come here." He bent and opened his arms. She went into them, all warm and sweet. He would miss this. He would miss her.

Pulling her inside, he closed the door. "They're parting?" he said, though he had already surmised as much from the duke's foul mood.

She nodded against his chest. "I don't know everything, but I know my mistress found her daughter. She can't take her back to London, and we're staying here." She looked up at him. "Has the duke said anything?"

"He said to pack and then said he wasn't leaving."

Her eyes narrowed. "He'll fight for her?"

"You didn't think he'd just walk away." Reynolds gave her a meaningful look. "He doesn't give up that easily."

"But there's no hope. She can't marry him. They can't be together."

"Oh, I have a feeling they'll find a way."

Meg arched a brow. "Are we still talking about the nobs?"

"Why would I waste my breath on them? It's you I care about, Meg. It's you I want to be with."

She stared at him, unbelieving. "You'll just leave His Grace's service? For me?"

"Of course, I will."

"Reynolds." She took his face in her hands and kissed him. After a moment he pulled away.

"Come here. If he comes back, we'll be caught." He tugged her into the dressing room. The duke had been given the best chamber in the inn, and it had its own dressing room, where Reynolds had stored the luggage and His Grace's clothing. It also currently housed one small brown rabbit who looked up from a bowl of assorted vegetables and sniffed when the two of them stumbled inside. Reynolds closed the door. He kissed Meg again then pulled back before he was tempted to do more. "I'd be a fool to walk away without making plans. I have to find other work so I can support you."

"Are you saying—"

"That I want to marry you? Yes. Would you have me, Meg?"

"Reynolds!" She kissed him again. He sank to his knees, and her arms wrapped around his neck. Her kisses were passionate, but he was not so drunk on them that he didn't realize she hadn't accepted his proposal.

"Meg, is that a yes?"

She squeezed her eyes shut, and he sat back on his heels. So she *had* come to say good-bye.

"I can't leave her. Not now. She needs me."

"*I* need you."

"And you'll really walk away from him? All those years of service?"

"I have to find something else first and give him time to replace me. Say you'll be waiting for me, Meg."

She looked down. "I don't know. She's all alone. I can't leave her, not now. Maybe not ever. She saved me, Reynolds.

In some ways we saved each other. I can't turn my back on her."

He blew out a breath. "I'd really thought, after that last night they were together in Wiltshire…"

"I know." She threaded her hands through his hair. "I thought so too. She loves him, you know. That's why she's letting him go."

"I'm not so sure he wants to be let go. I know I don't."

"Come here." She pulled him against her, and his lips found her warm ones. The kiss was sweet and a bit desperate. Perhaps if they tried harder to reconcile the countess and the duke, he wouldn't have to let Meg go.

He heard a sound and pulled back. Putting a finger to his mouth, he rose and peered through the sliver of space between the door to the dressing room and the bed chamber. The duke was back. He stomped into the room, stripped out of his coat, and ran a hand through his hair before swearing then stalking to the window and back across the room again.

Meg tapped his arm, and he turned and looked at her.

The duke? she mouthed.

He nodded.

She winced, and he understood the sentiment. She shouldn't have been in the duke's chambers with him, and even if that could be explained away, the two of them hiding in the dressing room could not. But Reynolds was nothing if not resourceful. He leaned down and whispered into Meg's ear. "I'll go out and distract him. When he's not looking, you slip away." He straightened, but she tugged him back down to her level.

In his ear, she hissed, "Are you completely daft?"

He scowled at her. She scowled right back. He leaned in close to tell her it was their only hope, and then someone knocked on the duke's door. Reynolds put a hand over his eyes. Meg covered her mouth, which was open now in horror. The duke swore and then moved, boots clomping, across the floor to open the door.

***

"Goddamn it all to hell," Phin said as he stalked to the door. It had better be Reynolds. Phin had told the man to pack, and now he'd disappeared. Phin had to admit he might have given the valet some other directive. Damned if he could remember. For the first time in a very long time, Phin didn't know what to do. Stay? Leave? Pick Annabel up, throw her over his shoulder, and run away with her? He didn't like any of the options.

"What do you want?" he said when he opened the door. And then he blanched. Annabel was there.

"I'm sorry to—"

He pulled her into the room, kicked the door shut, and stared at her. "You changed your mind."

Her gaze dropped. "No. I haven't. But I didn't want you to leave without saying good-bye."

"I'm not leaving."

She sighed. "Phin, you can't stay with me. We've been over this."

They had been over it, at least she had. And she was correct. He did have duties to see to. He did need to marry a young woman and produce heirs. He couldn't stay in Berkshire and live with her. He couldn't even stay in Berkshire and not live with her—not without causing a scandal.

"I don't care," he said.

"What do you mean?"

"Exactly what I said. I don't care about any of it. I don't want to be a duke. I don't want to marry some chit with breeding hips. And I don't bloody well care if I ever sire any offspring. I want you, Annabel."

"No. You're not thinking clearly."

But he was thinking clearly. For the first time since Richard had died and the dukedom had been thrust on his shoulders, Phineas Leopold Duncombe, ninth Duke of

Mayne, was thinking perfectly clearly. He knew exactly what he wanted and how to get it.

"I am thinking clearly, and it's so obvious I don't know why I haven't thought of it before. I want to marry you, Annabel."

Something thudded in the dressing room, and he glanced at the door then remembered Twitchy was in there. The rabbit had probably knocked over his bowl. He looked back at Annabel, who was staring at him as though he'd gone mad.

"You can't marry me."

"Why?"

"I'm a widow."

He grasped her hands. "Which means you're free to remarry."

"Yes, but I'm the Wanton Widow. You can't marry a scandalous woman."

He shrugged. "Everyone has a scandal these days. Ever heard of Lord Byron? The Duke of York and his mistress? Nelson and—"

"I don't want to be the woman who ruined the Duke of Mayne's reputation."

"Then be my wife. No one will dare say a word about you if you're the Duchess of Mayne. And if they do, I'll throttle them myself."

"Phin, you need an heir. I'm almost seven and forty. I can't give you a child, even if I could"—she swallowed—"you saw Theadosia. I may not be able to produce a healthy child." Tears sparkled in her eyes and Phin pulled her into his arms. To his surprise, she allowed it.

"I don't care about all that. I have a nephew and uncles with offspring as well as more cousins than I can count. The line will not die if I marry for love."

She stiffened and pulled back, her gaze flicking up to his. "You're not thinking."

He smiled. "You'll make me say it, won't you?"

"Say what?"

"That's fine. I'll say it."

"What are you talking about?"

"I love you, Annabel. I. Love. You. If you love me back, even a little, then say you'll marry me. I'll make you love me if you give me a chance."

She stared at him, and in her silence, his worst fears were confirmed. She didn't love him. It was too soon for her to trust him enough to give up her freedom to marry another man. Or perhaps she just didn't love him. She wanted him, but he knew as well as any man that lust was not love.

"Love isn't something you can make someone feel," she whispered, and Phin felt his heart thud into his belly. "It has to be freely given."

"Annabel, give me—" But he didn't know what he should say. Give him time? Give him a chance? Give him her heart?

A knock sounded on the door, and he clenched his jaw. "Bloody goddamn hell," he muttered. Toward the door, he called, "Come back later, Reynolds."

"It's not Reynolds."

It was John. Wat the devil? Why was he still in Berkshire? He'd obviously come to press the duchess's case again, but Phin couldn't understand why he was so determined. "I told you the conversation is over, John. You can go back to West Sussex."

"The conversation isn't over, Duke." His brother-in-law sounded strangely resolute. "And if you don't open the door, I'll tell the innkeeper I fear for your well-being and have him open it for me."

"What should I do?" Annabel whispered.

Phin wanted to curse again. It was bad enough that John had interrupted the moment when he was declaring his love—something he'd never done before and never intended to do again. But even worse was the fact that Annabel was in his bed chamber, alone with him. That certainly would not help her reputation, and while Phin couldn't have cared less, he knew she cared.

"Go hide in the dressing room while I deal with him," Phin murmured.

She nodded, turned, opened the door, and stepped inside. When she was out of sight, Phin went to the door and pulled it open.

John stepped inside and raised his pistol.

Nineteen

"My lady?"

Annabel almost jumped out of her skin at the whispered words. She covered her mouth to keep from screaming when she turned and saw not only Meg, who had spoken, but Reynolds standing behind her in the dressing room.

"What are you doing in here?" she whispered. Then realizing she probably knew the answer to that, waved a hand. "Never mind. I'll deal with you later." Not that there would be any great punishment. What crime had they committed that she herself was not guilty of? Hadn't she just been alone in Phin's bed chamber?

She turned away, her cheeks burning as she realized the valet and the housekeeper had overheard her private conversation. They'd heard Phin say he wanted to marry her. They'd heard him tell her he loved her.

He loved her! Phin *loved* her.

Annabel still couldn't quite believe it. She couldn't quite believe him. No man had ever told her he loved her. She had never before wanted a man to love her. But she wanted Phin to love her. She wanted to be his duchess.

She heard a man's voice in the bed chamber and tried to focus her thoughts. She leaned close to listen, and Reynolds and Mrs. Slightley leaned close as well.

"What's this?" Phin asked on the other side of the door. "Some sort of game?"

"Yes, that's right," said another man. "A game. I've been playing it for years. I'm rather good at it now, you see."

Annabel glanced at Reynolds in confusion, but he shook his head, clearly as bewildered as she. He pushed the door slightly, opening it a bit further. She peered through the crack then moved back so Reynolds could do the same. She didn't recognize the well-dressed man with the light brown hair standing with his back to the dressing room, but she could see from Phin's expression that he was not welcome.

"It's Mr. Clare. He's married to Lady Anne, the duke's sister," Reynolds whispered. Clare had come from the sanitarium to continue his discussion with Phin then. But that didn't explain why Phin looked so concerned.

"I don't understand," Phin said, and Annabel could tell he was deliberately not looking at the dressing room, not wanting to draw his brother-in-law's attention to it.

"No," Clare said. "You never did understand. And I admit I liked that about you, Phineas. You didn't want to be duke, and I liked that about you, in particular. I had hoped you would die in the war, but against all odds you returned home."

Annabel covered her mouth and shot Reynolds an alarmed look. Reynolds pointed to the crack and moved aside so she could look. Annabel's heart rose to her throat.

Mr. Clare was pointing a pistol at Phineas.

Annabel heard Phin's voice as if from far away. He was asking why his brother-in-law had wanted him dead. She didn't know how he sounded so calm with a pistol pointed at his chest, because she was certainly not calm. Not at all.

"What should we do?" she hissed at Reynolds. "I have to go out there."

"No!" He grasped her arm, which was an enormous breech of conduct, but she understood he was just protecting her. "Stay here!" he mouthed.

"Isn't that obvious? I didn't want to have to kill you. But you've left me no choice," Clare said.

Annabel's eyes widened as she stared at Reynolds.

"Oh, my God," Phin said, his voice full of horror. "They weren't accidents, were they?"

"And Anne always says you are the clever one in the family. No, your brothers' deaths weren't accidents. Actually, Phillip's death was an accident. He truly did drown, but that gave me the idea."

"What idea?"

Annabel clenched her hands together. "His Grace is trying to stall for time. We have to help him," she whispered.

"How?" Meg mouthed.

Reynolds gestured for both women to stand back. Annabel shook her head, but Reynolds just shouldered his way in front of her. Now she couldn't see the bed chamber, only hear Mr. Clare.

"George was easy to kill. He had such a short temper; I knew it would only be a matter of time before he was involved in another duel. It was an easy matter to go along and make sure his pistol wouldn't fire."

"You bastard."

"Oh, he would have been a disastrous duke, and you know it. Now Ernest was the best of all of you. But one small push and down he went. The fall on the ice wasn't enough to kill him, so I had to bash the back of his head in to be certain."

"And Richard, I suppose you broke his neck and made it look like a fall from his horse."

"I would have killed him before that, but you were always at his side."

"I was trying to keep him alive. How will you explain my death? Everyone knows you're in Berkshire. Won't it seem suspicious if I'm shot?"

"Perhaps. But the rumor is that you are rogering Lady Longstowe. With her reputation, who would be surprised if a lover's quarrel ended in violence? I'll testify I heard you arguing."

"You leave her out of it."

"I may. What do I care who takes the blame? My son will be the duke." His voice rose with triumph.

"And that's what this was about? Making sure your son inherited the title?"

"And the wealth. You don't know what it's like, having to scrape by. Having to ask for an allowance every month."

"You have Anne's money!"

"A pittance!" Clare waved the pistol. "I deserve to hold the purse. It was me who was always at your mother's side, me who oversaw the estates when Richard was whoring or George dueling or you pretending to be a hero during the war. I deserve to be duke!"

"You'll never be the duke. And when Anne finds out about this, you'll be hanged, and your own son will despise you."

"Then we will make sure she never finds out."

Meg gasped, and Annabel tried to push past Reynolds. "Now!"

But Reynolds burst into the room. Annabel saw nothing but the back of Reynolds's coat for a moment, then the sound of a pistol firing. She screamed as Reynolds went down. But then she saw Mr. Clare swing his pistol back toward Phin. "Phin! Watch out!"

The duke leapt forward and caught Clare's arm, swinging the pistol upward so it was pointed at the ceiling. Mr. Clare grabbed Phin's other arm, and the two men grappled for a long moment. Annabel stumbled out of their way, dimly aware Meg was kneeling on the floor beside Reynolds. She could see the spill of crimson on his shirt.

Clare shoved the duke against the wash table, and the pitcher and basin overturned, smashing to the floor with a crash. The noise gave Annabel an idea. "Help!" she screamed. "Murder! Help!"

Mr. Clare gave her a warning look. "Shut up!"

The distraction was enough to give Phin the chance to throw his brother-in-law off balance. They lurched across the floor, like two drunkards locked in an embrace. But Phin gained traction and thrust Clare against a wall. Hard. The pictures rattled and Annabel gasped as Phin slammed Clare's head hard against the plaster. Mr. Clare kicked out, just missing Phin who jumped back. And then he moved forward again, pressing Clare's hand against the wall and squeezing his wrist until Annabel swore she heard a bone crack. Mr. Clare howled and dropped the pistol. Phin dropped his arm, which Clare immediately cradled to his chest. Phin clamped a hand on his brother-in-law's neck and shoved his head back against the wall again. This time plaster dust rained down and Clare visibly slumped.

Pounding sounded on the door, and someone yelled, "What's happening? Your Grace? Do you need help?"

"Yes!" Annabel cried. "Hurry!"

The door burst open, and the innkeeper and two other men shoved into the now quite crowded room. The innkeeper took one look about and said, "What has happened?"

"Never mind that," Phin said, releasing Mr. Clare, who slid to the floor. His gaze slid to Reynolds, whose breathing was labored. Annabel could hear it from across the room. "Fetch a surgeon. Hurry!"

***

Meg's hand was covered in blood. She'd pressed it against Reynolds's abdomen to stop the bleeding. Then she'd pressed a handkerchief to the wound. But the valet's shirt and the handkerchief were soaked through. Now her hand was wet. She didn't look away from Reynolds's face, though. His light brown eyes were on her, though they had grown a bit dim. His face was rather gray now too.

"Meg," he said.

"Don't try to talk," she ordered. "Save your strength for the surgeon."

"I want to say something."

She shook her head, struggling to keep the tears from falling. Tears would not save him, and she didn't want his last view of her to be sniffling and red-faced. "No, I want to say something," she said. "And you're to listen to me, do you understand that, Mr. Reynolds?"

"Yes, my love," he croaked.

"I was wrong," she said, her voice hitching. "When you asked me to marry you, I didn't say yes."

"You didn't say no," he pointed out. His hand moved to cover hers, and his skin was as cold as ice.

"But I should have said yes. I should have said I would marry you today. I will, Mr. Reynolds. I forgot how precious love is. I forgot we don't find it every day, and I swear on all that is holy that if you will just live, if you will just stay with me, I will marry you."

"So this is what it takes to convince you." His voice grew fainter.

"I was an idiot," she said then leaned close to him. She couldn't stop the tears from falling now. "I promise, I'll never be an idiot again. Just live, Reynolds. I love you."

"Barnaby," he whispered.

"What?"

"My name. Barnaby Reynolds."

She kissed his cheek. "I love you, Barnaby Reynolds."

He smiled and closed his eyes.

***

Phin paced the common room, which had been emptied of patrons so that he, Annabel, and Mrs. Slightley might wait here until the surgeon was finished with Reynolds. He'd arrived just as Phin feared he would be too late, and they'd all been shuttled out of the room. The innkeeper and Phin had dragged John out and locked him in the cellar. Annabel had directed the other man to fetch Twitchy from the dressing room, and the countess had gathered her housekeeper in her arms and all but supported her as the women walked to the common room. Now Mrs. Slightley sat with an untouched cup of tea before her, staring blankly at the wall. Annabel held the rabbit, stroking his fur and rocking slightly.

The door opened, and Phin spun around to face the innkeeper. "Any word?"

"Not yet, Your Grace."

"Bloody hell! How long does it take to remove a bullet and sew a man up? It's been hours."

The innkeeper opened his mouth, but Phin shook his head. He knew it could take an inordinate amount of time. He'd known men who had been hurt in the war and it seemed like days until the surgeon was finished with them. He tried not to think about those the surgeon had sighed over before pulling the sheet to cover their pale faces.

"All you can do now is say good-bye, lads."

Phin did not want to say farewell to Reynolds. He owed the man his life.

"I wanted to tell you the constable is here. If you agree, he'll take Mr. Clare into custody."

"Good. Where is the magistrate?"

"He's been summoned, but he was overseeing a case in another town today, Your Grace. It will take time for him to ride back."

"I want to see him as soon as he arrives."

"Of course, Your Grace." The innkeeper backed out of the room.

Phin paced back and forth, watching Mrs. Slightley with concern. She didn't move, didn't even seem to breathe. Finally, he whirled toward the door. "I would go see what's taking so long."

Annabel rose, placing the rabbit back in his crate. "Phin, wait."

He looked back at her, his impatience rising.

"Step outside with me a moment," she said, looking over her shoulder at Meg. He nodded and opened the door, waiting for her to pass through before stepping outside the common room himself and closing the door.

Annabel looked up at him, her bright blue eyes rimmed with red. "Stay here, please. If you go upstairs, it will only distract the surgeon from his work."

"I know." He raked a hand through his hair. "I just can't stand not knowing what's happening. How do I even know if the man is worth his salt?"

"What other choice do we have?"

He shook his head, and he felt the lump rise in his throat. "Come here." She opened her arms, and he went into them willingly. His head dropped to her shoulder and he inhaled her musky scent, now so familiar.

"If he dies, it's my fault. It will forever be on my conscience."

"No." She stroked his hair. "It's Mr. Clare's fault. Reynolds only wanted to protect you."

"You warned me," he murmured. "You said I should consider the possibility someone was trying to kill me. I dismissed the idea. Even when I'd been hit on the head and shot at, I didn't believe it. It was John all the time."

"I didn't really believe it either. I was only speculating. And your own sister's husband! How could you have known? How could anyone have known?"

"I *should* have known!"

"Why?" She pulled back and cupped his face. Tears were in her eyes, and he couldn't hold back his own tears. "Do you think being a duke gives you some sort of omniscience? No one knew, not even his own wife." She caught his tears with her thumbs. "You can't blame yourself. I forbid it."

He smiled. "How can I argue?"

"You can't and you shouldn't." She pulled him close again. God, he needed her. He needed her now, and he needed her tomorrow. And the day after that. And the next day and the next. But now was not the time to bring up marriage again. She didn't love him. She'd said love wasn't something someone could be made to feel. He couldn't make her love him. But that didn't mean he intended to give up trying. She had to fall in love with him…eventually.

"He won't die, will he, Annabel?" Phin whispered.

"Of course, not. Did you hear what Meg told him? How could he die after that declaration?"

She was so strong, so strong. "You should march up there and order him to live."

"If I thought it would work, I would. All we can do now is wait."

They stood embracing for a long time, and when the innkeeper brought food, Annabel told everyone to eat and ignored her own directive. Mrs. Slightley didn't eat either. By midnight, both women had fallen asleep out of sheer exhaustion. The housekeeper had curled up on a bench, and Annabel had laid her head on a table and not lifted it again.

Phin sat silently, willing the door to open. When it finally did, he half thought it must be a hallucination. But the surgeon looked too young and too weary for him to imagine the man's presence. Phin rose slowly.

"Your Grace," the surgeon said with a perfunctory bow.

"How is he?"

"He's alive," the surgeon said.

Mrs. Slightley let out a small cry, and Phin looked at her, not having realized she'd woken when the surgeon came in.

"When can I see him?" the housekeeper asked.

"He's resting now," the surgeon said as Annabel raised her head. "I was able to remove the pistol ball and repair the damage it did. I won't be too specific with the ladies present, but Mr. Reynolds is resting."

"I want to see him!" Mrs. Slightley said.

The physician held up a hand. "My nurse is with him, and I will go sit with him as well. If he is still resting comfortably in the morning then you may see him for a few minutes."

"What about fever?" Phin asked. He'd known men who had survived being shot only to die of fever days later.

The surgeon gave him a pained look. "It is a concern, of course. I hope if we keep the wound clean and irrigated, we might avoid infection. But unfortunately, only time will tell. Now, I suggest all of you go to sleep. I'll wake you if there is any change."

"Thank you, sir," Phin said.

The surgeon bowed again. Phin didn't mention that he had nowhere to sleep as Reynolds was in his chamber. He'd slept in worse places than the floor of a common room. "Annabel, take Mrs. Slightley to your chamber."

"I'm not tired, Your Grace."

"No doubt, but you should both lie down for a few hours. I'll wait here in case there is any change."

Annabel looked as though she wanted to argue, but Phin gave her a hard stare, and she gathered her housekeeper up and the two women followed the surgeon out of the common room.

Phin took a look at the floor then cleared off one of the long tables. He settled himself on it, stretching out, and staring at the ceiling. Above him, Reynolds fought for his life. "You're a fighter, Reynolds," Phin whispered. "Don't give up now."

Twenty

Reynolds opened his eyes slowly and stared at the face of a man he did not know. The man smiled at him, but Reynolds did not smile back. "Who the devil are you?" If he was the man responsible for the excruciating pain in his belly then Reynolds had a few choice words for him.

"I'm Mr. Bash, your surgeon. How are you feeling?"

"Like shit."

Someone giggled and Reynolds swung his gaze toward the sound. Lady Longstowe and Meg were across the room. Meg was smiling at him, and Lady Longstowe looked down, pretending she hadn't heard. The duke was in the doorway. He looked rather irate.

"Your Grace," Reynolds said, trying to sit. The surgeon pushed him down again.

"None of that, Mr. Reynolds. You've not the strength yet."

The Duke of Mayne came into his line of vision. "Listen to the surgeon, Reynolds. You've earned a long rest."

Reynolds looked about. "I'm in your chamber, Your Grace. In your bed."

The duke waved a hand. "I'll make do. You're to stay here until you're well again. And then, it's my understanding you have plans to retire from my service?"

"Your Grace, I—"

The duke gestured to Meg, who came to sit on the bed beside Reynolds.

"I'm sure you'd much rather look at her face than mine, Reynolds. And when you two marry, I'll give you a comfortable wedding gift. Now, I think a few minutes alone is in order."

The duke withdrew, taking Lady Longstowe and the surgeon with him. Reynolds smiled wearily up at Meg. "That went well. He didn't seem cross at my leaving at all."

"I'm cross enough for the entire village." She slapped him on the arm.

"Ow. What was that for?"

"For almost getting yourself killed. What were you thinking?" She slapped him again.

"Ow! I was thinking that if I didn't do something, the countess would. I couldn't very well let her be shot."

"You had no business being shot either!"

"I can promise you I won't repeat the experience. It hurts like the dickens."

Her expression turned instantly concerned. "What can I do? Should I call the surgeon?"

"I need something the surgeon can't give me. A kiss."

She rolled her eyes. "Go on, now."

"You'll deny a dying man a kiss?"

"You're not dying anymore." But she leaned down and kissed him gently on the lips. "There."

"You'll marry me, Meg?"

"I will."

He gave the ceiling a speculative look. "Did I imagine it, or did you tell me you loved me right after that bastard shot me?"

"You didn't imagine it."

"Then tell me again."

"I love you, Barnaby Reynolds." She kissed him again and lay her head on his heart, just where he wanted her.

***

Phin had just returned from escorting Annabel to Brookside Place, along with Twitchy, who had become not only a favorite of Theadosia but many of the other residents as well. Instead of going to the new room Phin had been given, he veered toward the common room and asked for a pint. The innkeeper handed it to him, and he sat on a stool.

The man beside him looked over. "Long day?" he asked.

"Long week. I really would rather something stronger, but..." He trailed off, narrowing his eyes. "What the hell are you doing here?"

Colin FitzRoy raised a brow. "Having a pint, same as you. Took you long enough to recognize me."

"I'm distracted or I would have known you earlier. You're not even in disguise."

"Draven sent me to see that your Mr. Clare makes it back to Town without issue."

At the mention of his former commanding officer, Phin straightened slightly. "Draven? What's he to do with this?"

"When someone tries to kill one of his men, he doesn't take it kindly."

"Tell Draven I won't be needing my dancing shoes just yet."

Colin smiled at the reference. When they'd been in a difficult position in the war, the men had cheered each other by saying, *Put on your dancing shoes* because there was the risk that by the end of the night they'd be dancing with the devil.

Colin sipped his ale. "I'm to make sure Clare arrives at the Tower to await trial. Also, your mother wants to see you."

"Is she in Town as well?"

"She is, but Draven persuaded her to wait for you at Mayne House. That took some doing on his part. The duchess is convinced you mean to marry someone called the Wanton Widow."

Phin took a deep drink from his glass.

Colin took a drink of his own ale. "Somehow mothers always know."

"Yes, well mine needn't worry. The lady won't have me."

Colin looked about, probably hoping to find someone else to intervene. He was known for his aversion to emotional scenes. In fact, he was perpetually stoic. Seeing no one else he could recruit, Colin sighed. "I'm no good at this sort of thing."

"Neither am I."

Colin swallowed. "Do you"—he swallowed again—"love her? Just nod yes or no."

Amused, Phin nodded yes.

"Does she—er, reciprocate?"

"I think so. She—"

Colin held up a hand. "Don't expound. For the love of God, don't expound. Is she vital to your happiness?"

"She is."

"You can't just find another widow or drink yourself into a stupor or hit some man senseless at Mostyn's Boxing Studio?"

Phin shook his head. "Temporary cures, all of them."

"Then I suppose you had better do what you must to win her over."

"Good advice, FitzRoy. Remind me never to ask you again."

Colin finished his ale. "I'll tell Draven to hold your mother off a bit longer. You can thank me later." He rose. "The men dispatched to ride back to London with Clare and myself are waiting. Do me one favor, Phin."

"What's that?"

"Don't invite me to the wedding."

"But you're such a good matchmaker!" Phin called after him. Then he set his unfinished ale on the counter and trudged up to his small, lonely room.

***

Annabel turned when the door opened. The room was small, but she hadn't parted the curtains, and she could tell Phin didn't see her at first. He closed the door and took a step then froze.

"It's just me," she said, moving out of the corner. "I've been waiting for you."

"I see." He gave her a wary look, that of a man not certain what comes next.

"I went to see Mrs. Slightley and Reynolds when I returned."

"How are they?"

"Exceedingly happy. Reynolds offered to help me find a small cottage nearby once he's on his feet again. Meg said she would interview housekeepers for me. So you see, I am well taken care of."

He leaned an arm against the fireplace. "Is this my congé?"

"No. But I didn't want you to feel as though you had to stay to take care of me."

"You can take care of yourself, is that it?"

"I can."

He nodded, and she held her breath. This was it. He would leave now, pack his things and ride back to Town. She'd probably never see him again. She'd only read of his marriage and the birth of his children. Her heart felt as though someone had reached in and grasped it tightly. It hurt more than she had imagined.

"And what if I don't wish to leave?"

Her breath caught. "But you have duties in Town and at your estates."

He waved a hand. "Those mean nothing to me if I don't have you."

"Your Grace—"

He moved forward, toward her. "I know you don't love me. Not yet. But I'm not about to give up."

She took a step back, her heart hammering in her throat. "You're not?"

"No. If you want to be close to your daughter, then I'll find a cottage here too. I'll spend a week in Town and a week here. A week at my estate and a week here."

"That sounds like anything but a life of leisure. You are a duke."

"I want to be your husband. And if it takes me a year or five or ten to woo you, to prove I love you, to show you that you can trust me with your love, then I will take a year or five or ten." He was right before her now, but instead of boxing her in, he lowered to one knee. "Just give me a chance, Annabel. That's all I'm asking."

She stared down at him, her fear and her love warring for control. And wasn't it time that war ended? Wasn't it time she believed the man on his knees before her could handle the disapproval of Society and knew, better than anyone, what he wanted? He wanted her. Life was short, and she had already had so much of it taken from her. Why not reach for happiness?

"I was terrified for you when I hid in the dressing room," she said.

Phin's expression turned from hope to confusion. "I was terrified for me too, especially when I realized what he intended."

"No, you weren't. I could see you through the crack in the door. You weren't worried about yourself."

He stood. "The hell I wasn't."

"You were worried about me. You made sure not to look at the dressing room. You didn't want him to suspect anyone was inside. You didn't want to endanger me."

"Little did I know a valet with a death wish was also inside."

"And if you had, you would have protected him too. That's why I love you, Phin. You always think of others."

"I'm a duke. I'm plenty—wait, what did you say?"

"I said you always think of others."

"No, the other thing. Right before."

"I said, that's why I love you."

He took an audible breath, and she couldn't make him wait any longer. She went to him, wrapping her arms about his body, which was stiff from surprise. "I do love you, Phin. I do want to be your wife. That is, if you'll have me."

He started violently, like a dead man reanimated. "If I'll have you? Annabel, the only question, ever, was whether you'd have me." He twirled her around, barely keeping her feet from hitting the edge of the bed. "Annabel, I love you. You'll marry me?" He looked down at her, concern furrowing his brow.

"I'll marry you."

"Now? Oh, that won't work. As soon as I get the special license?"

"Yes, as soon as you like."

"I'll go now." He started away, but she grasped his coat and held then reeled him back.

"You can go tomorrow. That's soon enough."

"There's plenty of daylight left."

"And I intend to make full use of it." She stripped off his coat and loosened his neck cloth.

"It's the middle of the day. We'll scandalize the servants passing by."

"Not if we're quiet," she said, reaching for his trousers.

"What's the fun in that?" And he swept her off her feet, making her squeal and then moan when he set her on the bed, coming down over her and kissing her. Unfastening her bodice with one hand and sliding the hem of her skirt up with the other, he murmured, "Let's see just how wanton you truly are."

Twenty-One

"What do you mean he's married her?" the Duchess of Mayne, now the Dowager Duchess of Mayne, asked. Her voice was imperious, and though she was a good deal shorter than he, Colin FitzRoy winced.

With effort, the former soldier resisted the urge to shift from one foot to the other. "I just received word, Your Grace."

"And why have I not received word?" She waved a hand, pacing from one side of the grand drawing room to the other. Colin hadn't ever been to Mayne House. Though he was the third son of a viscount, his family had not been wealthy, and he was unused to such opulence. "I blame that Lieutenant Draven. He told me if I stayed here everything would work out for the best."

Colin didn't reply. He supposed Phin was of the opinion everything had worked out for the best. Colin was just happy the couple had married by special license in Berkshire. He hadn't had to attend the wedding.

He detested weddings. Not simply because of all the women sniffling and the men smiling and giving hearty congratulations, but because they reminded him of a wedding he would rather forget.

"If there's nothing else, Your Grace, I'm needed—" Where the hell was he needed? Surely somewhere? Perhaps there was another war he could fight? The battlefield at Waterloo was preferable to this assignment.

"There is something else, Mr. FitzRoy." The duchess stopped pacing and looked at him.

Colin sighed. He was beginning to despair of ever making it out of this house. "Your Grace?"

She lifted her chin and closed her eyes, as though pained. "Answer me one question."

"If I can."

"Does he love her?"

Colin refrained from rolling his eyes. Love. Why the hell was everyone obsessed with love? Love was just a feeling people attributed to lust or strong friendship or comradery. It came and it went, and it couldn't be relied upon. Someone might say they loved you one day and then claim to have fallen out of love the next. Did Mayne love the Wanton Widow? Yes? No? For the moment?

Colin went with the least controversial response. "He said he did, Your Grace. And he seemed quite…" What was the word? Daft? Mad? Idiotic? "Sincere."

She nodded. "Then I suppose I had better send congratulations to him and felicitations to her."

Colin blinked. He had three sisters, so he was familiar with feminine mood changes. But even by those standards, this was abrupt.

"That is good, Your Grace," he said carefully.

"I'm not happy," she said, pointing an accusing finger at him.

"No, Your Grace."

"But I do love Phineas, as frustrating and headstrong as he is. Do you have children, Mr. FitzRoy?"

"No, Your Grace." The question had surprised him. And it saddened him a bit too. He liked children.

"One day you will, and you will understand."

Colin didn't bother to argue. He was not so foolish as to argue with a duchess who was in a mood like the Dowager Duchess of Mayne.

The duchess went to a desk in the corner and ran a finger over the polished wood. "Do you think she makes him happy?" She gave Colin time to consider before looking up at him expectantly.

Colin had no idea, and he didn't really want to think about the matter. "Yes," he said, as it was the simplest answer.

"Then I am happy." She nodded. "Go on then, Mr. FitzRoy. I have a letter to write. And if you see the duke before I, tell him I want to wish him"—she pressed her lips together, her next words requiring obvious effort—"and his new wife happiness"

"I will, Your Grace." Colin bowed and backed away.

He was down the stairs and out of Mayne House within five minutes, which was quite the feat considering its size. God save him from duchesses. He'd escaped one. Now if he could just escape another. The Duchess of Warcliffe had requested an audience with him. Colin was putting it off as long as possible. He did not want to see her. He had nothing to say to her.

But he supposed it was only a matter of time before she had her way. After all, she was his mother-in-law.

About Shana Galen

Shana Galen is three-time Rita award nominee and the bestselling author of passionate Regency romps. "The road to happily-ever-after is intense, conflicted, suspenseful and fun," and *RT Bookreviews* calls her books "lighthearted yet poignant, humorous yet touching." She taught English at the middle and high school level off and on for eleven years. Most of those years were spent working in Houston's inner city. Now she writes full time, surrounded by three cats and one spoiled dog. She's happily married and has a daughter who is most definitely a romance heroine in the making.

Would you like exclusive content, book news, and a chance to win early copies of Shana's books? Sign up for monthly emails at her website for exclusive news and giveaways.

Want more of the Survivors series? Read a Survivors novella in the anthology, The Bachelors of Bond Street, on sale October 11, 2019.

Enjoy an excerpt.

Thomas Gaines was in a hurry. The hackney he'd hailed at his home in Cheapside with plenty of time to spare had been caught behind a line of carts and other hackneys waiting for an overturned carriage to be righted and cleared from the busy London street.

In the hackney, Thomas had fumed. He fumed now as he took long-legged strides down Bond Street, passing Madame LeMonde's modiste shop, The Hungry Mind book store, and a boy who waved a copy of *The Midnight Cryer* in his face saying it had all the latest scandals for only a penny. Thomas declined.

He skirted around the crates stacked at the door of a shop, around the cluster of servants gossiping on the corner, shook his head at the apple seller calling out, "Apples! Get yer fresh apples!" Two children ran past, knocking into him. He put his hand on his pocket to keep it from being picked and stepped over a puddle of liquid dumped out of an upper window. He almost wished he hadn't jumped out of the hackney early, but he could walk this last quarter mile faster than a vehicle could traverse the congested streets. Sometimes he missed Wapping.

Sometimes.

Today was the one day he absolutely must be on time. His shop on Bond Street had been open less than a week and today he would receive his first bulk shipment of coffee and tobacco. He knew what he had bought. Knew what it was worth, and he wanted to be certain that what was delivered was what he'd paid for. The merchants in Wapping knew him, but London was a different animal. They'd see a black man and think him ignorant and an easy mark. But Thomas was far from ignorant. In fact, when it came to coffee and tobacco, Thomas probably knew more than almost any other man in England.

His shop wasn't yet open, so he entered through the back door. He didn't need his key as his manager, Alfred, a trusted man he'd brought from Wapping, was already there and had the door unlocked. As soon as he entered, Thomas heard the men speaking.

"If that's all then," the delivery man was saying.

"That's not all," Thomas said, his deep voice cutting through the room and causing all three men to turn and look at him. Alfred nodded at him, but the two delivery men frowned.

"Who's this, then?" the taller of the delivery men asked. Both men were tall and lanky. They didn't have the kind of profession that lent itself to stoutness. The one who spoke wore a brown cap over his brown hair.

"This is Mr. Gaines," Alfred said. "The owner of Bond Street Coffee & Tobacco."

Both delivery men looked him up and down, probably not used to a black man owning a shop on Bond Street. Gaines wasn't quite used to it either. But there were upwards of twenty thousand black men and women in London, and just like the rest of the populace, some were wealthy, others poor; some lived to serve and others to be served.

"A pleasure, Mr. Gaines," the brown-capped delivery man said with a nod of his head. "We've finished unloading your goods. All we need is a signature and the payment." He gestured to the paper Alfred held.

Gaines took it from him. "I'll just have a look first."

"Your man already approved it," the other delivery man said. He wore a black cap dusty with soot.

"No one is paid until *I* approve it." Thomas made his way to the large sacks holding the fragrant tobacco leaves. The scent was so familiar that he felt a rush of confidence. In Virginia he had been a slave on a tobacco plantation. He'd planted, tended, reaped, and dried tobacco. He knew good tobacco.

He opened one of the bags and lifted out a handful of the leaves, holding it up to the light of one of the small windows in the back room, which was stacked with bags of coffee and now tobacco. In a few hours, the space would be bustling with his workers, sorting and packaging the coffee and tobacco for sale in the shop. Others would grind the coffee beans for the coffee room.

Gaines examined the light brown leaves. He held them to his nose, inhaling the earthy scent of them overlaid with just the slightest hint of spice. He could imagine the leaves as they had been when picked, bright green in the black hands that had plucked them. These leaves had been hung to dry and cure, then carefully bundled and packaged and sent on a ship to England. It was good tobacco. He could tell by the feel and the smell.

He dug deeper into the sack, pulling out more bundles, making certain what was underneath was the same quality as that on top. When he finished one sack, he went to the next.

"Is he planning to look through every bag?" one of the delivery men asked. "We have other stops to make."

"It won't take long," Alfred said. "Mr. Gaines is particular."

The deliverymen grumbled but waited.

Finally, Thomas had gone through the bags and returned, paper in hand. "I'll sign, but I'm not paying this price." He pointed to the total at the bottom of the invoice. "That bag over there is only three-fourths full and the leaves at the bottom are old and crushed. I'll pay half for that one or you can take it back and I'll just take the others."

"What are you talking about?" the brown-capped delivery man said, looking offended, though Thomas had seen the slight twitch of his lips. He'd known that bag was poor quality. It was why he'd put it in the back.

"That's my best offer. And tell your employer if he wants my business, he'd be wise to send his best from now on. Alfred, I'll leave the details to you." Thomas handed his man the invoice and strode to his office. It was on the first floor of the shop and could be accessed from stairs in the back room. It had a window that looked out onto Bond Street and Thomas went straight to the window as soon as he'd closed the door behind him. Thomas opened the shutter on the window and peered down at the street, just now beginning to bustle with shopkeepers sweeping their stoops and rolling down awnings. Across the street and diagonal was The Greedy Vicar, a pub where Thomas had eaten a few times. His coffee room served lighter fare, but he liked to sample the competition. It was a pleasant enough place, but he had the advantage of novelty on his side. At least for now.

He heard a tap on the door and turned as Alfred entered. "Sir, I want to apologize for not—"

Thomas waved a hand. "Come look out this window, Alfred."

The manager crossed the room, past the desk with its teetering papers, the assortment of chairs, and the cold hearth. "What is it, sir?"

Alfred stood at his side, his pale hands clutched together. He was an older man of perhaps fifty, and he was intelligent and trustworthy. He'd lived in Wapping all his life and had a wife and four children there. He had two days off a week and would go home at every opportunity. Gaines had rooms in Wapping as well, but he didn't care if he ever went back for more than the time it took to look in on his businesses there.

"Did you ever think we would be here, Alfred? That we would have our own shop on Bond Street? This is the most famous street in the world, and here we are."

"It's quite an accomplishment, sir, but I can't say I'm surprised."

Gaines looked at him.

"Ever since you first hired me as a waiter, I knew you weren't like other men. You're shrewd but kind."

Thomas made a hissing sound. "Don't spread that rumor about."

Alfred smiled. "No, sir. I suppose it helps that you know your tobacco so well. And your coffee. I've never known a man to take such a keen interest. So I can't say I'm surprised."

The two men stood at the window, looking out over their little square of the street until Thomas's eye was drawn by a bright blue turban. Most of the bonnets were white or drab, dull colors, but this turban was blue as the sky on a clear winter day. He watched the woman in the turban move closer until she stopped across from the shop—his shop—and paused. She looked up at the sun, perhaps gauging the time, and Thomas felt his brows arch.

She was a lovely shade of umber, her eyes wide-spaced and inquisitive. She had a long neck and, now that he was looking, a long slim body as well. It was hidden under a blue serge dress that was too big for her, but he could imagine her long legs and small waist.

"I'd better go down, sir," Alfred said. "Our people will be here soon."

Gaines nodded then forced himself away from the window and the lovely young woman just as a group of Mrs. Sinclair's students passed by, obscuring her from view. He had a stack of documents to read and organize. When he sat at his crowded desk, he did miss Wapping. He'd had a filing system in place there, but here he'd had to start over. Right now he had everything in three piles—important, very important, and extremely important. He needed a clerk to come in and file everything for him. But he'd have to worry about that another day. He didn't have time for clerks and filing when his extremely important stack was so tall.

He lifted the first document and began to read.

***

Raeni smoothed the clean white apron over her blue dress and tried to keep up with the woman behind the coffee room's counter. Mrs. Price spoke quickly and moved even quicker. She rattled off instructions that made Raeni's head spin. Although, her head might have been spinning simply from hunger and exhaustion. She'd slept on the floor of a church last night and had nothing to eat since yesterday afternoon when she'd spent her last penny on an old bun.

She struggled to listen carefully to Mrs. Price's directives. Raeni couldn't afford to lose this position. It didn't help that Mrs. Price had tried to turn her away when she'd applied. It had been the kind manager, Alfred Miller, who had given her a chance.

But Mr. Miller oversaw the coffee shop, which sold coffee by the pound and tobacco as well. Raeni was stuck on the other side of Bond Street Coffee & Tobacco, and in a few moments her side, the coffee room, would open and begin serving. Despite the fact that Raeni had grown up around servants, she had not much experience serving herself. Her life in Jamaica had been so different from life here in England.

"Did you hear me, Miss Sawyer?" Mrs. Price asked sharply. The use of her formal name tore Raeni's thoughts away from her reminiscences.

"Yes, Mrs. Price. I'm to seat customers and allow Caroline to serve."

Caroline was a white woman in a gray dress and stiff apron. She was young and pretty and poured coffee with a flourish.

"Then go stand by the door," Mrs. Price ordered. "And stand up straight. Mr. Gaines doesn't like his employees to slouch."

Raeni hadn't met this Mr. Gaines, but she didn't like him already. Mrs. Price had a long list of things he didn't like. In addition to slouching, Mr. Gaines did not approve of tardiness, loud voices, smiles that showed too many teeth, or dust. The coffee room was immaculate, so clean in fact that Raeni wished she'd been able to sleep on this floor rather than the dusty old church floor. But beggars couldn't be choosy, and right now she was one misstep from beggary.

Raeni took her position at the door and not a moment too soon as two men approached. She opened the door, causing the little bell above it to tinkle, and said, "Welcome to Bond Street Coffee & Tobacco."

The men, dressed in the clothing of clerks barely acknowledged her, but followed her to a table, their conversation about Old Man Lofton barely slowing.

"Enjoy your coffee," she told the men, as she had been instructed. The next two hours passed similarly. There was a steady stream of men, and a few ladies, in and out. Raeni sat the ladies well away from the shop area, which was separated from the coffee room by a partial wall, and sat the men closer so they might wander over to purchase tobacco after their refreshment. Her head had stopped spinning, but her throat was dry from repeating the same phrases time and again.

Caroline moved efficiently and her smile never faltered, but Raeni could see the tables were almost all taken. Caroline was looking about with an expression bordering on panic. At that moment, Mrs. Price beckoned to Raeni, who left her post and rushed to the counter where Mrs. Price took the customers' orders and relayed them to the cook. Very little needed to be cooked. Most of the items offered were pastries and biscuits, which were made ahead of time, but Mr. Gaines had also added soup to the menu and that must be kept warm. And then, of course, there was the constant brewing of coffee.

"Yes, Mrs. Price?" Raeni asked.

"Go see to those men over there." Mrs. Price pointed to a table of three men Raeni had seated a few minutes before. Mrs. Price turned and went back into the kitchen, and Raeni stood still for a moment, unsure of what she was to do.

She took a calming breath. She'd been watching Caroline all morning. It seemed easy enough. She plastered a tight smile on her face and made her way to the table. The men were speaking, and she wasn't certain if she should interrupt or wait until there was a pause in the conversation. She stood awkwardly at the table. It seemed so easy for Caroline. Mrs. Price came back out and glowered at her, her dark skin shiny from the heat of the kitchen. Raeni cleared her throat. When the men paid her no attention, she cleared it again.

One of the men looked at her.

"Oh, hello," she said. "What would you like?"

He gave her a slow smile. "What are you offering?"

She ignored the insinuation behind his words. "We have coffee, pastries, soup, and bread."

"Just coffee," the man said. The other men said they'd have the same and went back to their conversation.

That had been easy enough. Raeni moved to the counter where Mrs. Price waited. She had to dodge Caroline, who carried a tray heavy with a silver coffee pot and several pastries. "The men will have coffee," she told Mrs. Price.

The little bell above the door tinkled, and Raeni glanced at a group of four women who had entered.

"What kind of coffee?" Mrs. Price asked.

Raeni furrowed her brow. "I don't understand."

"Do they want milk in it or chocolate? What about sugar?"

"Oh." She hadn't thought to ask. Raeni didn't drink coffee, and though she knew it was not always taken black, she hadn't thought to ask.

Mrs. Price waved a hand. "Go seat those ladies and then ask. Hurry now!"

Raeni rushed to the entrance, weaving past Caroline, now returning with a tray, which was stacked with dirty plates and cups. "Miss Sawyer, can you clear that table when you have a moment?" She gestured to an empty table stacked with used dishes. "Mr. Miller was supposed to send one of the men from the back to clear, but he must have forgotten or he still needs them all."

"Of course." Raeni was beginning to see why Caroline had looked so panicked. She greeted the women at the door and led them to a table but just as she was ready to return to the men whose coffee order she'd taken, two more men entered. She seated them and started back to the first table of men.

"Where's our coffee?" the man who'd given her a smile earlier asked, his tone slightly irritated.

"It will be out in just a moment. Did you want milk, chocolate, or sugar?"

The men detailed the way they wanted their coffee, and Raeni nodded and hurried toward Mrs. Price. She passed Caroline, carrying yet another heavy tray. "Miss Sawyer, I thought I asked you to clear that table."

"I will. I'll do it right after this."

The bell at the door tinkled again. Raeni blew out a breath. Mrs. Price gave the door a pointed look, and Raeni glanced over her shoulder to see six men crowding into the room. Where would she put them? The coffee room, with its polished brass and dark paneled walls, had plenty of light from the large front windows, but though the light gave it a spacious feel, it was all but full now. The tables had four chairs. How could she find a place to seat six?

She gave Mrs. Price the gentlemen's order then rushed to seat the newcomers, managing to push two tables together. She was sweating now, and the coffee room was out of tables. Caroline gave her an exasperated look and Raeni rushed to clear the dirty table so the next set of customers could sit there.

Unfortunately, she didn't have a tray, which meant she carried the dishes in several trips to the kitchen. Then she had to ask for a clean rag to wipe the table. Rag in hand, Mrs. Price stopped her. "The coffee is ready. Bring it to those gentlemen before they leave. They've been waiting almost a quarter of an hour."

"But I was to clean the table."

"In a moment," Mrs. Price said. She gestured to a tray on the counter. Raeni eyed it with no little trepidation. A coffee pot sat in the middle surrounded by empty cups and saucers of milk and chocolate. Raeni approached the tray and wondered how she was to carry it across the room without tipping it. She tried to remember how Caroline had done it, the tray balanced on one shoulder. Carefully, Raeni hoisted the heavy tray and balanced it on her shoulder.

It wasn't so difficult. She couldn't see past the tray, but it would only be for a moment. Most of the room was still visible to her. She started toward the table of men, walking quickly but carefully, and just then the bell above the door tinkled. Raeni glanced in that direction. A man entered, and for a moment he looked so much like her father's overseer that she stumbled. She managed to keep the tray steady long enough to realize it wasn't him after all, but by then her legs had gone to jelly out of fear. She lurched forward, the tray making it impossible for her to see the man in the expensive coat who had stepped into her path until it was too late. She plowed into the man, her tray crashing down, the coffee on it splashing over him. He yelped and jumped back as the hot beverage scalded his skin. Raeni tried desperately to right the tray, but she could do little but watch it slide as her own momentum carried it and her into the man.

He tried to catch her, and she tried to step back, but the wet floor was slippery and she lost her footing. She went down and the man went down beside her. From the floor, Raeni looked up at the dark beams running along the ceiling. She'd be fired now. She'd probably be let go without even the day's wages. The coffee, milk, and chocolate on her gown were as close to a meal as she was likely to have today or in the foreseeable future. But she wouldn't give up that easily.

Perhaps if she sought out Mr. Gaines, stood straight and begged—without showing too many teeth—for him to give her another chance, he might take pity on her.

Mrs. Price's face came into view, but she wasn't looking down at Raeni. She was looking at the man Raeni had taken down. "Sir! Are you injured?" Mrs. Price asked.

Obviously, no one cared if Raeni was injured. Still, Raeni thought a better question for the man might be *where did you come from and why weren't you watching where you were going?*

"I'm fine," he said, his voice a low bass.

"Oh, I do apologize," Mrs. Price was saying. Raeni wanted to roll her eyes. Why was she apologizing when it had been his fault? She'd better apologize too, especially if she hoped to beg Mr. Gaines for her position.

She pushed up to her elbows just in time for Mrs. Price to toss her an angry look. "This girl is new. But I'll let her go right away. This won't happen again, Mr. Gaines."

The words were like a cold bucket of water tossed over her. Raeni wanted to sink right back down, curl up on the floor, and close her eyes. The handsome man before her, with his mocha-colored eyes and walnut skin, was Mr. Gaines. *The* Mr. Gaines. She was doomed.

Buy it now!

Printed in Great Britain
by Amazon